THIS
LOVE STORY
WILL
SELF-DESTRUCT

THIS
LOVE STORY
WILL
SELF-DESTRUCT

LESLIE COHEN

GALLERY BOOKS

New York   London   Toronto   Sydney   New Delhi

G

Gallery Books
An Imprint of Simon & Schuster, Inc.
1230 Avenue of the Americas
New York, NY 10020

First Gallery Books trade paperback edition January 2018

GALLERY BOOKS and colophon are registered trademarks of
Simon & Schuster, Inc.

For information about special discounts for bulk purchases,
please contact Simon & Schuster Special Sales at 1-866-506-1949
or business@simonandschuster.com.

The Simon & Schuster Speakers Bureau can bring authors to
your live event. For more information or to book an event, contact
the Simon & Schuster Speakers Bureau at 1-866-248-3049 or
visit our website at www.simonspeakers.com.

Interior design by Bryden Spevak

Manufactured in the United States of America

10 9 8 7 6 5 4 3 2 1

Library of Congress Cataloging-in-Publication Data is available.

ISBN 978-1-5011-6853-6
ISBN 978-1-5011-6854-3 (ebook)

THIS
LOVE STORY
WILL
SELF-DESTRUCT

EVE

Part of me wanted to drive him a little crazy, to see how far I could push before sending him screaming for the hills. Only this was New York City, so by "hills" I mean that minuscule square of green shrubbery outside your apartment building that passes for a front yard. Was I innocent? Not entirely. But *let us not judge hastily the actions of the young for fear of neglecting the importance of the journey*, said forty thousand fortune cookies, and forty thousand fortune cookies cannot be wrong.

I still pass them by sometimes: the streets, apartment buildings, bars, and restaurants, all a part of this story. And, while they are unremarkable to most, they possess the unique ability to stop me dead in my tracks. I think to myself, somewhat irrationally, *What is going on here?* I get philosophical, and yes, a tad self-centered. Does an apartment still exist once you no longer live there? Why does a restaurant continue to operate once you've paid the bill and walked away, the door swishing closed in your wake? I can't fully acknowledge that the place has moved on. Without me.

A part of this story will always remain in those places, as if stranded in time. I like to revisit some of them and enjoy the nostalgia. The memories are still so vivid. Others are best left alone, to fade over time. Looking back, I can see how those places were leading us somewhere. We were drawing lines from a series of scattered dots, hoping to see a picture emerge. It took time to put it together. The dots existed all over the city—and not in a way that made any sense or always felt good. But we should have known. And whenever I find myself passing one of these places, I can't help but think, *What took us so long?*

BEN

- - - - - -

"What took us so long?" Did she really just say that? I'll tell you what took us so long. The ratio of irrational to rational thoughts inside her head was about twenty to one. That was her first mistake (there were others). To get from point A to point B, most people take a straight line. Not Eve. She zigzags; takes several steps backward; loops around; launches into deep contemplation at every turn, twist, and fork in the road; circles; hovers; eventually lands. And I could have walked away from the whole mess. I could have said, *Good luck to you, Eve. See you in ten years, when you finally decide what you want.* But I didn't. Because the thing about Eve is, when she does land, she sticks that landing something hard, and suddenly, walking away is the very last thought on your mind.

part one

SPRING 2005

EVE

AN ASYLUM IN MORNINGSIDE HEIGHTS

It was senior year. We were having a party. The theme was trash.

In preparation, we decorated our suite with black garbage bags and blinking Christmas lights. The letters *T-R-A-S-H* hung from the ceiling.

We were all looking to make something happen that night. Each of us felt like something big was *right there*. And it didn't matter how many times we'd been disappointed in the past, how many times we'd dressed up and then fallen into bed hours later, with zero to show for the night but a faint dizziness, an imminent headache, a morning of recovery. We were resilient enough to bounce back. We didn't even have to think about it. As the sun went down, a greater power took hold of us. It pushed us to close books, to shake off the haze from our afternoon naps, to get dressed, plan, send messages out into the ether, and hope, with a little luck, to get a few back.

It was the power of possibility, that feeling of boundless potential that occurs late in the afternoon in New York, when the sun goes down and all the windows in all the buildings look asleep; before darkness rolls over the city like one long sheet and the lights come on. It could terrify me, all that vastness just waiting to be filled. But not that night. That night, I was ready for it. *Lights on, Manhattan!* I thought, clapping my hands together, standing at the window of our suite, as if I alone had the power to bring light to all those tiny square boxes out there. The illusion of control was tempting. *I am not afraid of you*, you had to say to yourself, when you looked out at the city. *I am not fucking scared of you*, you had to say. And you had to really believe it, or you were toast.

I lived with three other girls in a four-bedroom suite in East Campus, a dorm between 117th and 118th Streets that housed most of Columbia's upperclassmen. From the window of our suite, I could see the whole campus, the Hudson River in the distance, the chemical pink clouds descending into the granite dome of Low Library. In our world, Low was the Pantheon, and beyond Low, there were only buildings—mysterious, anonymous buildings. We had a panoramic view of the city that stretched from nearly one wall to the other and yet went largely disregarded. Everything that mattered seemed to happen within the walls of Suite 1603. Every now and then, we did peer out at the rest of the universe. We liked to pretend, sometimes, from our high-up fortress in Morningside Heights, that we were running this town.

I'd invited Jesse Prescott to the party, a guy from my Poetry and Place in the Modern Landscape class with whom I'd been flirting for months. "Happily Ever After." That was the title of the poem that I'd read out loud to him—well, to my entire class, actually. Yes, that's right. I read it *out loud*. To people. With ears. It was still haunting me. Luckily, it wasn't my first time. I'd done this to myself hundreds of times before, over the past few years of writing classes at this establishment. I'd learned to persevere. There are survival mechanisms that kick in, in a situation like that. *I am not afraid of you*, you had to say to yourself, before you started reading. *I am not fucking scared of you.*

I was stunned that he wanted to talk to me afterward, that he *still* wanted to talk to me, even after hearing that overly emotional drivel:

> *And then, she sees everything with a stunningly harsh*
> *   clarity,*
> *the kind of clarity that makes reality seem hopeless,*
> *which makes you wish for an entirely new reality,*
> *something with reliably brighter thoughts.*
> *She wonders if everything in the world is fleeting.*
> *Love fades.*
> *The seduction of expectation crashes.*
> *Reality throws her into a strange, unpossessed place of*
> *   which she has no bearing.*
> *Everything seems as far beyond her grasp as the yellow*
> *   lights,*
> *spinning and dashing behind the man . . .*

"I liked it," he said, when called upon by Professor Rosario to offer his thoughts, and those words were enough to earn him one invitation to our trash party. As a self-protective measure, I told myself countless times that he might not come. Yet somehow, his presence had become critical. In the days before the party, when I thought of it, everything inside me jumped. I looked down at myself, thinking, *How did you get to this place?*

But before anything could happen, he would have to actually

show up that night, to the sixteenth floor of East Campus, a dorm that used to be an insane asylum, and in many ways still was.

- - - -

"It's party time! It's party time! Tell everyone it's party time!" my suitemate Scarlett sang. "I want to meet someone tonight who will *crush me*. And then I want to *break his heart*. And then I want to fight to win him back. And then I want him to break *my* heart. And then I want to burn all his possessions to the ground!"

I laughed. "That's quite an agenda," I said to her as she balanced herself against the wall in our living room with one hand, sliding on black, shiny, five-inch heels with the other. They looked much nobler on her feet than they did in their usual position—cradled in her hands at the end of the night as she stumbled home barefoot.

Farther down the hall, I could hear the sound of a phone beeping. The noise reverberated, echoing deeply throughout the entire suite. Within a few seconds, there was the faint sound of my suitemates discussing it.

"It's from a 917 number."

"Ugh, but the voice mail is only thirty seconds long. It can't be important. He's obviously bailing."

"How do you know?"

"It's only thirty seconds long! What can he say in thirty seconds that isn't him bailing? And why else would he call this late? If he were coming, he would have called earlier. And he wouldn't have left a message."

"Just check it! Just call the number back! Why are you being so negative?"

"I'm going to! I just want to wait a few minutes! I need to think about it. I can't just *call*."

Suite 1603 was a frenzy of emotions. Basically, it was a place for emotions to go on spring break. Like, when they wanted to run wild and really enjoy themselves and not be contained by things like logic and good judgment. Those downers.

And this was especially true before a party. Clothes went flying. Anxieties ran rampant. By the time the first guests arrived, I was somewhat surprised to be still standing.

I heard the sound of my name being called. *"Eve!"* I walked toward it, down the stairs from our living room to a hallway leading to several bedrooms. I went to my suitemate Maya's room, slowly, warily. One never knew, with Maya.

I stood at the doorframe.

"I have a question for you, Evelyn J. Porter, MD, PhD," she said.

I smiled. "Just Eve. No *J*. And *barely* going to graduate with my bachelor's."

"I was trying to make you sound more official. I broke up with Todd," she said, and then, before I had the chance to respond, "Do you think I'm a selfish person?"

I paused before I answered. Maya was the most volatile of my friends. A beautiful Indian girl who wore Converse sneakers and oversize black-rimmed glasses, she was known to ask for advice, all sweetness and soft-spoken, and then explode at you if she didn't like what you said.

"What?" she said. "I really want to know what you think. Give me your most honest opinion." Her big brown eyes appeared to be quivering. She was intimidating, this one-hundred-pound girl sitting in front of me on a purple comforter, next to a framed picture of an ice-cream cone.

"I don't think you're selfish," I said. "Not any more so than anyone else."

"So do you think he'll call?"

"Well, if you broke up with him . . ."

"You don't think he'll call?" she snapped, her eyes zeroing in on me. I stared at her blankly.

"Sorry. I didn't mean . . ." She was turning on me. *Abandon all honesty and placate! PLACATE!*

"I'm sure he'll call in a few days," I amended quickly.

She sighed. "I wish I had a test to study for." She stood up and walked over to her closet. Tests were Maya's version of therapy. She was one of the few people for whom being in the library all night studying provided a profound sense of well-being.

"There will be another test," I said, trying for comforting.

"Maybe I need to just sleep with someone else. . . . The theme for the night *is* trash."

"That's true," I said. "That would be very trashy of you!" Her face lit up. We started to laugh.

"Thank God we didn't pick a theme like *the age of innocence,*" she said. "Can you imagine how hard that would be for us to pull off?"

"We'd still be able to have the party," I said. "We just wouldn't be able to attend."

We knew from experience that when choosing a theme for a party, it was best not to be too specific. We didn't want to get hemmed in by thematic restrictions. Those were for amateurs. We were sophisticated city girls. We knew what we were doing. *We* had bags full of lingerie from the ninety-nine-cent store, this magical place on Amsterdam Avenue where you could buy a year's worth of toilet paper, an assortment of vaguely religious lamps, and clothes perfect for theme parties but likely meant for prostitutes. At the store, we dug into cardboard boxes full of clothing, but it wasn't long before we got distracted by other items and decided that yes, four large potted plants, taller than we were, would be a smart purchase. They would provide *ambiance* for the party. "It'll be like a jungle!" one of the girls insisted. After some searching, I ended up with a black lace dress that was see-through but not totally see-through. So, tasteful. And since it was the classiest of the prostitute costumes, my friends declared, "Park Avenue trash!" That's what I would be.

For the next few hours, my suitemates came to me with fistfuls of necklaces—long strands of fake pearls, fake diamond chokers.

"Why?" I yelled.

"Because you'll under-accessorize otherwise, if we don't help you."

"'Park Avenue trash' is about collecting as much material wealth as possible and putting it into one ensemble. It requires attention to quantifiable possessions."

"You can't just wear a black dress and call it a day."

Our other suitemate, Kate, came into Maya's room and sat down on her bed. "Do I look under-accessorized?" I asked her. I put a few of the necklaces on and held the rest in my hands.

"It looks like a jewelry store threw up on you," she said.

"Thank you."

Kate was half Czech, half Chinese, and somehow managed to possess the prettiest features from both ethnicities. She had skin that was perpetually tan, visible cheekbones, *dimples*. Her eyes and hair were the same shade of perfect chestnut. Kate never bothered to use these occasions to put on a crazy outfit that just so happened to flaunt how pretty she was. She didn't need to. On Halloween, when everyone else wore slutty angel and fairy ensembles, Kate dressed up as the Unabomber.

At eight o'clock, the delivery guy from Hamilton Deli arrived—we could throw a stone from our window and hit Hamilton Deli, but that didn't stop us from ordering—with a crate full of orange juice, tonic water, ginger ale. We set up a "bar" in the corner, which was really just a desk covered in a black garbage bag, with red plastic cups stacked in a tall cylinder, bottles of tequila and gin, a half-gone bottle of vodka from our freezer, and the mixers from the deli. We placed the four plants we'd bought from the ninety-nine-cent store in the corners of the room and lit them up with the Christmas lights. When we were finished, we looked around.

"It looks *so* cracked out!" Maya said, giddy. In our suite, that was about the best thing you could say—that something was *cracked out*. It was most commonly applied to moments that combined alcohol, drugs, and nonsensical actions. For example, when, after a big night out, someone went on an instant-soup shopping spree at Duane Reade, or painted the bathroom doors, or started spraying people with a fire hose. "He was *so* cracked out!" we'd say, relishing the moment. *College!* We embraced it.

I made my first drink of the night and sat with Kate on my bed as our suitemates ran through the room in various outfits, occasionally stopping to ask things like: "Do you think Xanax and alcohol is a bad idea or a bad idea in a good way?" One of us would inevitably say no to something, but we didn't try very hard. We knew that nothing we said made any difference.

Suddenly, Maya burst in, looking like she had just received the best news of her life. Scarlett was standing behind her. I thought she was about to tell us she'd been accepted to med school, but instead, she said, "Scarlett found a plastic bag full of white powder in the back of a taxi!"

We looked at her, confused.

"What should we do about it?" she said, her arms stretched out to us, her palms turned up toward the ceiling.

"Let's snort it!" Scarlett shrieked.

"Are you insane?" Kate replied. "It could be anything! It could be *laundry detergent*."

"It won't kill us."

"Actually, it could kill us," Kate said.

It wasn't what you'd expect from two girls who were pre-med. Maya wanted to be a surgeon, often citing her prowess at fixing a stuck zipper five minutes before a party as proof of her qualification. Scarlett wanted to be an emergency room doctor, because being a surgeon required choosing one area of the body to work on and she wanted to be able to fix any problem at any time, rather than be so specialized. Needless to say, it behooved everyone to talk to each one, separately, regarding her medical aspirations. Kate, the constant voice of reason, was applying to work in finance but only the type of finance that required traveling regularly to Buenos Aires, which made her sound like a floozy until she started firing off facts about the South American markets.

By eleven, we were dressed to kill, amped up on either cocaine or laundry detergent, and looking around at an empty suite. Scarlett, wearing what appeared to be a one-piece bathing suit from the fifties and giant heels, went out to walk the halls.

"Are you guys coming to our party?" she said to the guys on our floor, who received this question silently but then followed her back to our suite, as if possessed. With our new friends in tow, my suitemates insisted on shots. I finished the first easily and then started on the second, after which I immediately felt the rush of alcohol hitting my bloodstream. By the third, I felt sick. *They were going by too fast.* I already needed a break, but still I was lifting the glass from the kitchen table, watching the shots go by. It wasn't so bad. *People did this all the time!*

"Is that guy from your writing class coming tonight?" Maya asked. "What's the deal with you guys anyway?"

"No deal," I said. I pushed away my shot glass, until it was removed from sight. Maya handed me a wedge of lime and I sunk my teeth into it. "We walk together after class."

"You *walk* together?"

Sadly, that was the most accurate description I could muster. We walked from class to the pizza place, from class to Duane Reade. I'll admit that I invented scenarios to throw us together, but so did he. We basically took each other on errands. At one point, I accompanied him to the computer lab so that I could watch him send an e-mail. Our conversations drew all my attention. I only wanted the walks to be longer. The campus was designed so that anything you needed was within a few blocks, which was doing me a great disservice. I stood at the counter of Duane Reade and talked to him about Reese's Pieces versus M&M's, but could only do it for so long. I was fixated on making him like me, but it was also clear that I was succeeding, and without much effort. Each time, just before we were supposed to part ways, one of us would come up with a reason to continue walking. He'd touch my wrist as we stood on the partition between the two parts of Broadway. "I think I need a coffee," he'd say, after he'd slowed to a stop and smiled. "Oh, of course," I'd say, relieved. "I could use one too." And then we'd start walking again, each of us pretending not to understand what the other was doing.

"So you *walk* together? That's it?" she questioned, still at a loss.

I was about to respond, but Kate waved Maya's incredulity off. "Don't listen to her," she said. "They're in love."

I laughed. "How is it that we're *in love?*"

"Okay, so," she said, preparing for a recitation of the facts. "They make goofy expressions at each other in class. The guy comes up to her when class is over and makes up some ridiculous excuse to hang out like, 'Uhhh, uhhh, my roommate and I ran out of Skittles yesterday so do you want to, uhhh, go to CVS with me and then um help me carry the bag back to my room?'"

"Well, this is exciting!" Maya said.

"It's nothing," I told her. "And there are a few potential problems."

"Yes." Kate stood up straighter and took on a serious, professor-like tone. "From his poems, we have discerned that he may be mentally unstable, but he's a musician, so that's probably standard."

I had told Kate about the song lyrics he recited in class, about a poem that he wrote entitled "O Captain! My Captain!" "The title alone," I'd said to her admiringly. The fact that it had been used before didn't ruin it for me in the slightest. From what I could decipher, it was about someone laboring under pressure to move his life in a certain direction. Graduation was looming, two months away. The real world was no place for an aspiring musician. I read between the lines, as our writing class wore collective looks of concern. At first, he seemed to be explaining what it would feel like to catch yourself on fire while wearing a perfectly tailored suit. Then, there was something about going home for Thanksgiving and getting buried alive by his parents and a psychotic dog. So there were some red flags. But, of course, instead of getting scared off like a normal person, I found him insightful. Okay, *intriguing*, at the very least. I sat there, mesmerized, interested in his words, and *what it all meant.*

"A mentally unstable musician? That is *so* your type!" Maya said optimistically. "He fits in perfectly with your history."

It seemed to amuse my friends that I had this whole other circle that they were not allowed to be a part of, and it was true, I suppose, that when I hung out with people from my writing classes, I didn't want them to come along. They would refer to them as "artsy," and maybe they were, but they were also just glamorous to me, pursuing things that were almost impossible to carry on after college, in the real world. These people stayed up late to work on projects with no specific purpose other than that they loved to do it, and how could they possibly not? It was foreign to me. I grew up in the Bronx with a father who installed windows for a living and a mother who forbade me from watching the Muppets as a child because they were, in her opinion, a bunch of troublemakers.

In college, I was this walking, talking well of feelings. All you had to do was press gently, and there was a tenderness inside of me, a prickly feeling. *Just press slightly*, and everything would come spilling out uncontrollably. There were no parameters, no telling what I might write or say, or how long I might be feeling it. Writing classes were both this wonderful and dangerous opportunity for me to tap into that place, to be a ball of emotions without judgment. Okay, with *some* judgment. But it wasn't like the people around me were saying, "Don't have feelings." *God knows*, they had feelings. They were mostly saying things like "Could you have feelings but in a less confusing, more narrative-driven, punchier-dialogue type of way?"

"He does fit in perfectly!" Kate agreed with Maya. "Let's see . . . there was the playwright with the high school sweetheart down in Florida."

"I just thought that he should see other things!" I yelled. "Plus, I didn't know his girlfriend in Florida was a *cheerleader*. I would have given up more easily. I can't fight that."

"And then there was the photographer who was addicted to cocaine," Maya added.

"Only on the weekends!"

Kate rolled her eyes. "Then there was that reclusive drummer guy who lived on our floor freshman year and never left his room and wore exclusively white T-shirts with holes in them. He was very sexy though. I'll give you that. Ugh, *those T-shirts*. Remember when he got drunk and ripped his door out of its socket and replaced it with caution tape?"

"At least he was being honest!"

"What we're saying is that this particular guy fits right in. You've never dated someone normal."

I glared at them. "What is normal?"

"Ugh, you sound just like them," Kate said.

"You know what's funny about Eve?" Maya turned to Kate and spoke as if I weren't in the room. "If you saw her walking down the street, you'd think, *Totally normal person*—wouldn't you?"

"Totally." Kate nodded profusely.

"*Maybe* you'd be like, *Oh, she's pretty!* But that's about it. She's got her straight brown hair, she's average height, those little turquoise earrings. . . . But then she puts on the slightest bit of eyeliner and starts talking about her feelings. . . . And it's like, oh, she's a freak."

"*A freak?*" I exclaimed.

"And that's why you like them."

"Like *who?*"

"The other freaks," Kate clarified. I put my hands on my hips and made a drawn-out huffing noise. They laughed. *Yes, come one, come all, to see the girl with the sad parental situation and the stepfather who bought us a lava lamp and an* Animal House *poster to increase the "cool" factor in our suite.*

"But! You also look normal and wear normal clothes and like to eat frozen yogurt and watch *Project Runway*, which is why you're friends with us."

"*Used to be* friends with you," I added.

Maya's eyes widened. "So is it going to be one of those situations where you go to see his band and he stares at you as he's playing and then you have this moment where you realize that *Oh my god, this song is about me?* And then you go to see him after the show and there are all these bitches everywhere vying for his attention but you're like, *Move over, ladies, that shit was about me.*"

I started to laugh. "You are about one romantic comedy away from losing your fucking mind."

"Answer the question!" she said, like a judge on daytime television.

"We haven't been on a single date yet, so I can't foresee that situation at the moment . . . but the night is young." I smiled.

Once we stopped staring at the door, people began showing up, funneling in by twos and threes, like very strangely dressed moths to a flame. One of us made sure to always be behind the bar, doling out drinks with a minimum level of concentration. Everyone who entered appeared to be in a daze—as they took in the plants, the blinking lights, the trash bags. They entered into a suite that looked like a cross between a really fun jungle and a dark alleyway filled with garbage.

After the first round of cocktails and conversation permeated the crowd, people started to sway to the music, obligingly at first, then with more dedication. My job was to arrange the playlist for the night. I had decided on all jungle-related songs, because of the potted plants we'd purchased, but once I got through "Welcome to the Jungle" and "Jungle Love," my options became more limited than anticipated. So I purchased a few songs from an album called *Sounds of the Jungle*. Birds chirping. Rain trickling. Crickets. It was either going to go over very well at this party or very badly. Time would tell.

My suitemates and I got together for another shot, excluding all others. This was the party within the party, and it was just for us.

"To bad decisions!" Maya cried, and then the clinking of glasses.

I pretended not to look for Jesse, but I did. My spirits began to drop as I met people I'd met a thousand times before. I started to get nervous that this would be like every other night—no new arrivals, the same faces and voices we'd been socializing with for years, but in weird clothes. I pictured myself hours earlier—putting on the black lace dress, a furtive glance in the mirror, my insides bubbling away. Right then, I was asking for trouble. *It happens the same way every time. Why do you do this to yourself?*

As the party went on, I noticed myself sinking into a sadness that wasn't comfortable. Some guy wearing a T-shirt with a piece of masking tape attached to it knocked into me and spilled my drink. Worse than the vodka pooling around my ankles was that I would have to talk to him.

"Hey," he said. "Sorry about that."

"It's okay," I said, irrationally annoyed. "Nice to meet you."

"Actually, we've met," he said. "I'm Ben. Julian's roommate."

"Oh yeah." I nodded, pretending to have just come to the realization. I stared at the words on his chest, TACOMA NARROWS BRIDGE, written on masking tape with a Sharpie. He was tall with light features, fair skin, almost but not quite blond hair.

He looked down at them, following my eyes. "It's a bridge

that collapsed . . . so it's trash," he said, looking for my approval. "I'm in the engineering school," he said, by way of explanation. "I don't know. I tried." He shrugged. "I've actually been to all your parties."

"Really? Cool." *It wasn't cool. It was the least cool thing I'd heard all night. And was I supposed to laugh at that bridge joke?*

"They're always fun. What was the one . . . with all the red martinis?"

I looked at him like I wasn't sure, even though I was.

"Valentine's Day!" he said.

"Yup."

"And you guys served only red drinks, right?"

"Yeah." I nodded slowly. "We did."

It wasn't that there was anything wrong with this guy. It was just that he was yet another acquaintance I'd been bumping into for years—outside the library, by the elevators, in Hamilton Deli—hello, good-bye, *should I keep walking or do I have to stop this time?* I wanted something more that night. My hostility was zeroing in on this awkward social obligation obstacle. *Where was Jesse?*

"Okay, well, I'm going to go get another drink," I said. Another drink. That was always a decent exit strategy. Not good per se, because everyone knew what you were doing, but decent. I turned away and went to the kitchen, where my friends were drunk and talking in low voices. I pretended to listen. I would deny this vehemently to anyone who asked, but I was agonizingly aware of every person who was in my vicinity. I was staring at the door, lingering in conversations without looking directly at the person I was talking to.

There was no question that I would know it, the second he walked in. And when he finally did, I spotted him before I even knew what I was looking at. We made eye contact across the room, exchanged smiles. He dodged bodies left and right. Relief was coursing through me as he got closer.

"You came," I said, trying not to sound surprised.

"Of course!" he replied.

I explained my outfit, that "trash" was the theme, as if he couldn't see that on his own, and then told him that this would not be my personal choice, under other circumstances. All intelligent thoughts had spilled out of my brain at this point.

"You look good," he said. "You should wear that to class." He smiled and pushed his dark, almost black hair out of his green eyes. His hair was messy, stood up in places, and flopped down across his forehead. He wasn't wearing the glasses that he wore in class.

"Um . . ." I laughed.

We talked a bit about the other kids in our class. He kept remembering lines from their poems, and every few minutes he would bring up something else, in amused disbelief. I stopped craning my neck toward the door and looked up at him, stood closer, laughed at everything he said, my eyes bright. I asked him questions, touched his arm whenever he said something funny. I was being *fun*!

At some point, Maya came over and required my attention. Jesse and I lost each other in the crowd. I went to the kitchen with Maya and attempted to defuse whatever was bothering her. She showed me an empty bottle of freezer-burned vodka, a hysterical look on her face. We searched the kitchen until we found espresso vodka that somebody must have brought. It was in a pyramid-shaped bottle and lit up neon green when we picked it up from the counter. We lifted it and put it back down several times, thrilled by our finding. "The enchanted vodka bottle!" we decided to call it, for marketing purposes. We started pouring it directly into people's mouths. It was too exquisite for a glass, we told them, too prized to spare a drop. As soon as I had some myself, I became hyper immediately, laughing and smiling so widely that I felt it in my eyes. I had an insatiable need to socialize, and started babbling to strangers about their outfits, the party decor, a weird thing that happened to me in a dream once.

I kept checking on Jesse, spotting him in various positions across the room. At one point, I saw him standing a few feet away from a blond girl who had her hair tied back in a loose ponytail. He looked over at her a few times, briefly, discreetly. She noticed him as well, appeared all smiles, nodding at him and laughing with her friends. She was wearing a black halter top that she'd fashioned out of a garbage bag. *Pretty and resourceful! Damn it, the cards were stacked against me.* It was cropped and tied together with a string at the neck. I examined her face, as if trying to make sense of it. She was looking at her friends, but also somehow at Jesse. Then, she turned. They knew each other. I watched him lightly grab the back of her neck and cup his hand right around the spot beneath her ponytail. He mouthed something at her that I couldn't decipher. She whispered in his ear. There was some kind of understanding exchanged, though I had no way of knowing. *Oh, so there were others. Of course there were others.* This party was rife with options. Girls were there for him, for whatever reason.

I kept shuffling things around in the kitchen, pretending to be very busy—more booze, back and forth to the freezer, moving a stack of cups, tossing a bag of chips. I talked to Maya. Minutes later, out of the corner of my eye, I spotted him with another girl—this one not trying to hide it. Her face lit up as he touched her hoop earring, ran his finger along the large gold circle. She was emitting a glow that conventional wisdom would lead any-one to believe she was the happiest person in history. She flicked her wrist against his stomach, sipped from her plastic cup, and looked at the ground with a kind of intensity. My eyes darted back to him again. *I like this man very much.* He was even better than before, as he put his hand on her arm and smiled. *No danger with this one, of him wanting to form—to begin forming—some future "how we met" story. Just specifically for this night, he is perfect, all things considered.*

Eventually, I could sense Jesse staring at me from across the room. *What is happening? Is it my turn?* He whispered into the ear of the guy next to him, and something about the way his eyes stayed locked on me as he talked gave me the distinct feeling that he was talking about me. I had a sudden idea. The guy next to him was a friend of Kate's. I made my way through the crowd until I located her.

"Can you go find out what Jesse just said?" I said to her, my voice unusually loud.

"Right now?" she replied, carelessly.

"Yes! Right now."

The second that Jesse and his friend separated, I hustled Kate along. I stood away, allowed her to do the talking. After they were done whispering, she looked at me and then grabbed my arm. We walked to the other side of the room.

"He said, and I quote, 'See that chick? I want to suck her brains out.'" She wrinkled her nose, as if grossed out by the words as she said them.

"What?" I said, stunned.

"He wants to suck your brains out."

"You mean 'fuck'?"

"Huh?"

"'Fuck' would make more sense. Less zombielike."

"Oh," she said. "Yeah. Fuck. Probably."

The whole party seemed to come to a pause. At that moment, all my ideas, all the games that I had played with myself about how this night might go, promptly went to shit. I turned serious, all of a sudden. "He said that?"

She nodded, disinterested. I had the wrong audience. While Kate was good for a down-to-earth assessment, my other friends were better for blindingly supporting something for no sensible reason.

"Are you sure?" I said.

"Yes," she said, irritated. "I thought you said he was a poetry major."

I smiled. "That *is* poetry."

I was in that state of intoxication where you become very direct, very to the point. You tell people how you feel. You grab things that you want. There was more dancing now, a crowd in the middle of the room, circles of girls leaning into one another closely, bursts of male laugher. As I made my way across the room, I could feel something rising higher in my throat, making me tremble a little. I met Jesse's gaze as I walked toward him. It was one of those rare moments of understanding. Eventually, I'd feel tightness inside of me, an abrupt rigidity, an inability to move further. But for now, I could enjoy myself.

"Can I see your room?" he said to me as soon as I was within shouting distance.

"Absolutely," I replied, and then slipped in front of him. I walked toward the staircase that went down to our bedrooms, knowing that he was following me.

My bedroom was a menacing shade of dark red, the result of a painting expedition with my suitemates in which we painted all the rooms different colors, each more brutal than the next, not providing for the fact of hangovers. I often thought of repainting it in the middle of the night, like I couldn't sleep there a single second longer. I lay in bed thinking about whether red walls were enough of a reason to have a nervous breakdown. I fell back asleep trying to decide. I didn't decorate the room otherwise. Room decor in college was all about what you hung on the walls, and I could never find the right poster to attach to my identity. At the store, faced with five to ten images—a girl with an umbrella, the Brooklyn Bridge, Central Park in the fall—I crumbled under the pressure. Instead, I relied on the bed being the centerpiece, my white sheets with tiny pink hearts on them. The sheets were for me to look at, in case I ever felt like I was living in hard times.

In our house growing up, my mother bought cheap furniture and spent her allotted money on soft sheets. She insisted that all that mattered was having a nice bed. Each year in college, as I went about setting up my dorm room, I imagined her walking into my new room, looking around at the bare, paint-chipped walls, the cold floors, and that dreaded blue mattress, the tag wrinkled and the stuffing jutting out in places. She'd cheerily insist, "Let's make up the bed!" She'd unpack freshly ironed lavender and pale green sheets, and by the time she'd finished fluffing the last pillow, things would be looking up.

Jesse walked around my room, examining everything. Meanwhile, I was sitting on my bed, trying to gather myself. I was feeling my heart beat, a prickly sensation on my skin, the bitter taste in my mouth. It was the result of having him in my room, plus whatever espresso vodka could do to a person. He leaned over my desk, scribbled something on a piece of paper. He took the paper and taped it to the wall above my bed. I looked up. It had the words WALDEN POND on it.

"Walden Pond?" I asked.

"It's a joke," he said.

"A very English major–y joke."

"You don't get it?"

"I hate to admit this, but I've never actually read *Walden*."

He gave me a surprised look.

"What? Is that bad?" I cringed.

"Kind of! It's a classic. It's about simplicity. Blank walls. You're a very straightforward person. I like that about you."

"*Excuse me*," I yelled, jamming my fists into the bed. "I am *complex*."

"Mmmm-hmmm," he said, looking me up and down. "These walls are very blank for someone who wants to write about music. Where is your Rolling Stones poster?"

I should have said: *I want to write about music not because of any one band or song but because music* transformed *situations and people and molecules inside of you.* Instead, there was a brief silence and I said nothing.

"Thanks for coming to my party!" I said finally, with an enthusiasm that wasn't natural. *Thanks for coming to my party? What are you, eleven?*

He looked at me curiously. "I was happy to come."

More quiet filled the room, as he continued to look around.

"Nice hat," Jesse said, pointing to the green-and-pink shower cap that lay on top of my bookshelf. I got off the bed to grab it, but he snatched it before I could, examining it with firm concentration. I sat back down, defeated. My friends had been trying to get rid of that shower cap for years, often sneaking into my room and hiding it under tissue paper in a bag they knew I intended to throw away. It was impossible to hide anything around here.

"It's cool, it's cool," he said. "Very Martha Washington."

"Thank you very much," I said, with a smile. "That's just what I was going for."

"Can I confess something?" he asked.

"Okay . . . ," I said, a caution in my voice. I stared at the square of carpet between my feet, which appeared to be moving. My eyes were playing tricks on me. The thread of the carpet was like quicksand, sinking further and further down into a single point. *It happens the same way every time. Just for the night? It's never that simple. This could really end badly. This could really end very badly. Why are you setting yourself up? What are you even doing here? Why did you invite him? So that you could sit here and let someone disappoint you? Good job! Go ahead! By all means! Get all excited and then* thud. *It'll be over.*

"I really like having class with you," he said.

"You do?" I looked up at him.

"Yes," he said, laughing. "Why? Is that surprising? You look like I just told you that your dog died."

"I don't know!" I said quickly.

He reached for my hand and pulled me up. I stood next to him as he wrapped his arm around my waist and turned toward my bookshelf. He asked if I wanted to read something with him. I stood there for a few seconds.

"I think I'm going to be sick," I said meekly, stepping away from him and covering my mouth with my hand.

"From the alcohol?"

"No," I said, shaking my head. "From that suggestion."

I stared at the bookshelf and started to smile. I *had* him. He laughed.

"You're such a nerd," he said.

"I'm a nerd? You're the one making *Walden* references and suggesting that we read together."

"It was a romantic gesture."

"I don't like romantic gestures, typically."

"Oh, please. Yes you do," he said, rolling his eyes. "Don't tell me you're some sort of exception. I won't buy it for a second."

"I don't. I really don't."

He immediately lifted me off the floor and then placed me down onto the bed, his body hovering on top of mine, his face inches away. He was waiting for me to look at him. I knew that, but I don't give in easily. So I darted my eyes everywhere but up. *I will not look. I will not look.* I looked. He leaned down and kissed me. *Gone.* My head was spinning. The room was shifting out of focus.

There was a loud knock at the door.

"You guys!" I heard Kate yell and Maya laugh. Then, I tilted my head back and saw Kate's hand reach across the doorframe and turn off the lights. She slammed the door closed and held it shut.

"We'll leave you alone once we hear the sound of you guys *fucking!*" she yelled.

"Your friends are out of control," he said.

Neither of us went to turn on the lights, and for a few minutes, we kissed in the dark. Then he got up, and I heard him walking toward the door. *Is he trying to open it? Is he leaving?* He locked it.

The sound of the lock prompted something within me. I sat up, shifted my dress so that it went farther down my legs. He came over to me and I tried to settle down. He began removing the necklaces I was wearing, one by one. I could feel his fingertips against my neck. When he was finished, his arms tightened around me.

"What is this thing that you're wearing?"

"I thought you liked it."

"It's not very you," he said.

"Thank God," I said, smiling. "I need a break from that girl."

I saw him reach into his pocket, the flash of his phone next to me. Then, suddenly, the light came closer to my dress.

"What are you doing?" I said. He groaned.

"Nothing," he replied, and then the light disappeared. "Shit. I have to go."

"What?" I immediately thought of repeating the news to my suitemates, with a gust of emotion. *He just* left!

"I have something that I have to do," he said.

"Okay . . ."

"Don't get insulted. Let's just say I make deliveries, but it's the type of thing where when someone wants what I have to offer, I have to be available to bring it to them, at all hours, even if I'd rather be . . . doing something else."

"Do you mean . . . What do you . . . How did you . . . What?"

"Pick a question, darlin'."

I managed to spit one out. I had a feeling he was talking about drugs and the distribution thereof, but I couldn't bring myself to ask. I didn't want confirmation, so I talked around the subject. "How did you get into this?"

"Craigslist."

"Really?"

"No." He laughed.

"Oh."

"Same reason I work at the library. I need the money. I'm a poor kid from Nebraska and I'm about to become an even poorer struggling musician. Whatever. Boring story. You've heard it all before. I'm sure you can figure it out."

Oh, how he overestimated me. I hadn't the foggiest clue what he was talking about. I watched him get ready to leave and then stood at the doorframe with him, prepared to say good-bye. I pictured myself rejoining the party upstairs until everyone left, coming back downstairs and peeling off my dress, going back upstairs and eating a bowl of cereal to sober up. But then, we started kissing again. He broke away. "*Where am I going?*" he said.

"I don't know."

"I don't want to leave you," he said. "Can I interest you in a walk across campus?"

I smiled. "Is this another one of your romantic gestures?"

"Definitely not."

"Okay, then I'll go. But if you say one thing about the moonlight, I'm leaving."

"Deal."

The night started to go by quickly after that. I remember asking him to pick out a coat for me because I couldn't go outside in just my dress. "Which one of these coats looks like it's ready for a night on the town?" I said.

"You have a personification problem," he replied. "But probably this one."

I ended up in the hallway, carrying my polka-dotted raincoat. We were upstairs, telling my suitemates that we'd be right back. On my way out the door, I looked back over my shoulder and saw Maya in the corner of the room, moping. "Give me a second," I said to Jesse. I went to her.

"What's wrong?" I asked.

"I'm sad about Todd," she said to me, turning her bottom lip over.

"Okay. You need to get your mind off this. Just hook up with someone else," I said, in my infinite wisdom. "How about that guy?"

"Which guy?"

"That one." I pointed to the guy with the bridge name on his T-shirt, the one who I'd seen at a hundred other parties and whose presence had irritated me earlier. He now seemed utterly harmless. In fact, I was feeling magnanimous—I was about to do this guy a favor.

"Why him?"

"Because he's cute, and who cares?" I gave her a long look.

"Okay, fine," she said. I grabbed her by the arm and dragged her over to him, made a quick introduction, and then fled, leaving the two of them midsentence.

- - - -

Once outside, with the fresh air blowing in my face, I felt like I could breathe again. I wasn't totally aware of where we were going, but I didn't care. When we got to the steps of Low Library, they were empty. Everyone was at the bars on Broadway. We had the whole place to ourselves. I flew down the steps, going faster and faster. Whenever my suitemates and I crossed campus at night, we always ran down the steps of Low as fast as we could, our hearts pumping with adrenaline and alcohol.

I stopped at the bottom of the stairs. Jesse held my hand as my body sprang forward, almost falling, laughing. He yanked me back to standing. "You're a mess," he said, shaking his head. When we got to the cobblestone path that bisected the campus, he dropped my hand.

"I love this campus at night," he said, looking around. "Without all the people."

At night, the campus did have an adventurous, romantic feel to it. It was just the northern edge of Manhattan, but it felt like a modern-day Athens. This enclave of lofty institutions—a theological seminary, a music college, the Cathedral Church of Saint John the Divine, Grant's Tomb—and Columbia was the center point, an elevated plateau.

"What's wrong with all the people?" I said.

"Everything." He shuddered.

"What's everything?"

"Don't you see how people walk around here? Like they're in the darkest state of their lives, like they're so terribly burdened?"

"I guess."

"And I'm just here to help them have a good time."

I didn't say anything in response. All I could think was: he sure doesn't *look* like a drug dealer, with his preppy clothes, tortoise-rimmed glasses and button-down shirts. There was innocence to Jesse, to the way he raised his eyebrows in class whenever somebody said something of interest to him, the way he ordered a scone at the coffee shop and then looked at it curiously and said, "Call this a scone all you want, it seems very muffin-like to me." But then there was this.

"Hey," he said, with restraint in his voice. "Can I ask you a question?" He touched my wrist, and we stopped walking.

"Okay . . ."

"That poem you wrote? Was that about your mother?" His eyes were looking so acutely into mine that I almost felt like I didn't have to say anything.

Almost.

He knew. Of course he knew. Who was I kidding? It happened senior year of high school, but everyone here knew. I was the girl whose mother died on September Eleventh. Most people didn't bring it up directly. Most people simply assumed that I'd rather not talk about it, that I was okay with being silently de-

serving of their kindness and left it at that. They didn't want to get into it. They treated me like a bomb that might explode at any moment. It was too sad, too impossible to confront fully, so why mention it at all?

"My mother died when I was ten," he said. "That's why I'm asking. I know it's none of my business, but . . . I guess I'm always looking for someone to talk about it with, as lame as that is." He started walking again, vaguely shaking his head at the ground.

I stood there for a few seconds and then ran to catch up to him. I grabbed hold of his hand. He sort of smiled, but there was weight to his expression, an understanding. I felt a thrilling sensation in my chest. There is something so damn attractive to me about someone who has been in pain. It makes that person seem strong and capable of handling all the shit that life can throw at you. When my sympathy kicks in, so does my fantasy that I and I alone can take care of and repair this person. Somehow, I feel uniquely qualified to do this. Other girls don't know. They don't understand. *I* know. *I* get it. I want someone who's been tossed around a bit, who has made mistakes and paid the consequences. They just seem more qualified for the job. Basically, I have no desire to be the first thing that messes up someone's life. Give me someone who has suffered, like really suffered, and then it'll be easy for them to deal with me. They'll say "*Her?* Oh, dating her is nothing, compared to a funeral."

We kept walking. All that could be heard was the gentle sound of running water from two fountains on the steps of the library. No noise from the rest of the city was permitted to creep in. The only light was emanating from lampposts dotting the campus. They lit up the columns in front of every austere building, the flagpole with its pale blue banner waving.

The wind picked up. We were leaning against each other for

support. I was feeling like something significant was about to happen, or maybe I'd walk back to my suite alone, stop and get pizza along the way. Anything was possible.

We passed a sculpture of Alexander Hamilton, the facade of the library, with its arcade of columns, the names of writers and philosophers etched onto it—Homer, Sophocles, Plato, Aristotle, Virgil, Shakespeare, Milton, Voltaire. In the silhouette of famous names, collegiate life had its own traditions, oddities, mischief. Yes, along with the greatest thinkers of history, there I was. In the middle of a drug deal. Maybe.

"So you don't like anyone here on this whole campus, huh?" I said, giving him a light shove. He fell dramatically to the side.

"I like you," Jesse said, and then turned to me. "Clearly."

"You're only saying that because you want to sleep with me."

"That is one hundred percent my motivation in saying that." I couldn't tell if he was being sincere.

"I knew it!"

"Get out of here."

"I wish I could."

"I bet you do," he said. "*Hey*, the musician and the music writer. That's pretty cute, huh?"

There was a lot of nonsense flying around. We walked until we got to 114th Street, a tree-lined row of town houses. I could see taxis shooting up and down Broadway, the backbone of the area—where bars, dusty stationery stores, understocked pharmacies, upscale and dilapidated eateries lined up next to one another, where books and cheap prints were sold on the street along with socks and electronic gadgets ten years past their prime.

I could see a group of people lighting cigarettes outside a dorm on the corner. They were sitting on the sidewalk, but I could hear laughter and see the shadow of their forms. Morningside Heights was an assortment of oddballs—a middle-aged man with newspapers in his pockets, an older lady with a brush stuck midway through her hair. You had to be nice to these people, despite their quirks, because it was nearly impossible to distinguish the run-of-the-mill eccentric who lived in the neighborhood from the—surprise!—it's your philosophy professor.

"Wait here," he said, standing in front of one of the town houses. He put his hands on my shoulders. "Don't move from right here, okay?"

I nodded.

I watched as he ascended the stairs. When he got to the top, he stopped and looked back at me from the arched doorway. He rolled his eyes. *Go!* I mouthed. *Hurry up!* The house was dark, save for the three windows on the third floor, which were lit up. I tried to get into the moment. It was exciting! It was dangerous! I was the lookout!

But I was scared. To calm down, I told myself, *You can always walk away.* But then, what would happen if he got caught? I imagined going to class on Monday without him there and had an intense reaction to that notion, like I'd be alone, without a friend in the world.

I walked up to the house, examined the plaque next to the door: SIGMA DELTA TAU. I peered in the window, but there was nothing to see but an empty gray garbage can. On the street behind me, a guy walked by, on the phone. His voice was loud, but then disappeared as he continued on down the street. All I heard was "She was so fucking wasted that she . . ."

As I stood there, I watched the wind rearrange a stack of empty pizza boxes and shuffle along a copy of *Herodotus* with the cover ripped off. I didn't know what was going on up there. I could have said, in a jokey manner, "So what are we delivering? Pot? Coke? LSD?" But I didn't. I guess I still wanted the whole thing to exist in vague, amorphous terms. I was already mentally cutting this part of my evening from the picture, stitching together the party scene with whatever would happen between us after he came down those stairs.

Twenty minutes went by. I kept waiting, getting increasingly agitated. A car passed and someone popped their head out of the window and yelled something at me, and I was so startled that it might be the police that I almost threw up. I started to tie up my hair and almost went to lean over the garbage can on the corner. Suddenly, I stood up straight. A bad feeling crept over me. All the fear and alcohol in my system was affecting me, catching up to me now that he was no longer there to distract me from it. I looked up at the windows on the third floor, reassuring myself with the idea that Jesse was watching me. But the longer I stood there, the more I started to panic. I felt like I was falling. I took as much breath into my lungs as I could and exhaled. The square of sidewalk that I stood on no longer felt secure. The world was starting to spin and slip away. I looked around, scanning for something, anything, to ground me. I looked up at the windows, but I could see nothing.

It happens the same way every time. You obsess and fixate over it, but then you realize that you have to let go eventually, so why not now? It's time to let it go. Invite him to the party, be cool about it, what's the worst that can happen? You get hurt. That's the worst. What's the big deal? Plus, there are a lot of worse things out there. Think about all those things. Feel better about yourself. Be a little bit tougher than you really are. Confidence breeds confidence. Believe in yourself. Release it!

You let it go. Of course you let it go. It takes guts, but you have guts. You tell him you'll be his girlfriend; you say "I love you too"; you invite him to the party. You breathe. You walk away. You're tempted to analyze his response, but no, that will only make things worse. Keep walking. Make a clean break. It's too late now anyway. You commence waiting for the results, waiting to make some progress. You've done the hard part, and now he determines whether you get to move forward. It's entirely out of your control. Relax, people say. There's nothing more you can do.

This is wrong. There is something more that you can do. There is something more that you will do. You will worry. It's something you're familiar with, from life. It's not like, Oh, worrying? What is that? Is that what I'm doing right now? I'm not familiar. *No, you've done this before. It's something of a side profession for you.*

At first, there is this feeling of vulnerability. You want to take it back, to crawl into a hiding spot, to hug yourself into a tight enough ball that it disappears. But then you settle into it, you adjust, you decide, I'm the type of person who can do this. I've moved on. I'm not some damaged girl. My father left and my mother died, so I'll always be fucked-up about relationships? No thank you. I'm the type of person who moves on. I'm the type of person who is out there. *And once you settle into it, it's kind of like a drug. You think,* What else can I do? What else might he want to know? I bet he'd be interested in this or that story. *You tell the stories to yourself first, correct the grammar, improve the dialogue, save it all for use at a later date. The high has kind of a manic quality to it. It's as if your mind might spin away from you. Your imagination is running faster than you can keep up with. So you start to get cautious. You realize you're paving the way for disappointment. You think that if things go too well, you will cross the street and get hit by a truck. To keep your head down, you change gears; you start anticipating the worst, which puts you in a somewhat gloomy state. But it's a relief, really. What were you doing before? You have to protect yourself! But then after a while, you realize that you're too down. You can only keep up this doomsday approach for so long. You meander back into cautious optimism because you have no control anyway, so what's the point of feeling bad all the time?*

Eventually, the ball drops. He wasn't what you thought he was. And the fact that the ball drops is kind of hilarious to you. Well, not the fact itself. What's hilarious is that you thought that it wouldn't. You actually threw that thing up into the air and expected it to stay there, or maybe come down a little, but certainly it would not thud on the floor. No. Never. For the ball to drop would so fly in the face of the fundamentals of physics. HA.

And then, it is as if someone took all those exciting moments and flipped them around. The same ache that had you soaring now has you in despair. There's a fair amount of tears, body hunched over and shaking, head in hands, palms pressed hard against your forehead tears. It's all coming back to you in short, gasping breaths, the kind that pushes your insides further in, that turns your inhales into short puffs. Every single time you have felt good about this in recent memory is coming back to you, and you feel the reverse side of it. The exact amount of pleasure is now pain. But it's worse now because the pleasure was spread out over time, thinly distributed, whereas the pain is happening all at once, crashing down on you like a heavy rainstorm. You're choking on the words that you told yourself, those ridiculous words that you told yourself, how you said, Keep going, you're doing so well! You're finally over it! *It's all turned to poison. It's rotting before your eyes, and there is absolutely no way to reverse it. That's how final and penetrating the damage is going to be. Attempting to reverse it doesn't even occur to you.*

I looked up at the town house. The lights on the third floor clicked off. I waited for several minutes but heard nothing.

Where is he? Will he be okay?

Will I?

Anything was possible.

part two

FALL 2007

EVE

- - - - -

FEAR AND LOATHING ON THE LOWER EAST SIDE

He wasn't picking up his phone, so I decided to risk it. Taking the subway to his place had become a ritual, and Jesse, of all people, would understand that some habits are hard to break. I had an *addiction*, I'd say, if he ever questioned it. It was just too damn easy to go to his place, to get on the roller coaster, to throw my hands up and close my eyes and *whoosh*, let it take me.

There were no cars, few people. I allowed the glow of the street lamps to guide me. From the Second Avenue subway stop, I walked down Houston Street, with the faint, salty smell of pastrami in the air. I made a right on Ludlow, a narrow passage of fire escapes scaling the buildings on both sides. If I lifted my head, I would see a store selling wholesale hardware, another selling electrical supplies, an awning with Chinese writing on it. But I wasn't looking up. Nope. I was going straight ahead, deliberately. There were a few people hanging out on their fire escapes. One leaned down to ask me if I knew what day it was. I felt a hand graze my shoulder. I flinched and kept walking and spoke to myself in a reassuring voice. *You are so close. You are almost there. Jesse is just a few blocks away. Nothing bad can happen to you.*

I kept having the sense that someone was behind me, kept hearing footsteps, stopping, turning. It was getting to be that time when the area turned over, morphed into something else. And I knew what this place was capable of doing to me. To deal with the postmidnight scene around here, I had to be in that particular state of Zen, where I was so composed that I could look at someone and say, *Oh, you have a black eye and a pet parrot that you carry around with you? That's cool! Whatever floats your boat!* If I felt a little weird in any way, this neighborhood only brought that feeling to the surface.

I took out my cell phone and called my sister, Emma, which I often did on my late-night walks to Jesse's apartment from the subway. I was half interested in chatting and half afraid of walking to his apartment without some form of armor.

"Just so you know, your so-called protection is lying on the couch, wearing Cookie Monster pajamas, and at least seventy blocks away," she told me.

"That's fine," I said. "It makes me feel safer to be on the phone. It sends a message to potential murderers."

"And what message is that? 'Don't kill me because I have friends'?" Emma laughed. She talked to me about her night for five minutes. And then, she promptly ditched me for another call.

Shit. On my own again.

I took Orchard Street. It was less abandoned. I'd decided, at some point, that Orchard Street was safe. A red sign for a tattoo parlor was the only thing lighting up the block. I peeked as far down the street as I could, to make sure there was nothing lurking behind a pile of garbage bags. I walked, almost running, in a diagonal dash toward his building, a white brick walk-up. I punched the button on the intercom next to 4A, and then stood there. The sound of the buzzer scared me right out of my skin. "It's me," I said, as soon as I heard the static.

"Hey, sweetheart," Jesse said. I exhaled, imagined all the ghosts in the neighborhood that would now leave me alone. A few minutes later, he was flying down the stairs and opening the door.

The entranceway was dreary, with damaged walls and a buzzing coming from the broken lamp half hanging from the ceiling. I dropped my stuff on the floor in front of him—a laptop case, a small duffel bag. I gave him a fatigued look. He was wide-awake, in a T-shirt and jeans.

"Long night?" he asked, picking up the bags from the floor.

"Yes," I answered.

"Were you at Nobu this whole time?"

After flitting between a few odd jobs, I was now working as a hostess at a restaurant in midtown, where my job was to stand for six hours (surprisingly strenuous), walk around the restaurant while crying out *Irasshaimase!* ("Welcome" in Japanese), and lead people to their tables with a stack of menus in my hands. My function at Nobu, as far as I could tell, was to manage the dining room, to keep people from killing one another, and last, to keep them from killing me. I'd never worked in a restaurant before, and that first month, man, I was happy. I became friends with everyone, the bartenders and waitresses. I ignored the busboys hitting on me as we dried off glasses with a towel. That night, one of them had offered to take me out to the Red Lobster in Times Square.

One year in, and the job was starting to wear on me, but it

had a greater purpose. I was attempting to make it as a music writer, which, in New York, is such a preposterous notion that I said it to a friend on Houston Street and a stranger who was walking by us actually started to laugh—this disturbing, high-pitched cackle of a laugh. When I recounted the story for Jesse, he acted unfazed, like *of course* that happened. "Don't say that shit out loud," he told me.

So far, I'd only found one magazine that was willing to pay me to write for them, and it had nothing to do with music. It was called *Outdoor World* and was mainly about hunting and fishing. I'd been freelancing for them for a few months, and it was going well; the only *slight* hitch was that I knew nothing about hunting or fishing, but I needed the clips, to show someone, someday, that I was remotely in the realm of journalism. Nobody I knew had heard of *Outdoor World*. I didn't care. I wrote about a fishing competition in Vermont, different brands of beef jerky, how to keep camouflage clothing from fading. I wasn't writing about music, but I was writing about *something*. I had a few hundred words to write every week. I was ecstatic.

Working at Nobu was about ten times less exciting than writing but paid me ten times more. When my stepfather, Arthur, inquired, in his typical good-natured, jokey fashion, why the Columbia degree that he'd paid for had landed me nothing more than a restaurant job and an exposé on safe bugs and how to eat them, I had to explain that the two positions went hand in hand. Almost everyone who worked at the restaurant was an aspiring artist of some kind—actors, mostly, but a few more grungy-looking photographers and cheek-boned models also roamed the premises. I pretended that it was a social experiment, not so much a way for me to pay for things, something that writing might never allow me to do. I dressed like a bohemian—with long, flowing skirts and turquoise bracelets. I got into it—serving the high-class, business crowd of midtown by day, walking among the wackadoodles of the Lower East Side by night.

"They had a big party in the private room that just *would not* leave," I explained.

"*So tired* and yet she made it all the way downtown," Jesse said, smiling behind me, as we walked up the stairs. "Yet again."

At the end of the night, when faced with the choice of Arthur's apartment on the Upper East Side or here, I always chose here. It was a pretty easy decision, a way to feign the adulthood I hadn't earned. Jesse and I were in a real relationship. He called most nights. We didn't "go out for dinner," but we got burritos at three o'clock in the morning. We ate scrambled eggs standing over his sink in our underwear. He read all my articles, and I knew every one of his songs, that the one about the extra toothbrush in his bathroom was really about me. *Take that, ladies.*

As I walked, he grabbed at the fabric of my skirt, tugged at it.

"I just wanted to see what you were up to," I whispered, looking back at him with a wry smile. He reached for me again, and I hopped up a few steps farther, out of his reach.

"Okay. Okay," he said. "I'll be more civilized."

I looked at the closed doors to other apartments as we ascended the stairs. We actually knew some of his neighbors—not their names, but their routines, their occupations. There was a film professor who lived on the second floor, with two sons who smoked pot every Sunday (the scent came in through Jesse's windows about twenty seconds after they started). There was a masseuse who lived on the third floor, who got late-night visits from men who looked like they'd just been at the gym. There was the twentysomething woman whose friends arrived every Saturday night, carrying pillows and candles, brown paper bags filled with candy and beer. All evidence suggested that they were having some kind of séance. The building's superintendent always seemed to be pacing the street outside the building. He was friendly, very social, as he watered the sidewalk. Most days, I found myself torn between talking to him about the weather and telling him my innermost thoughts.

Each time I climbed the steps to the fourth floor, I learned a lot about what people were up to. None of it was a secret. None of it was "what people do when nobody is watching." There was no shame around here. The only shame was in *not* having late-night visitors, in having nothing to hide.

In his building, all Jesse had to do was sneeze and people were fascinated. He'd tell them about his band, about his stint playing the Coke bottle as a trumpet at an art installation on Rivington. He was instantly accepted, invited over for dinner, even, in the case of the elderly Italian lady who lived on his floor. When I encountered these same people, they couldn't even look at me, for how naive I was. They looked off to the side right away, as if blinded by my inexperience. I had yet to harness my edge. But Jesse was covered, with his music and his stories of drug dealing in the Ivy League.

"I didn't know if it was too late," I said. "And you weren't picking up your phone. As per usual."

"It's never too late," he said. "I'm always up. You know that." Each stair creaked when I stepped on it, but to an unsettling extent, like it was a risk, like I might continue to fall down, down, down, all the way through it.

"Hungry?" he asked.

"Always."

"You should really eat at the restaurant," he said.

"I did eat. But that was at four o'clock."

The staff dinners at Nobu, which took place at the beginning of each night, were, to me, what I imagined it would be like to live like royalty. The food was mediocre, but I didn't care. I piled chicken and stir-fried vegetables onto my plate. I took five cookies and stuffed them into my apron and ate them outside in the alleyway, before one of the waitresses informed me that I didn't have to be so sneaky. "They don't serve those. They're for the staff. You can eat as many as you want," she said, with some combination of kindness and condescension. I looked down at the cookies, flat cylinders with specks of brown, and felt a sense of shame, that I'd actually thought they were a precious commodity.

"Why didn't you eat . . . at the end of the night?"

I sighed. "I can't bring myself to eat what people leave on their plates," I said. "We've talked about this."

"Amateur."

"Troglodyte."

"All right, Porter," he said. "No prehistoric insults after midnight."

"How was your night?" I asked.

"Eh. Fine. I met up with Ian and Chris for a bit."

Ian and Chris were Jesse's bandmates. They got together to practice a few times a week, at a studio they rented. They had performed together in college, at small venues in Brooklyn and on Thursday nights at "partios," a.k.a. parties on the Columbia Business School patio. They were now self-producing their debut album, and once it was finished, they planned to circulate it online.

I was winded by the time we got to the fourth-floor landing. I wasn't sure how much of it was attributable to the steps and how much was because of his hand, going for my skirt, over and over again. He pushed the door, and I looked around at the familiar scene—the leatherlike sofa, a kitchen with a mini fridge, a two-burner stove, and a mattress on the floor. He had left one lamp on. A window that looked out onto the street was slightly open—that damn window, which caused nothing but trouble. One morning, I woke up to find an ant line marching from the window, across the apartment, and to a spilled scattering of Cheerios on the kitchen counter. The ceiling was low and cracking, on the verge of collapse. The floors were uneven. The only thing that provided any brightness was the bookshelf, which was spilling with colorful books, the books of the scholarly male—Hemingway, Pynchon, Carver, McCarthy.

Jesse closed the door and put his arms around my waist. I closed my eyes. "I have to pee," I said, as he kissed the side of my head.

I went to the bathroom and then stood there, in front of the mirror, looking at the mildewed walls. I needed a second to collect myself, to get ready for the Jesse portion of my night. Without thinking, I started scrubbing away at the walls with a wet square of toilet paper, but I couldn't make much progress. I started on a large stain on the shower curtain.

I washed my face in the sink. The cold water felt good, and I tried to ignore the fact that the water was a little bit brown against my hands. *Okay. Okay.* It was all starting to fade—the chaos of the restaurant, the subway ride downtown, the brief walk through the Lower East Side. I closed my eyes and listened to the sound of the running water, the quiet hum of the fan that Jesse kept in the corner of his apartment.

I hovered over the sink, splashed my face one final time. Through a small hole below the faucet, I saw a pair of antennae move back and forth. I froze. I shut off the water. A large cock-roach came crawling out of the hole. I gasped and ran out of the bathroom. I opened the closet and flung a broom at Jesse.

"We have *company!*" I said dramatically. "The bathroom. GIANT cockroach. Kill it. *Kill it please!*"

He took the broom and stood there for a second. Then, he rested it gently against the wall. He went into the kitchen and came back with a paper towel. He walked toward the bathroom and, a few seconds later, I heard the sound of the toilet flushing. He came back into the living room and shook his head.

"This is what you give me?" he said, laughing, lifting the broom. "What, was an AK-47 not available?"

He imitated my voice: "We have *company!* Jesus fucking Christ."

"But I—"

"I'm going to use this on you instead." He pointed the broom at me, smiling. "Let's see how you like it." He chased me around the apartment. I ran for my life, until I was backed up into a corner and out of breath. He came toward me with a heavy stare, closer and closer to his surrounded prey. I pushed him away with a shove in the chest. He kept sweeping at my feet, running me around until we both fell onto the bed, exhausted.

"What happened to *Outdoor World*?" he said. "I thought that you were pro-bug these days."

I laughed. "Well, then you were mistaken."

After we'd lay there for a few seconds, Jesse said, "Speaking of your job . . ." and then he told me he had a "sort of" present for me. He unzipped something at the foot of the bed. I sat up. He handed me a long and slender black box. I opened it care-fully, as if there might be something living inside of it. I still had cockroaches on the brain.

"A pen?" I said, staring at the shiny, silver object.

"Yeah, but it lights up." He pressed a small button on the side of it, and the tip gave off a yellow light.

"It's for writing your articles," he elaborated. "I found it at that weird vintage store on Houston. I figured you could use it when you go night fishing and you have to write stuff down but you can't because it's too dark."

"I'm not going night fishing!" I said, grinning widely. "Oh my god. Is that a thing? Do people go night fishing?"

"It exists, and you might," he said. "You are an outdoorsman now."

"I'm not an *outdoorsman*. I'm just faking it for the byline."

"I don't know. . . . I think you're going to get hooked. I can see you now, asking me to go camping on the weekends."

I shook my head. "I'm from New York. We sleep indoors."

"I'm just messing with you," he said, looking down at the pen. "It's for shows . . . music shows, you know? Because it's also dark, at shows, in my experience."

"Oh!" I gave him a hug on the bed, my knees digging into the mattress. "At shows!" I said. "Of course! Thank you. Yes. A girl can dream."

He pulled off his T-shirt. "Fuck, it's hot in here." He moved back to lean against the wall, grabbing me along the way. He had a rubber band around his wrist and his feet were tan and kind of dirty. We kissed to the sound of people yelling on the street, and then the sound of horns being blown. Neither one of us flinched. He twisted his legs tighter around mine. His skin was warm and smelled like cigarettes.

"You're not seeing anyone at the restaurant, right?" he said breathlessly.

"Are you kidding?" I said, clearing the hair from my mouth and face. "I'm here almost every night!"

"I know, but I don't want you to fall for some guy there, someone who thinks your jokes are funny and who walks you home because he's pretending to be worried about your *safety*." He said the word *safety* with unqualified derision.

"I actually do have a boyfriend at the restaurant," I said, leaning my head against his chest. "His name is Joseph. He's from Poland. He wants to take me out for seafood."

I knew that I had to milk this for all it was worth. I had to *really* enjoy myself. Jesse almost never spoke about our relationship. But those few moments when he did—they were glorious.

"Does he?" he said, taunting me.

"He doesn't seem as antagonistic toward me as you are though, so our relationship is really missing that special something."

He put his arms around me and put his face against my neck. "Yeah, is that what makes ours special? That antagonism?"

I tilted my head toward him. We started kissing again, which quickly turned urgent. He slid down on the bed and pulled me with him, so that we were lying next to each other. He took my wrists and put them together, pulled them over my head. He kept them there with one hand, as we kissed, his other hand removing my clothes. I helped him. Then, he stopped, as if a sudden idea had come to him. He lifted me up off the bed and carried me toward the window.

"Put me down!" I shrieked. He opened the window with one hand.

"I will," he said, and he placed me on the sill with a mix of care and disregard. I was naked, sitting on the edge, my legs wrapped around him. I hugged myself, arms covering my chest.

"What are you doing?" I said.

"This is the best thing to do at this hour."

We entangled ourselves on the sill, and in truth, I really didn't care where, at this point. I was glad he didn't ask me. I was glad when he told me what to do, how to lean back, let my head and chest go out the window, how to hold myself up. I didn't want any of our time together to be any less than it could be. I wanted to embrace it all, to experience it to the fullest. His choices were never predictable, never awkward. It made sense. The windowsill was hip height. After a few seconds of adjustments, one thing became clear: he'd done this before. I wasn't his first. I didn't dare ask. I never asked.

"I'm going to fall," I said, as he put his hands against my lower back.

"You won't."

In the beginning, there was something funny about it, to be having sex above all these people in their apartments, not looking up. It was a rush, knowing everyone underneath us was none the wiser. I couldn't see any passersby. I looked around, thinking, *Someone has to look up. Does this happen all the time? How many times have I walked underneath people having sex on a windowsill? Everyone is at the mercy of me, and I am at the mercy of everyone else.* I noticed the city differently, in that moment. I always felt like I was the one spying on everyone, but I realized it then: they were spying on me too.

"Say something," Jesse whispered. I hadn't realized it, but I'd gone silent. "It's no fun if you don't say anything, sweetheart."

I shook my head, but then let out a small moan. My voice didn't sound right, as I released it into the landscape. *Everyone must do this, right? People must do this. Why don't I see it? Everyone is having sex. Everyone's got windows. This is the easiest way to fuck somebody. There is no out. And you offer them a nice view.* It was hard to concentrate on the sex, because it was so extroverted, but I did the best I could. I felt a new vulnerability in the city. I was a part of it now. I was a new fixture, an ornament on a building. *Where is everyone? Why aren't they looking out their windows?*

Jesse's foot was on the radiator. I heard his knee crack the window. I shuddered, held on to the fire escape. There was broken glass everywhere. I glanced down and saw the building super, looking up at us. "I'm not replacing that!" he shouted.

– – – –

We were in bed for two minutes before Jesse stood up and crossed the room, went for his guitar. He came back and asked if he could play a song for me that he wrote that day. He played it, in boxer shorts, cross-legged on the bed, and then waited for my reaction. It wasn't his best, but I didn't know how to tell him that, so I sat there, in silence. The moment after he finished playing always felt loaded. I had learned to tread lightly. I could sense him holding his breath. I didn't want to ruin the night. I said: "Is it about springtime or . . . California? In the spring? Sorry, you know how bad I am with . . ." When I spoke, my voice was low and sweet. But he got agitated anyway, and stood up and put his guitar in the corner of the apartment, then snapped it back into its case.

"Just explain it to me," I said, pleading with him, but he was already gone.

"Forget it."

"I'm just trying to understand. . . ."

"Let's forget it, okay? Let's talk about your night some more."

I sighed and dug my fists down into the mattress. He watched me closely, his neck red. For the past few weeks, Jesse had become increasingly touchy about his music. I got the sense that he wasn't being too productive and was looking for someone, anyone, to blame. At first it was his bandmates—they were lazy, he said, procrastinating, never showed up to practice on time—but lately I felt the blame had shifted squarely onto my shoulders. Half the time, I had no idea what we were even fighting about.

He'd say something like: "You don't *really* get me though, do you? And it's not your fault. I don't think you have the emotional capacity to get me."

I'd respond to this maturely. By yelling. "Say what you want about me. But *do not insult* my emotional capacity!"

"Maybe our relationship is the problem," he'd said once, pacing around his apartment, talking to himself more so than me. "Maybe being around someone who is *so stable* is messing up my ability to write anything remotely interesting."

Then, the shit really hit the fan.

"You think *I'm* stable?"

"You just want me to be dark for a few minutes! And then you want me to get over it and get myself together!"

"That's not true! I want to be your source of comfort in the world!"

He'd start shuffling things around in his apartment, slamming drawers with too much force, kicking the mattress with all his might and watching it move a whopping two inches farther away from him. He never hit me, but he came after me a few times, like he was about to do something. I always felt like he would have, if I'd only stuck around a little longer. But I ran away fast, every time, at all hours of the morning, my fear of what remained inside for once outweighing what lurked outside, out of his apartment and down the stairs, down the street, always shutting the door to his building behind me with a sense of panic and relief, like I'd made it out just in time. Sometimes he followed me outside, and we screamed at each other on the street, loud enough to wake the neighbors.

Sometimes, after a fight, he'd leave in the middle of the night to go out, when I was too tired to protest or to really process the whole thing in the first place. He'd come home at around five with glassy, bloodshot eyes, in a semiconscious trance. We'd talk about how much he'd had to drink, his songs, the gloom that would come over him sometimes and cause him not to sleep. I was his girlfriend/full-time therapist. Every time he came home, I would sit up in bed, wide-awake, as I listened to Jesse in the bathroom throwing up. "Are you okay?" I said, in my hazy state. His response to this was to run the water so that I wouldn't hear anything. When he got into bed, he passed out, but I got up every half hour to make sure he was still breathing.

One morning, I woke up to find that he wasn't beside me. I found him asleep on the couch. I tried to ask him why he wasn't in bed, but he didn't seem to hear me. I leaned over him and listened for his heartbeat. He started rocking his body back and forth. On the carpet next to him was one thumb-size clear plastic bag. I said his name. His legs started shaking, like he was warding off bad energy that was inside him. I remember how worried I was, how I couldn't feel myself move around the apartment. "Jesse," I said, and then my voice grew louder, tougher, more insistent. His eyes opened. When he looked at me, the person I knew seemed to be far away. Hours later, he told me he did some drugs that night, and that he'd slept on the couch because he didn't want to be close to me. He was too ashamed.

That morning, at a park on Essex and Canal, he finally explained himself. He told me how he'd done a few drugs in college but nothing crazy, just to experiment, then he sold them to make money, and maybe he had a few dalliances now and then, post-college. He told me that it started when his ten-year-old brother was diagnosed with bipolar disorder. His family was devastated. He said that it was genetic, and that he worried about himself sometimes. He said that drugs were a classic thing that manic and bipolar people did. Their personality gave them this high of happiness and mania, but there were also lows, and when you got into the lows, you wanted to get out of them. He told me that in college, one time, he went up to the roof of Mudd, the engineering building. I told him that he didn't have to take any engineering classes if he didn't want to, which made him laugh. He said it wasn't his style, truly, the drugs, the self-destruction. At his core, he said he liked it best when we were listening to music in bed together, and he was making fun of me for having bad taste. He called it *recovery*, to be with me, after a long night out. *Recovery* meant me being there, with him, holed up in his apartment. It meant us together in the dark, watching movies, getting takeout from the Chinese restaurant where Jesse was greeted by the entire staff. I swear, they threw as many complimentary fortune cookies as could fit in the bag. Each night that he slept soundly, I lay next to him in silence, feeling satisfied. It was a refuge, for me as well as him. It stopped me from worrying about other things. All that drifted into the background. Nothing was as pressing as keeping Jesse alive.

I got up and started getting dressed, readied myself for a battle. "I liked the song," I said. "But it's not my fault if *you* don't." After a few minutes, he appeared to calm down, came over to me, just as I was putting on my shoes, pressed his cheek to mine. He wrapped his arms around me and lifted me up so that my shoes fell off, and then carried me back over to the bed. "Don't go. Don't go," he whispered. I grabbed hold of the back of his neck.

The musician and the music writer.

"You know what?" he said, once he'd released me down onto the mattress. "Let's go out. We gotta get out of here." What he meant was that we needed to step out of ourselves, whatever happened to us when we fought. He had a mischievous look on his face. He stood, went to his closet, looked back at me.

"Okay," I said. *I was far from sleep anyway.* I could never drop right off to sleep after work, not before 3:00 a.m. Something inside of me refused, would not give way. But I was more comfortable at his place than anywhere else. When he wasn't in bed with me, I had this phantom image of him. I imagined pulling him toward me, curling up beside him and feeling that I'd come to a safe place. *When everything in your life is so uncertain, you cling to clarity where you can find it. You cling to anything you can find that feels good or familiar. Did he know that I dreamed about him five nights a week? That every song was about him?*

I couldn't let him go out without me, then come home, barely conscious. It broke me to see him like that—unable to walk, speak, hold up his head.

"I'll go with you," I said.

"Where should we go?" He came over to the bed, kissed the top of my head. "How about PKNY?" Jesse said. He put his hand on my shoulder.

"What's PKNY?"

"Seriously? Painkiller New York? You've never been? I'm sure you've seen it. It's that tiki bar a few blocks away? Apparently, they have a new drink with rum and banana colada in it that will not only kill your pain but make you forget how to speak."

"Sounds perfect," I said, half sarcastically. I got up, made the bed. I smoothed the comforter evenly over the mattress, fluffed the pillows, as always, for my mother. As soon as I was done, Jesse took one hand and pushed me lightly so that I fell back onto it, ruining everything. I sighed.

"I hear that piña coladas are making a comeback," he said.

"You know what," I replied thoughtfully, staring at the ceiling. "Good for them."

"I'm feeling the need for some Polynesian and Manhattan fusion."

"That's not a need."

"Get *excited!* *This is why we live in Manhattan!* This is why we pay a ridiculous amount of money in rent. Well, this is why *I* pay a ridiculous amount of money. You are just a freeloader. But this is why we live here, man! To go to a tiki bar in Chinatown at one o'clock in the morning."

"Agreed," I said, sitting up.

"All right!" Jesse said, and then gave me a high five. He stood in front of his closet, scanning his options.

"So are you going to wear a plaid shirt? Or a plaid shirt?" I said, smiling.

He gave me a death stare.

"You know what, I hardly ever go out in a T-shirt," he said, with great interest, as if someone were interviewing him on the topic.

He put on a shirt, plaid, just as I'd predicted, and looked in the mirror. He closed his eyes slightly and fiddled with his hair. I flinched and looked away from the mirror. He was good-looking, but he knew it, which made him a little bit less so.

Once out of the apartment, he seemed to be in an extreme hurry to get there. I walked behind him, looking down and trying to figure out what clothing I'd put on, I'd been in such a rush. When he stopped walking, I looked up. There was no awning, no name. It was a tiny place and looked like it used to be a one-car garage. I could see the silver grates, up top, waiting to be pulled down at the end of the night. On the wall next to the bar, someone had painted a green palm tree against a sky-blue background.

"This is it," he said. He opened the door and allowed me to walk in first.

Inside, there was a bamboo-paneled bar, naturally. Colorful drinks were everywhere, with umbrellas and cherries stacked on a straw next to a wedge of pineapple. A few people had ordered flaming shots, which came in a half shell of coconut. Bowls of watermelon with neon straws sticking out of them were passing us by. I turned my attention to the crowd, barely listening as Jesse talked to the bartender, who he knew, of course. He knew every bartender within a five-block radius.

I spotted Kate across the bar, and I couldn't believe the luck of it. "Kate's here!" I yelled, tapping Jesse on the shoulder repeatedly. She was wearing a gray tank top tucked into black pants, a long necklace with a crystal dangling at the end of it. I pointed, standing on my toes to see over the crowd. Jesse looked at her and then looked back at me, rolling his eyes.

"Hey, don't do that," I protested. "Kate's my friend!"

"I'm the only friend you need."

"That is *not* true," I said.

He grinned. "I'm gonna go downstairs," he said.

"What's downstairs?"

He shrugged. "Some of *my* friends."

"But I have to say hi to Kate!"

"Feel free."

"Okay . . . so, I'll, um, I'll meet you down there in a few

minutes?" He nodded, and part of me was relieved to be able to catch up with Kate without him there. I hadn't seen her in a few weeks. When we met up then, we hadn't had the best dinner. Usually, our dinners were perfect conversational harmony. From the second we sat down, the drinks started flowing, the bread was torn into, we talked so much and so quickly that we didn't even notice what we were eating. But the last time, we were being too formal with each other for some reason, or she'd been in a lousy mood because of work, or something was off. I hadn't felt the same connection with her. But now, as I made my way toward her, I was ready to rectify the situation, to get back to our usual way. I realized how much that one mediocre dinner had caused me to miss her.

I went up to her with a huge smile on my face. There is something about accidentally running into a close friend that is as thrilling as anything.

"What are you doing here?" I said.

"I'm with some random people," she said, less thrilled. "You do not even want to know the night I've had."

I looked behind her at a booth where four guys we knew from college were seated, Glick, Ben, Danza, and Julian. *Ah-ha*. "I see Juuuuuulian is here," I said, drawing out his name in a singsong voice. "Why are you torturing that poor boy?"

"That poor boy has a girlfriend," she replied. "But I think I might try to seduce him anyway." She half smiled, half winced. "Is that bad?"

"For his girlfriend? Yes. Definitely."

She rolled her eyes. "Tell me what's going on with you and Jesse," she said, taking a sip of what appeared to be a strawberry daiquiri.

I stared at her for a few seconds. The truth was I didn't like to talk about my relationship with Jesse with my friends. I never knew what to say.

"It's going really well. . . . ," I said. "Except for when it's going really badly."

She nodded. "Standard Eve."

"I know."

"How bad is bad?"

"There's a fair amount of alcohol and drug use."

She didn't blink. "But when it's good?"

I took a long inhale. "Fireworks."

"Standard Eve."

"But it changes constantly. I can't trust it."

"Do you even want to?"

I stared at her.

"Eve. I think if you dated someone and everything went smoothly, it would blow your mind."

"That's . . . not true. It's not about highs and lows. It's just about the person. Jesse and I . . ."

She smiled and rolled her eyes. "*Ohhhh* yes. You and Jesse. I know. I know. You're about to tell me about this unspeakable bond that I couldn't *possibly* understand. You guys *get* each other. Go ahead. Carry on. Have an *experience*. Do it. *Vaya con Dios.* By all means. Hey, I'm seducing Julian for no apparent reason. I'm not exactly in a position to judge."

"Here's the thing though . . . I think I might be in love with him." I winced.

"Seriously?"

"And isn't it bad to love someone who will ultimately hurt me?"

She started shaking her head. "I love pink drinks. That doesn't make them good for me, and yet." She stuck out her tongue. It was bright red.

"So you think I'm setting myself up?"

"*Of course* you are setting yourself up. Look, just be careful. I'm not going to judge you or tell you to stop, but be careful. That's all I ask."

"I'm going to go get him."

I went to find Jesse, down the staircase in the back, to the basement. There was a long, mahogany hallway with small rooms every couple of feet and two larger rooms at both ends. The larger rooms were dark, with only a table visible in one and a black piano in the other. I walked to one of the smaller rooms that had its door shut but a light glowing from underneath it.

I knocked. "Come in!" Inside, there were six or seven people huddled around a mirrored coffee table streaked with white powder. Jesse looked up and smiled at me.

"Sit down," he said. I watched him clear room for me. I sat next to him, quietly observing. A girl in a red dress, with a flower in her hair, offered me a line. "No, thanks," I said, shaking my head. Jesse smiled at me and played with my hair, pushing away the strands near my face. He moved the pieces into a ponytail that he held in his hand behind my neck. "I think I'll pass," I said.

She did a line. He did a line. I stared at the floor. Eventually, I was able to get him away, to lead him back upstairs. He was rubbing my elbow with his fingers as we walked. I tried to get him to talk to Kate, to change her mind about him, about us. I tried to sit at the table and make conversation, but Jesse's hands were on my skirt, my thigh, under my skirt. He was gradually making it more and more impossible for me to talk. That seemed to be his goal, as he sat next to me, to get me to leave with him as soon as possible. Flashes of the windowsill were coming back to me. I was giving distracted answers to Kate. She could probably tell.

"Remember what happened earlier?" he whispered into my ear, while I was talking.

I took his hand in mine and tried to move it away, to put it back in his own lap, but it was a waste of time.

"I'm not really capable of socializing right now," he said into my neck. His fingers were fully up my skirt now. His fingertips were sliding beneath my underwear, moving it sideways. I started to laugh. I felt a little bit dizzy. I thought, for a second, about the streaks of white powder, but then I pushed that thought away.

When Kate got up to use the bathroom, Jesse dragged me outside by the arm and kissed me against the blue wall next to the bar, under the palm tree. I felt like I'd never done it before, like we were inventing something new, that nobody had ever thought about. He pressed me against the wall and when his lips left mine, I exhaled so hard that things started going blurry.

"Can we go home and fuck now?" he said, smiling, his wet mouth next to mine.

"Wait a second," I said. "I want to ask you something."

"What is it?"

I stood there quietly for a few seconds. "What do I . . . mean to you?"

"What?"

"You heard me. What am I? To you?"

"Come again?"

"Don't be an asshole."

"Seriously? This is what you want to know right now? While I'm high and fuck-drunk on you?"

"Is there a better time to ask?" I smiled.

"Ahhhh, see. You told me that you weren't one of those girls. But you are. You lured me in under false pretenses!"

"One of what girls? I just want to understand what's going on."

"Of course you do. You probably have a whole staff of people working on this issue as we speak."

"I don't. Fine. Look. You don't have to answer that. But, can I just ask you for one thing? When you're ready to break up with me, can you just tell me as soon as you know? Like, don't wait, don't drag it out, don't make me guess. Just do it."

"You're borderline insane."

"And you're not answering my question!"

"I just want to have a good time, man."

"What does that mean though?"

"It means—" He took a long, annoyed breath and ran his fingers through his hair. "Jesus, Porter. You kill me, you know that? You're *killing* me, even just by saying that, in that way that you say things. You and I both know that I can't even see straight right now. We fucked earlier, but it doesn't matter. That doesn't cool me off toward you. It only makes me hotter. It's like a cycle and I'm never satisfied. I'm in a state of pining for you, right now, that is probably bad for my health. If you walked away right now, I think I would die. I think I would literally stop breathing. I would do *anything* to stop this conversation and take you home right now. Literally. Anything. I want you so badly that it hurts, it fucking kills me."

"You know," I said, looking up at him. "I don't enjoy hearing you say these things."

"You *certainly* enjoy hearing me say these things."

I started to smile. "I'm just worried that . . ." He picked me up off the ground, his hands clasped around my legs. My little half yelps half laughter filled the air. He carried me down the street, with his arms still around me. It required an unnerving amount of energy. Once we were in front of his building, he placed me down, and stood in front of me. He moved closer and closer. He touched his nose to my nose. He kept his face there. We both closed our eyes.

"Jesse," I whispered. I could feel myself resisting. When he hugged me, I couldn't sink into him. I knew that I could go upstairs with him, we could sleep together, we could sleep next to each other, I could press myself against him all I wanted, but somehow, it wouldn't stick. He could hold on to me, but I wouldn't feel it. Instead, as I stood there on the street with him, I felt the frailty of my body, on my skin, a flash of Kate's red tongue in my face. I'd left without saying good-bye.

"See," he said, his arms around me, pulling me in. "This is how we are. This is *good*. Can't you see that?"

I looked around, uneasily, at a neighborhood that wasn't mine. I felt like there was something missing, like there was meant to be something underneath me, but instead I was holding myself up, and not well. *Something more reliable was supposed to be there.*

My chest tightened and I let out a sound that Jesse seemed to take for lust but was really much more me on the cusp of a full-blown panic attack. This wasn't stable. I wasn't stable. Nothing in my life was fucking stable.

I closed my eyes as Jesse buried his face in my neck and, as I had done for the past six years whenever I was on the verge of becoming completely unmoored, I wished for my mother.

EVE

CHILDHOOD IN THE BRONX (OR: NEVER TRUST A MIDNIGHT SNACK)

It was the summer of 1997. I was on a mission and pedaling fast, one thought circling on an endless loop in my head.

I needed to talk to my mother.

The buildings were blowing by me, the tall brick rectangles, each the same: a semicircle driveway, a few errant bushes, two or three trees along the road, not close enough to touch. From the Kingsbridge Academy, a public school in our neighborhood, I had to bike only a few blocks to get home, and I knew them well. I could afford to be reckless. I wasn't looking out for cars, or any movement on the street, or watching for stop signs. It was all grayness anyway, nothing to see. The small knapsack kept bobbing against my back, as I pedaled my heart out. I only knew that I had to talk to her, before it was too late.

I made the right onto Blackstone Avenue, went to the end of our road, which looped in a circle and then spit back out. Our house was tucked behind the Henry Hudson Parkway, not on the parkway, but not so far away from it that we didn't hear the cars, at night, when everything else was quiet. We were the third attached house on the left, in a row of four, each with a red awning. The group was distinct among the surrounding buildings. It didn't belong. It was shorter and stubbier, disconnected from the landscape. Of the four, we were the house with sheer curtains in every window. It wasn't the best part of Riverdale, the part that was green and suburban and looked more like Westchester than the Bronx. It was the part of the North Bronx where people lived if they didn't have money, but it was still a bastion of shelter compared to the South Bronx.

I propped my bike against a row of garbage cans and let myself inside with the key under the mat. My mother's car was in the driveway, which was a relief. It occurred to me, on the way home, that there was a small chance she'd be at the grocery store. Once inside, I figured I had about fifteen minutes before my sister, who was three years younger than I was, would come trudging home. A mere fifteen minutes to recount what she'd done that day. It was the worst thing imaginable. Up until then, I'd thought the worst that weasel would ever do occurred when I was nine and she borrowed one of my stuffed animals and left it in the back of the BxM2 bus. But no, this was worse.

That summer, my sister and I went to Kingsbridge together every morning, where we spent an hour each day playing sports and the rest of it taking math classes because it was cheap and my mother somehow managed to convince us that this was camp. The silver lining was that they took us on field trips every few weeks, to the community center for swimming, to the bowling alley. A rumor was circulating that there would be a trip to a water park at the end of the summer.

Normally, the prospect of a water park would have been

enough for me. But that summer, there were more pressing matters to attend to. I was thirteen and I had a crush on a boy named
Jeremy. That day, I'd found out that, joy of joys, he liked me too.
I told my sister, in a fit of excitement. Normally, I pretended that
she didn't exist. I only paid attention to her in an emergency,
like when she left the water running in the bathroom and nearly
flooded the place, or when she jumped into the pool without
her floaties on and had to be rescued by the sixteen-year-old
lifeguard. Under those circumstances, with a teacher breathing
down my neck ("Your sister almost *drowned*!") I paid attention to
her, the little inconvenience. Well, I should have stuck to that
policy. She was to be dealt with only in an emergency. But I broke
down. And leave it to her to take that single moment where I
chose to let her in a little bit, and turn it into a public relations
disaster. She went straight up to Jeremy Robbins, under the lunch
tent, with all the other kids watching, and declared, "Welcome
to the family!" She wrapped her arms around him in a bear hug.

I nearly melted into my sneakers. She didn't know. She had
no idea that you couldn't say stuff like that to thirteen-year-old
boys without scaring them away. You just *couldn't*. Later that day,
the crush of the moment told me that our deal was off, that he
no longer wanted to sit with me on the bus to the movies, that he
would not be holding my hand in the dark during the frightening
parts. Well, he didn't say that last bit, but it was an implied part
of the movie-field-trip bus-ride-companion contract, as far as I
was concerned.

I didn't discuss it with my sister. I didn't go to her and say
anything. I merely left for home without her that day. *Let her
wonder why I'm not waiting for her! Let her think about her actions!* I had a better, more industrious plan. I needed an audience
who would understand the scope of the damage. I was going to

go home and scream at my mother. She was at least, in part, responsible for what had transpired that day. She'd created the little monster, after all.

The tears were in my eyes as I ran upstairs, breathing heavily, the words ready, just waiting to pour out, as I replayed the events of the day over and over again in my head. It wasn't just that my mom would hear me out and probably punish Emma—she would calm me down, make me see reason, give me some perspective. She always did when I was freaking out about something. "There will be other Jeremys," she would say soothingly, her calm seeping into me like a drug and making me a little more numb to everything. "Now let's go downstairs and eat Emma's favorite flavor of ice cream and not give her any."

But when I got upstairs, the door to my parents' bedroom was closed, which was almost never the case. At some point, they'd told us that if the bedroom door was ever closed, we shouldn't bother them, that we should leave them alone and that they'd open it when they were available.

I thought about this but knocked anyway. *This* was an emergency. My sister would be home any minute and I wouldn't have time to have the very adult conversation that I needed to have with my mother without some *ten-year-old* hanging around. I knocked and held my breath. Nobody answered.

Disgruntled, I went to the bedroom that I shared with my sister and locked the door. I would wait, but I wasn't going to wait with *her* around. I almost caved when I heard her little footsteps outside. She didn't knock, but she slipped a Fruit Roll-Up under the door, my usual afternoon snack that I'd skipped over in my enraged state. It didn't really fit, but she pushed and pushed, wedging it into the small gap between the carpet and the door, until it lay there, freely.

If you think a Fruit Roll-Up is going to solve this . . ., I thought, enraged, and almost slipped it back under the door, just to show her what's what. But then I decided to leave it there, to allow for the possibility that I might, at some point, get hungry.

Once she left, I kept peeking down the hallway, waiting. Minutes passed like hours, but the door to my parents' room remained closed. All that I could hear was the sound of my sister watching television in the living room. I walked back and forth down the hall. I put my ear up to the door. I figured that my father would be home from work soon. She'd have to come out then.

But by the time I got the courage to venture back out, it was ten o'clock, the house was dark, and my sister was curled up, asleep on the couch. There was no answer when I knocked at my parents' door. I waited, knocked again. I opened the door slowly. "Mom?" I said cautiously, aware of the noise that I was emitting into the silent room. I tiptoed inside. Her bed was made. All clothing had been put away. There was no sign of her anywhere. The bathroom door was closed. I said again, "Mom?"

"Eve?" she said, in a voice I didn't recognize. "Come in."

I opened the door. She was sitting on the tile floor, in her robe, looking up at me. I'd never seen her sitting on the floor before. Nothing about this scene looked right to me. Nothing about her face looked right to me. It was as if she'd lost all her color, all her defining features.

"Dad's gone," she said. "He left."

For some reason, I registered the full extent of what she was saying. I didn't say *But when will he be back?* or *What do you mean, gone?* I could infer from the situation, from the look on her face, that something had transpired. It wasn't like I was the most insightful kid, but I knew my mother. She didn't work, and was home with us whenever we were home. We did everything together.

The first thing I said out loud to her was, "Is it okay if we still live here?" which didn't exactly make sense, given the circumstances. It must have struck me that the rules could change now, that there was nothing that could be relied upon completely. If my father wasn't here, where was he? He had no place in the world, if not here.

"Yes, of course," she said, and then she started crying. I didn't cry along with her. I just stood there feeling like I had to do something to take care of her, for a change. I remember feeling deeply inadequate for that task. I handed her a tissue box pathetically.

I went to the kitchen and looked at the counter and noticed that the money was gone. *The forty dollars.* It had been lying in the corner, the bills just jutting out enough to be visible. My first crushing thought was that my father had taken it. It was his money, after all. He had this glass jar of change that he kept in his bedroom closet. He filled it every night, when he came home from work. Often, when I was lying in bed, that was how I knew that he was home—by the sound of the coins hitting the glass jar. That brief but jingling noise was how I knew that everything was okay, everyone was home, and it was safe to go to sleep. My sister and I often went into my parents' bedroom and tried to guess how much money was inside the jar. We'd try to lift it but it was too heavy. Based on height and weight and density, we figured it contained roughly a million dollars. We liked to talk to my father about what we could spend the money on, once he took all the coins to the bank. We weren't particularly eccentric in our requests—they mostly involved Disney World. For a while, I was obsessed with Minnie Mouse and certain that, upon meeting, she and I would become fast friends. We had a lot in common. We both liked bows. We both tolerated Mickey, though sometimes we felt that he was trying a little too hard. Then, one glorious afternoon, the jar was full and our father took it to the bank. He made a big deal out of it. We helped him transfer the coins into plastic bags. When he came home, he presented the forty dollars to us and then put the money in the kitchen, under the tissue box, where we could all see it, with a promise that one day, we'd use it to do something fun, all together.

When I saw that the money was gone, I buried all thoughts about it deep inside of me. I'd never ask my mother about it. I talked myself out of thinking that he snatched it on the way out. I said, *No he would never do that. He'd never take it just like that.* I convinced myself that if he did take it, it was only to spare our feelings, so that we wouldn't see it and get reminded of the promise unfulfilled. Later on, I decided that it was my sister who took the money; *of course it was her,* though I never asked, for fear that she would prove herself innocent.

The great irony, which occurred to me in that moment, was that I was scared of everything. A robbery, a fire, an earthquake— you name the disaster, I lay in bed worrying about it. I even had a fairly specific apprehension about a tree getting struck by lightning and falling on my parents' car. They'd be driving on the highway, in a thunderstorm, and mid conversation, lightning would hit one of the trees nearby and *bam*, tragedy. As a result, whenever they left the house to drive somewhere, if there was even the slightest threat of rain, I'd worry about it endlessly, wondering where they were, how far they were from their destination, how long until they came back home. I'd stare out the window at the threatening sky, willing the rain to stop, the clouds to break. A single streak of blue sent relief ricocheting through me.

But of all the things I worried about, I had never worried that someday my father would leave my mother, that he would leave us, without any warning. That, somehow, didn't make the list. I suppose that's part of the reason why, when it happened, I was hit so hard. I didn't expect it to occur, and I made it my business to expect everything.

It happened on a bad day that I thought could only get better. I was trudging around, angry that my sister had embarrassed me, as if that was what pain felt like. *This* was pain. I realized it then, how oblivious I had been. Why hadn't I ever thought to scrutinize my parents, to listen to the way they talked, to pay attention to the way they looked at each other? Maybe, if I'd been watching, none of this would have happened. I promised myself that in the future, I would be more careful. I would become the world's most vigilant observer. I would watch everyone and catch catastrophes before they happened. I started keeping a journal. I wrote everything down—details about my sister's friends, how many times my grandparents came over per week. I had a detailed record of what the weather was like every day for about a month in 1998, in case anyone was interested. When my mother was out of the house, I created an inventory of the items in her closet. I told myself that, in life, you couldn't just leave people alone.

After my mother peeled herself off the bathroom floor that night, after she put my sister to bed, after she mixed pancake batter in a bowl, she started analyzing with me at the kitchen table. Secretly, I was finding a bit of enjoyment in sitting there with her, in having a late-night dinner, a "midnight snack" she called it, as we discussed the situation. She'd never have allowed this kind of thing before my father left. Dinner was always at seven, and it was always a variation of the same: meat, vegetable, potato. It felt like we had a secret, at first, something important that was just between us. A resolvable wound that we could make better. She treated me like a friend that night, and not her daughter. I was feeling pretty grown-up, all things considered.

The analysis of "what went wrong with Dad" began slowly, at first. She said that she couldn't be sure of anything, but that she knew he'd been unhappy, that there had been some changes at work—a larger company had bought his. There was a new boss, whom he didn't like. This explanation seemed lacking to me. He wasn't one of those people obsessed with work. My father worked for a window manufacturer. The only thing I really knew was that the shop was on the Lower East Side, on Avenue D, and that each night, when he came home, he poured himself a glass of Scotch. The smell of it, a combination of wood and Band-Aids, the rattling of ice cubes, *that* was my father, in essence, at the end of a long day. But he rarely talked about work. He rarely talked about anything.

My mother said that he'd gotten so quiet over the past few years, quiet even for him, but that she didn't know to take that as a sign of his discontent. She said that he'd started drinking more than usual. It was all very vague and confusing, her explanations. It was clear that she didn't know what to tell us. Then one day, she stopped talking about it at all. I was the kid again, and she only talked about him over the phone with a friend, or to my grandmother at the kitchen table. I heard them talk about his mood swings. My grandmother said something to my mother about a celebrity she'd read about who had some kind of mental illness, but then my mother hushed her and they stopped talking when she spotted me across the room. They said that he might come back, that he would certainly regret this. It was the past fifteen years of his life, that they'd been married. My grandmother insisted that he wouldn't do well on his own.

While they were putting it all together in the kitchen, I was looking around a half-empty house. Even though he was no longer physically there, his presence was everywhere. I could see him in the lamp that he switched off every night before he went to sleep, in the hallway outside of my room. That light *was* him, still up, watching television, standing guard. Who would shut it off now? He was there each time I saw a yellow dandelion in our backyard. He once helped me assemble them into a bouquet for my mother, allowing me to pillage the neighbors' yards. I felt like we were doing something very mischievous together, stealing flowers from the neighbors. I didn't realize until I got older that I was not so much committing petty larceny as I was weeding their lawns.

At night, after my grandparents left, there was only silence. That was the worst part of all of it, I think. My mother stopped talking to me. Sure, she would ask me about school, what my friends were up to, listless questions asked in a half-present voice. But she wasn't present. She wasn't *there*. I'd never been so lonely.

- - - -

And then one day, I heard something unusual coming from her bedroom. It was a Saturday morning, and there was music. It was Paul Simon. "Loves Me Like a Rock." I peeked into her bedroom and she was dancing around the perimeter of her carpet. She looked genuinely happy, free of something, though I didn't know what. Yet again I didn't see something coming, despite my new resolution to always, always expect everything. I didn't know how this was possible. It wasn't like everything was perfect after that, but walking in on my mother, mid dance party—I remember feeling light inside, like I used to feel after school was over on a Friday afternoon, or at the beginning of summer, with nothing but relief and Popsicles ahead. I had the feeling that we had entered into a new phase, and there was no going back.

The house on 238th Street was suddenly a changed universe. My mother played music every morning. She made more of an effort to turn everyday activities into something exciting— the park, the bakery, a new dress, even the walk to and from school. "Last person home *loses!*" she'd say, dashing off ahead of us. *"Loses what?"* we yelled, mouths open and sprinting behind her. She was blonder and prettier and younger-seeming than before. She went to work, as a secretary for a law firm in the World Trade Center. Before my father left, she had always talked about selling the house. It seemed like a half joke that they had together, her nagging him about her big dream to move to Manhattan. Whenever we went into "the city," she needled him on the way home in the car, about how much fun we'd had, about how much better it would be to get out of this sleepy neighborhood. My father said he liked the quiet. And somehow, she never got any further with her plans. It always remained in the "idea" stage. I knew the reality: we couldn't afford it. That was the reality that my father knew, and probably told her when my sister and I weren't around.

It was even more of a reality now that he was gone. She was more fun, but she also had little patience, got irritated more easily. She didn't fill the fridge with groceries. She stopped cleaning the house. She let the toilet water go yellow. One time, I was hunting around for odds and ends to make me and my sister dinner, and I found green lumps inside a jar of tomato sauce. I was so stunned by what I saw that I dropped it onto the floor and the glass shattered.

"Evie, bring me that poem you wrote," she said to me once. "The one about the bowl that gets left out of the dishwashing cycle. 'The Lament of the Bowl'? I want to read it." She always told me that I got overly attached to things because my father wasn't attached to me, or to anything. He had an inability to attach, she said. She wanted to see the poem, she said, to remind her that I wasn't like him.

On Saturdays, she would drag us into the city for the day. We didn't go to museums or shows, but we walked. We took walks so long that on the way home, my feet were throbbing. It was the only thing that she really loved to do. "Someday, when you're the president of the United States and you're the president of Cuba," she said, to me and my sister, pointing to us in the back of the car with a short laugh, "I'm going to live in Manhattan."

I remember thinking, *I don't care where we live, I will still miss Dad*. I even said it to her sometimes, but only when I was mad at her, only when I was so desperate for a solution that I had to say it out loud, even though I knew it would hurt her. "Everything changes," she responded, as if it were that simple.

When I was really little, I used to mistakenly tell people that my dad was a window washer. The distinction between that and window *manufacturer* was not clear to me. The first time it happened, he'd found this to be so hilarious and endearing that he told the story to everyone he knew, all about how his daughter thought that he washed windows for a living. He told it with this look in his eyes, this look of pure happiness, like he might cry. There was a time when the story seemed as precious to him as anything. There was a time when it seemed like he'd never stop telling it. *Everything changes.*

And it was true. His possessions began to slowly disappear. The framed photographs were the first to go, just the ones of my parents together, without us. Then his sweaters and shirts vanished, then his shoes, and last, his coats. I had no idea where it all went. I wondered, but then stopped myself. The end result was a house that was exactly half-empty. I still felt him there, though. I expected him to walk in, at any moment, and for us to resume normal life. But he didn't. And eventually, I got it into my head.

Then one night, several years later, the phone rang. It was a 212 number, followed by a strange man's voice. Strange men didn't call our house. My ears perked up. He said his name was Arthur. My mother took the phone into her bedroom and closed the door. She stayed in there for a while, and when she emerged, she said something about him being a friend of a friend and then, "He lives in the city, you know?" And I smiled back at her, tried to share in the excitement.

I remember coming home from school a few days after the call and finding her all dressed up and sitting in the kitchen with a glass of Scotch. She never drank, especially not in the house, especially not that brown liquid so heavily associated with my father. But she looked to be in a state of contemplation, her eyes a little glazed over, clutching the glass. She told me she had a date with that man in the city. A few weeks later, I met him. He wore a collared shirt with short sleeves and stripes. He was fine. Nice. Not my father.

Nonetheless, we were treading water. We, as a family, didn't feel so sunk down anymore, could see the sun, the promise of dry land. After Arthur proposed to my mother, we sold our house in the Bronx and moved into Manhattan. Not just Manhattan. The Upper East Side. Arthur was a stockbroker who worked out of his very nice home on Park Avenue. He had a guest bedroom that Emma and I shared with two twin beds, yellow walls, and a flat CD player that hung on the wall and was so high-tech that it opened up when you walked by it.

My mother kept her job at the law firm. On Friday afternoons, she'd come home, all exasperated by this or that person. "I can't tell you how happy I am to get away from that place." But by Saturday afternoon, she'd be back to talking about her co-workers, all wistful, her voice brimming with affection, filling us in on nicknames, lunch preferences. Arthur told her all the time that she could leave. "Josie, I don't know why you put up with it," he'd always say. But she insisted. Secretly, I think she liked that even though she was living in his apartment among all his things and socializing with his friends at his favorite restaurants, living his life, essentially, she still had something that was hers. Or maybe it was a contingency plan. She was all too aware that not everything worked out as calculated.

Living at Arthur's place, at first, seemed exciting and mischievous. Arthur was very lenient, wanted us to feel at home. Emma pushed the boundaries, threw a party once when they were away for the weekend. She was so exhilarated by the fact that in the city, you could order alcohol to be delivered and not get carded. The only catch was that when trying to conceal the fact of a party, it was best not to leave the receipt from the liquor store on the kitchen table. God how I worried about her party while it was going on. I stayed home that night to police the situation, to make sure that none of Arthur's knickknacks fell over and that no glasses sat too close to the edge of the table. I made sure that when someone removed a sword from a silver statue of a knight, the sword eventually returned back to its sling. I didn't especially like Arthur, but I didn't want his antique sword to go missing.

But the good thing was, once we settled into Arthur's apartment, life started to become more normal. Life was about friends and other routine teenaged things. And the best part was my mother and I started talking again. Arthur had this small round table in his kitchen where she and I would sit and discuss everything. This table saw it all—the good, the bad. She and I developed a relationship that could be characterized as both wonderful and difficult at the same time. We discussed everything at great length, often astonishing Arthur with the sheer amount of time we could spend just sitting and talking. Most of the time, I enjoyed these discussions. Talking to her was like talking to a close friend who was more invested in the situation. She had a way of being very wise but also, now that we lived in the city, she could be carefree, childlike. She constantly used the phrase *totally cool* to describe things. She'd look at me in a pair of knee-high boots she was thinking about buying for me and she'd say "Totally cool! Nobody will have boots like yours," like some sixteen-year-old version of herself. She'd see a black-and-white photograph of a motorcycle in a store window and say "Totally cool. For your bedroom? Let's get it!"

We shared so much that I often felt like if I didn't tell her something, it didn't really happen. Running an idea by her was like logging it into some imaginary but very official journal of my life. Unfortunately for me, if she was any kind of bookkeeper, she was the most unneutral one that ever existed. She didn't just want to know the basics. She wanted to shape things, to inject her not-so-subtle opinion into everything. And most of the time, to be honest, I was grateful for the guidance. But every now and then, when a conflict arose, it was what Arthur called World War Three in his apartment. My mother would look at him when he said this, exasperated. Arthur was perpetually three steps behind. It was irrelevant that nobody ever bothered to catch him up. We firmly believed that he should have found a way to keep up with everything on his own. My mother and I screamed at each other, I slammed my door (an act that she loathed, which would only escalate the situation), but after about thirty minutes, one of us would come crawling back to the other. Usually me, for fear of losing my most trusted adviser. We would then discuss things more quietly. She would come around to see my side.

And then, September Eleventh happened. I expected a call from my father, but one never came. I remember the phone ringing at Arthur's just as we were leaving for the funeral. The three of us stood in the doorframe, holding our coats, motionless, letting it ring. Just as Arthur was about to go to it, I said, "Nobody answer it, *please*," because I wanted so badly to believe that it might be my father. I didn't want to ruin my own illusion that he'd call, that he cared about what was going on. But he wasn't at the funeral. Emma and I were sunk right back down, even further than we'd ever been before. And, in a way, I spent the next ten years waiting for that phone to ring.

BEN

That one night wasn't a big deal, or anything like that. There was a girl, Eve, who was familiar because we showed up at the same places, over the years, but it wasn't that I really knew her. I wasn't thinking about her at all. But this particular night ended in me feeling sorry for her. And that ended up being important for what happened later. So that's why I'm starting here.

The night began, as so many others did, with my friends at a bar. None of us had an apartment where it was convenient to drink, so this was a fairly regular occurrence. I lived in Hoboken, but didn't invite people over because I had this thing about not pissing off my roommate, even though he wasn't winning any prizes. He was a Korean kid studying to get a PhD in chemical engineering, and he did nothing but study and play video games and cook soup in the middle of the night that smelled like it could stop a clock. But most of the time, he stayed in his room with the door closed and kept to himself, and if I got bored, I would knock and talk to him about biocatalytic fuel cells.

Danza still lived at home with his parents in Connecticut. Glick was paying two hundred dollars a month to sleep on a couch in the basement of an apartment in Crown Heights. And Julian lived with his girlfriend, but she didn't like us. At all. She didn't take to us from the beginning. But then there was one time when she came home to find Glick taking a shower in her bathroom and that was the final nail in the coffin. Julian was still paying for that one.

So we went to this bar on Thirty-Fourth Street, which was centrally located and had cheap pitchers. As usual, I was late and coming straight from my office in the financial district. By the time I got there, they'd all been drinking for hours.

"This night is going to be huge," Glick declared, as I took my seat at the table, took off my coat, loosened my tie. "HUGE."

If there was one thing I appreciated about Glick, it was his deluded optimism. Call it delusion, naivety, or just a bloated sense of self-importance in the world. It was his way, before any night out, to set the stakes, and make them sky-high, didn't matter the details. And it was a good way to be, to have some enthusiasm. Why not?

"What's the plan, anyway?" I said, pouring myself a beer. "Are we actually doing Lower East Side?"

"Absolutely, we are," replied Glick.

"I'm down," Julian said. "Do we have an exact location?"

We were two years out of college, and now that we had jobs and a little bit of money to spend, the city felt brand-new. Every weekend, we found new places to go, discovered new neighborhoods. We wanted to make the most of it and do every fun thing we could. Yeah, we wanted to meet girls and get laid, but that wasn't our primary objective. Our number-one priority was to have a good time, to get drunk and do stupid shit.

"Let's go to Hair of the Dog," said Glick. "I hear it's good."

"Can we get in?" I asked.

"Benjamin, have faith," Glick answered.

"I don't want to go if we can't get in," I said. "We spent all last Saturday night waiting on line."

"We can get in," he said, with confidence.

"Then sold."

We wanted to take it to the city, but really, we were lucky if we got into a cool spot. We didn't have *much* money. We were always waiting on line. The problem was that we weren't going to anonymous, half-empty places, but we also weren't buying bottles or tables. We were always going to that elusive cool bar that was overflowing with people, but not too expensive or exclusive to let us in. To get into a "cool bar" was a special achievement.

"Kate texted me that she's going to some tiki bar on Essex. PKNY," Julian said. Danza started to laugh, making a clicking sound with his cheek. Julian ignored him.

"Kate, huh?" Glick said. "What else did she say?"

Julian replied, "She's a friend."

"I need to find myself a *friend*," said Danza, getting up to go to the bathroom. He was wearing a buttoned-down shirt that was too small. From the back, you could see his spine through the fabric. You could see his arm muscles too, but that was probably the point. "I'm down. Let's go."

"Whatever you say," Glick agreed, and then added, "boss," which made him smile. Every time. He'd given Josh his "Danza" nickname because he was the team captain, so he was the boss, which led to Tony Danza from *Who's the Boss?* When Glick came up with it, he was thrilled. You'd think he'd discovered plutonium. Every time he met someone new, he threw out the reference, hoping they'd bite and ask what it was about.

And oh boy, when they did, that made Glick's night. His eyes would widen, so excited to tell them the essence of the nickname. In his mind, the entire party was gathered around him, like he was some old storyteller getting ready to spin a tale for the ages. That was Glick's way, and we loved him for it.

"Are you crashing at my place tonight?" I said to Danza.

"No. I'm taking the five a.m. train back to Connecticut," he replied.

I laughed. "That must be quite a sight."

"Yup. Only winners on that train."

"All right, guys. Get your game faces on," Glick said, and then made a hand signal toward the waitress, indicating the check.

The four of us were on the hockey team together at Columbia, which wasn't what it sounded like. It wasn't playing against Yale or Brown on Saturdays with a filled stadium, with parents drinking hot chocolate and girls in knit hats pulled down over their ears cheering us on, making us feel better after, if we lost. Columbia didn't have an actual hockey team, so this was more like a club team where we played against SUNY New Paltz with nobody in the stands and spent hours in the damn van driving in the middle of the night because somebody left the equipment behind and we had to go back for it. I'd never admit it to the guys, but I think it meant more to me than it did to all of them combined—I'd played all through high school, and I was grateful to play in college, even if it was for a shitty pseudo team whose season got suspended junior year because we got caught drinking in the locker room and for recruiting new members with T-shirts that read DON'T BE A PUSSY. JOIN COLUMBIA HOCKEY. Like most bad ideas, it started with Glick.

"Let's get out of here," Danza said a few minutes later, downing the last of his beer. Julian started nodding. I poured a second glass for myself and then chugged it.

On the train down to Grand Street, Glick started badgering me about my job. He did this all the time, wherever we were. He could be pretty annoying about it.

"How was work today? Did they give you the full hour for lunch?" he asked.

"Yup," I said. "Got the full hour. Standard union rules."

"What kind of hard hats do they give you guys? Can you keep them at the end of the job? Or do they keep track of everything, and it all goes to the next job site? Swipe one for me next time. I'd love a hard hat."

I was a glorified construction worker to him. He made jokes about the union, as if he knew anything about it. In reality, I worked in the structural and civil engineering department of Skidmore, Owings & Merrill, an architectural firm that had won the bid to build the Freedom Tower. I was the lowest-level person there, but it was pretty exciting. To give you a clear picture of my place on the totem pole: I ran the numbers. I did the wind-speed calculations. I worked on the modeling, made sure the structure was capable of resisting things—the people in it, garage vehicles, snow, wind, and ice. These all stressed the materials of the building throughout its duration. It had to have the capacity to resist.

The fact that I was in the engineering school in college and my friends were studying liberal arts seemed to always be an issue. I didn't get it, but it was a big deal to them. They treated me like I was a different sort of person, like because I hadn't read *Infinite Jest* fourteen times, I wasn't being properly socialized. They asked me once if I knew how to build a boat out of firewood, as if being an engineer meant learning archaic survival skills and when you were done, you got shipped off to a *Survivor*-type island to see how you'd do. Once, I asked them if they'd ever thought about something for class that wasn't purely theoretical. I got a look of abject confusion, and I never asked anything like that again. That was not the way to make friends at Columbia. You had to be pro *Infinite Jest* at all times.

Everyone asked why I didn't become an architect. After all, I worked at a well-known architecture firm. I explained that architecture was the visual aspect of the building. Architects provided a new design, but they worked with civil engineers like me (read: my bosses), because we were the ones who knew the materials, the high beams, the glass, the walls, where everything went or didn't go. The architects came up with a general idea of what they wanted the building to look like. *Let's have it resemble a bird that's flapping its wings! A serpent rising up from the sand!* In this case, they wanted the Freedom Tower to combine the sense of a memorial with the city rebuilding itself and pushing toward the future. So we were always dealing with a lot of artistic mumbo jumbo and people having grand ideas and then we as engineers were tasked with making it all work. It had to be structurally stable without taking away from artistic purposes, and it had to be buildable. We designed the structure of the building to make sure that it didn't, you know, fall down. And while everyone agreed that our job was important, it was significantly less cool.

I always got the same puzzled response from people, something like, "Hmmm, that's interesting. I don't think I know any civil engineers." Conversation over. But Glick was more aggressive about it. He was probably just pissed that he didn't have his own thing. After getting rejected by every consulting firm in the metropolitan area, he ended up with a job doing marketing for his father's swimming-pool company. He said it was only temporary, but it's hard to get a better job when you don't apply for one. I watched him now, on the subway, cleaning his fingernails. He had a small piece of turkey on his cheek, from a sandwich, hours earlier. I was waiting for the right moment to tell him about it.

When we got out of the subway, we walked a few blocks. We passed stores selling restaurant supplies and food wholesale, awnings displaying vague names like INTERNATIONAL MEN'S CLOTHIERS and NEW ERA FACTORY OUTLET. Some had clothes hanging in the window, others looked to be filled with cardboard boxes and dry cleaning. We passed a T-shirt shop and Glick pointed to a yellow T-shirt in the window that read TALKING IS HARD, and said, "Hey, Ben, we should get that one for you." Julian and Danza laughed. Glick liked to call me boring. That was his big joke with me. I ignored him. Always. Maybe I didn't express myself well. But Glick had a ton of personality, and nobody was particularly impressed. I'd rather be quiet than full of shit.

It was grittier in this neighborhood. There was a sense of history. It was old New York, except that there were also a few pizza places, upscale cocktail lounges, and packs of young people standing outside bars. There was a disconnect between people and backdrop, as if we were all presupposed into this universe. It was modern-day life in an old setting, a taste of how New York used to be at the turn of the century. It gave us a chance to see what it was like, to feel like the city might actually be danger-ous, even though, in reality, it wasn't. It was just enough danger to be fun.

We passed a bar called Stanton Social, a more upscale es-tablishment. We tried to get in. But they turned us down, and I can't say I blamed them. We were a bunch of drunk dudes. *"Oh, I'm sorry I forgot to wear my blazer tonight!"* Glick yelled, as we were leaving. On the way out, he spotted a young couple eating with their teenaged children. *"I'm sorry that I'm not here trying to have a nice family dinner!"*

There was a coffee cup on the street. He kicked it, thinking it was empty, but it was full and splashed all over Julian. "Are you fucking kidding me?" Julian yelled, going after him. It was hilarious. As if everything had lined up perfectly for that one moment. Julian's entire back and pants were covered in coffee. And the rest of us didn't get a single drop. Danza bought a set of dice from some guy on the street.

Once we got to Essex, we spotted the tiki bar, wedged between 47 Essex Street, a sporting-goods store that sold team uniforms, and 51 Essex Street, a place called the Pickle Guys, which had two barrels in front of it and a banner that read, WE SHIP NATIONWIDE! There was no sign for PKNY, but we knew it from the sight of a palm tree painted onto a brick wall.

"X marks the spot," Julian said.

"Nice!" Glick said, snapping his fingers and pointing. "Now you know we're in paradise."

Whenever Glick snapped and pointed, he was giving his approval. It was his way of showing that something scratched him right where he itched. We walked in and did our standard surveillance of the situation, each focused on our own set of priorities. Glick wanted to figure out the quickest and most efficient way to get a drink. Danza wanted to evaluate the male-to-female ratio and where to stand for maximum exposure. Julian was focused more on the music and tended to judge bars based purely on their selections. He claimed to have a sophisticated musical palate, but as far as I could tell, he just wanted to hear Billy Joel.

The four of us sprang at an empty table across from the bamboo bar. The table had just opened up when we walked in, and it felt like the greatest luck. Finding an empty table at a hopping bar was gold. We set about deciphering the menu, smug with our seats, like we could order anything now, like we owned the place.

"Are these all drinks?" Danza said, flipping through the six-page menu of frozen cocktails, mai tais, highballs, Scorpion Bowls, Sipping Spirits.

"I don't even care," Julian said. "I just want something with rum. Nothing frozen."

"No, I'm not going frozen either," I said. "I think I'm going to get the Lei Lani Volcano."

"I'm getting the Kon-Tiki Tropical Itch . . . or the Sleeping Giant . . ." Danza squinted at the menu.

"Strong choices. I'm going to go with the Dying Bastard or the Dead Bastard. One of the Bastards," Glick said, delighted. He always chose his drink based on the name, and this place really catered to his sensibilities. Every time he picked a drink, he enunciated every syllable and got all excited. He said, "It's not just about the drink. It's about what the drink *represents*!" Few people loved to drink as much as Glick.

As we waited, Kate came over to talk to us, or rather, to Julian.

"Hello, boys," she said. "Michael." She gave Glick a proper nod and stuck out her hand for him to shake. She was the only one who addressed him by his first name. She must have been tipsy. The three of us usually got the freeze from her. Kate was very beautiful. And I mean, she was universally considered a knockout. She was half Asian and had this exotic look about her. And confidence. She had a lot of confidence. She was one of those women who could easily put out that "It's nice to meet you / hang out with you / talk to you, but I don't need you" vibe.

"Where's Ali tonight?" she said to Julian, with almost a smile. Julian used to hook up with Kate in college, despite the fact that she was way out of his league. They were never dating, but she used to keep him around so that she could call him at the end of the night. He'd literally go running to wherever she was. One time, we were sitting in the McDonald's in Times Square and she told him that she was at a bar near Columbia. He said he was too, and then made a mad dash for the subway. She instructed him that they were "FWB," or Friends with Benefits. And now that Julian was with somebody else, she seemed to be even more hell-bent on keeping him around.

"Ali's not feeling well tonight," he said to her, not looking at her directly, and Kate did a slow, satisfied nod and then twirled herself away, toward the bar. She'd gotten all the information she wanted. For now.

All of us watched Kate as she walked away. She found her friend, a girl named Eve Something-or-other, who we knew from college. Eve didn't turn to see us. And frankly, if she didn't come over, it was no big loss. I wasn't interested in our usual round of chitchat. "Remember me? I'm Julian's roommate." We'd had the same conversation at least ten times. I felt like I knew her though, because we saw each other all the time—mutual friends, parties, the whole thing. There was one summer where I went with Julian to meet her and her friends in Central Park for some concert and I remember seeing her on the lawn with a blanket spread out underneath her and two bottles of wine, a small package of crackers. She'd come prepared, and there was something sort of cute about it, how she was all set up like that. She made a big stink when Glick took out a forty of Pabst and started passing it around.

That group of girls was always funny in general. We didn't really know them too well, but we went to their parties. We were *around* them a lot. Everything they did was so incredibly girly. They threw Valentine's Day parties, talked about their outfits, and went to the bathroom in groups. All their conversations were conducted in a secret tongue, and, although I understood each of the words individually, when strung together at that voracious speed, the whole thing passed me by like a speeding train. I saw it happen, but if you asked me to describe it a layer deeper than that, I'd be at a loss.

"That is one quality FWB," Glick said, with a smirk.

"Not anymore," Julian said. "That ship has sailed."

The thing about Julian was this: he had the kavorka when it came to getting girls. Nobody knew exactly why. Whether he was extraordinarily good-looking, I couldn't say. But basically, he knew how to talk to them, a skill that the rest of us had yet to master. He knew what to say, how much to say. He had an easy way of asking them questions. He turned on the charm, but not so much that it seemed like he was actually turning on the charm. Whereas Glick had his own foolproof method. He would stare a girl down, eyes scanning her from head to toe, as she passed us by, and then he'd raise his chin slightly in her direction, at what he believed to be just the right moment. To say that it never worked was an understatement.

"No, man. She doesn't want to be FWB anymore," Glick said. "Now she wants to be MWC."

"MWC?"

"Married with Children."

As soon as we got our drinks, Glick turned to Julian and started on him about Ali. "So how's the girlfriend treating you? Why isn't she here again?"

"Ah, she wasn't feeling well. I told you. She didn't want to come out tonight," he said.

"Is she ever feeling well? What's the deal?" Glick was being an ass, but he had a point.

"She's never around," Danza chimed in, and Danza hardly ever talked shit about anyone. He played it cool. He didn't keep tabs, usually.

"It's been over a month since we've seen her." I decided to throw my hat in the ring, as long as everyone else was.

"Is she so disgusted by us that she can't even fake it?" Glick continued. "Or are we talking about more serious issues below the surface? Slow burn? *Attention ground control*, Julian is fizzling out . . . *we're going to have a crash landing here.* Clear the runway, make room, we have a goner!"

"So?" Julian said, getting fed up already. "What about you guys? Ben, you were lucky enough to hook up with that girl from Kansas? Or Kentucky? One of those. But then you went back to her place and she made you watch *Titanic* and you fell asleep and she threw you out. And, Danza, didn't the girl you hooked up with last weekend tell you that she never wanted to hook up with you again, but if she saw you, she'd say hi?"

Danza's face turned serious. "Cut it out, man. You're making us sound terrible," he said, looking around and over his shoulder.

"Or amazing," said Glick.

"And, Glick, seriously the last time you got any action was *at least* a year ago, and the only reason she agreed to go home with you was because you told her that you had pot, which you didn't." Julian was right about Glick, at least. His hookups were few and far between. Each time it happened, I half expected him to take out an ad in the newspaper.

Then, as was inevitable, the old stories started flowing. Oh, the enthusiasm that we could muster for stories we'd told and retold hundreds of times, but it was fun to remember. *College*, what a crazy time that was . . . all two and a half years ago.

"I dodged the ambulance service *multiple* times," Glick mused.

"They thought I was too drunk. *Girls*, man. Trying to help. Not realizing that a passed-out guy in the corner is not a reason to call an ambulance. Amateurs . . . I showed them."

"You did," Danza agreed. "Except that one time that they actually got you and you had to escape."

"I did. I had to fucking escape! I walked across campus in a hospital gown." He took a sip of his drink. "And let me tell you something. Those gowns are *breezy*. They provide very little protection."

"They're not meant to be worn outside," I reasoned.

"Let's be real," Julian said. "It's a step up from your usual clothes."

"What's wrong with my usual clothes?"

"It's sixty degrees outside and you're wearing corduroys," Julian said. "Those are winter pants, man. I don't consider myself an expert on fashion by any stretch of the imagination, but that much I know. Aren't you hot in them? Do you not just have a river of sweat running down your backside?"

Glick ignored us and ordered another drink. He did an impression of an exotic bird for the waitress. Glick was the butt of every joke, but he took it well because he knew. What would we all talk about, if not for him?

"You know what, let's get Danza drunk for once," Glick said, half to the unimpressed waitress, half to us. "I've never seen him drunk. Let's get him good and drunk and then you can all spare me your usual judgments. A round for the table, m'lady!" he cried with a wave of his arm. The waitress looked confused and vaguely pissed-off, but nodded and returned several minutes later with a tray full of alcohol.

So we drank. A lot. Julian spent a solid half hour talking in the corner of the bar with Kate, during which time we made fun of him mercilessly, for the way he was standing there with such a stressed-out look on his face, as if torn apart by some moral dilemma, and yet shamelessly watching her fiddle with the necklace hanging near her chest. "Your girlfriend is outside," Glick said to him, a lie that worked like a charm. He was back sitting with us in no time.

Danza took out the dice and we started playing c-lo. It was a game we played sometimes in the locker room with three six-sided dice where you kept rolling until two out of three dice matched and your score was the amount on the remaining dice. The person with the highest score won the pot. We were rolling the dice at our table, gambling, taking bets, involving the bouncer and making a huge scene, cash on the ground, cash on the table. We ended up losing about a hundred dollars to a group of girls, a bachelorette party. Then, Danza made out with the bride-to-be after using some stupid line like, "Aren't you supposed to kiss a stranger tonight?"

By one o'clock in the morning, we were stinking drunk. And hungry. We talked about going to a pancake place on Clinton Street.

"Isn't it closed?"

"Whatever, we'll start pounding on the door. I'm sure they get deliveries. We'll say, *The yeast is coming and so are we!*" Glick yelled.

"I'm not breaking into a pancake place," I said. "There's a diner on every corner."

"Yeah, dude, that is not the only restaurant in Manhattan to get food right now," Julian said.

"We are *doing this*," Glick insisted. "It's not about the fucking pancakes, it's about the fucking principle."

"*What principle?*" I shouted, eyes wide. The argument went

on for much, much longer than it should have. It somehow became a question of loyalty. Always. Everything was for the team.

"Guys. We set a goal and we have to achieve it," Glick said. "We shouldn't settle for anything less than that fluffy pancake in the sky!" He got all red-faced and fired-up. "We need to end the night this way. Don't you guys realize? This entire night has been leading up to these pancakes. Without these pancakes, the whole night didn't exist." He started shaking his head. "I'm not doing this for me. I'm doing this for *all of us*. I'm doing this so that tomorrow, you'll wake up and your stomach will be full and you'll say, *Wow, what an amazing fucking night*."

Glick was an idiot, and there was no way to reason with him once he had something stuck in his head. Julian was a free bird that night, with his girlfriend busy doing something else, "not feeling well" or "working" or whatever it was, and even though he was yawning like crazy, he wasn't going home a minute sooner than he had to. Danza could barely keep his eyes open, but he insisted that he was a "team player" and "taking one for the team," which meant never backing out of anything, ever. And you know what, good for him. I said good-bye and started to walk away from them. I guess I didn't possess the leadership qualities of a Danza, that diehard devotion. I left them all there, to the sound of groans and protests.

"Glick," I yelled, from across the bar. "You have turkey on your face."

Not everyone can be the team captain.

- - - -

The walk to the subway would be good with nobody around. I was hoping I wouldn't have to wait too long for the train. The streets looked different, now that the night was over. The Lower East Side had a coolness to it, but when you looked more carefully, there was a crustiness to everything too. A romanticizing went on, but in the end, it was a neighborhood of old tenements. There was a reason why everyone left before we got here. It was not one of the nicer parts of town. It was housing for the poorest class of people. Twenty years ago, a room probably cost fifty dollars a month. They say these houses have improved, but it was hard to believe that, from the looks of them. It was the least possible amount of light and air for tenants and the greatest number of people crowded into the space. I learned a lot about areas like this in an urban infrastructure class that I took in college, about tenements, the damage of congestion, the lack of park space and open areas.

The Lower East Side had an allure, but the more time you spent there, the more carefully you looked, you realized it. The cracks were visible. The allure dissipated. It was the complete absence of engineering. No engineer had ever looked at any of it. If you were to walk into any Lower East Side tenement and put a marble on the floor, it would roll down to one side of the room. The floors weren't level, and that drove me crazy. Not to mention the walls were not vertical, all out of plumb. Calculations were never done.

As I rounded the corner of Houston and Ludlow, I heard a guy talking. The voice got louder as I walked, but I couldn't see anything. I turned, like he might be talking to me. But then I looked across the narrow street and I saw Eve. She was standing next to this guy in a plaid shirt who looked familiar to me from college. He was in a band. Or something. I don't know why but this guy had this look about him, a look that screamed unemployment. But then, in college Eve was always with guys like that. Nobody really knew what she was doing. Anyway. Plaid Shirt was standing across from her. She was a few feet from him, arms across her chest. Something about him always irked me. He was the type of guy who wouldn't talk to you unless you had something for him.

"Jesus, what is up with you tonight?"

"I'm scared!" she said, and then caught herself yelling, lowered her voice. She sat down on a bench. "And I know people say that all the time, but I don't have parents, so cut me some slack, please, because sometimes, I feel completely alone in the world. And I know that people say *that* too, but in my case, it's actually true."

I felt glued to my spot on the street. As soon as I heard her say that, I had this strange feeling, like I was invested in what was happening.

"You're not alone," he said, and then he walked over, sat down next to her. He sounded calmer than I expected him to. I watched the wisps of her hair moving in the wind.

"I feel like I'm desperately trying to hold on to something or *someone*. And you're not . . . holding."

"Oh, really? Like how I held your head every night while you were sleeping?"

Oh brother. This guy.

"Look. Eve. It's not your fault. It's like there's this darkness inside of me. There's not a single day when I wake up and wish that it weren't there, but I don't know how to get rid of it."

"I know exactly what you mean though. Doesn't that help? Shouldn't that help?"

"No. Because your darkness isn't like my darkness."

It should be illegal for two English majors to date each other.

"I thought that it was," she said, shaking her head and staring at the ground. "I thought that . . . we were."

"I'm just tired, man, and I'm tired of talking to you about this and the reality is . . . *I will never have this with anyone.*" He motioned to the space between them and then stood up, started pacing around in a circle, moving around a lot. I was sure of it now. Something was amped up about him. Maybe he was high.

"Whatever I'll have with other people will be something else, and it's such a heartbreaking idea, isn't it? But we might be wrong for each other! Okay? It's true! We might be wrong for each other! And we could battle it out for months, years even, and you'll get mad and I'll be sorry and we'll both ultimately come up short. There is no doubt in my mind that some intangible thing connects us, and that we have become tied together in a way that I might never find with someone else. This alone could sustain us for a long time. I could stay with you just to avoid that endogenous and visceral fear of never finding it again."

Endogenous? Okay, now he was making up words.

She put her hand up to her mouth and looked like she was going to cry. Was she going to cry? I wasn't too sharp about this kind of thing, but she looked like she might cry. I took a few steps to my left, officially lurking in the shadows, but I didn't care if I got caught. She wouldn't care. I was just some acquaintance, though I felt some instinctual need to help her, not sure why, but there was nothing I could do, as she sat there, concentrating on him.

"What?" he said. "You don't like the drugs, right? The fact that I do drugs bothers you? Well, you are pretty and smart and there's no reason that you need to put up with someone like me. No reason, and you shouldn't. You just shouldn't. I would recommend against it. Go."

"But you're . . ."

"I'm WHAT?" he yelled.

"Nothing . . . it's just . . . I would never have had the guts to say all this to you. You may be right, but I would never have been able to talk about us like that, in the past tense. What you're saying sounds nice, they're nice words, but they sound a whole lot like good-bye."

"You know that you basically pressed me into this place, right? You forced a conclusion. This is what *you* wanted."

Then, she started to put her hand on her forehead, on her eyes, all over. He sat there, didn't move. What was the matter with him? What was the big deal that you couldn't just shut up and make someone feel better? No reason to torture each other. With an upset girl on my hands, my tendency was always to back down, to be quiet, overly agreeable. I was never overtly mean. Or maybe I was and I didn't realize it. I guess there have been times of drunk fighting when things weren't totally talked out but then we had sex and forgot about it. I was once seeing this girl who annoyed the hell out of me, but the sex was fun because I was sort of perpetually mad at her. Controlled doses of pain or anger could be good, I guess. But this was too much.

I started to walk again, leaving them to their conversation, in all its glory. I was feeling bad for her, but also, frankly, glad not to be involved in that kind of mess. I had no desire for a girl-friend, then, but at some point, I probably would. And when I did, I knew one thing for sure: I wanted a relationship that wasn't a lot of drama.

It was time to get the hell out of there.

EVE

The sky was darkening, in the middle of the day, which brought on that looming feeling, those ominous clouds. And then suddenly it was pouring rain and I was caught on the street with my lunch, headed back to the asset management firm where I'd been working as an assistant for the past few months because Arthur had a friend who worked there and at the point when he asked me about it, the thought of a steady paycheck had become blindingly appealing. Plus Nobu reminded me too much of Jesse, of coming home to him smelling like a plate of chicken teriyaki. I decided that I needed a clean break from that entire part of my life. It didn't fit anymore. That was the *other* Eve. The new, adult Eve was going places, like to and from the copy room. I could still write, I told myself. If I could pretend to know what asset management was, I could certainly pretend that I was still writing.

There were people all around. The streets near Bryant Park were more congested than any other part of the city. I couldn't get any clearance for myself, within the stream of bodies. And so, of course, some guy in a suit knocked me out. He hit me so hard that I fell onto the street and so did my salad. Most of it burst out of its plastic container, so it looked like it was raining fucking lettuce for a while and I had to gather the rest of it up off the ground with my hands to throw it out. Fuck. It was a thirteen-dollar salad, supposed to last for two meals.

Oh you're so busy! I wanted to yell after him, from my squatting position on the street. *You're soooooo busy!* And then, some lady walked by while I was on the ground trying to salvage some of the salad, and she knelt down and got in my face and said, *"Are you kidding? Are you kidding?"* She told me that I was disgusting, like I was homeless and eating from the garbage can in front of her, like whatever happened on the street was her personal fucking business.

And so I got fucking upset. Because sometimes a stranger getting in your face and telling you that you're disgusting is fucking upsetting. I ran after her.

"HEY!" I yelled, at the back of her head. She turned. "You know you really upset me just now. You have no right to confront someone so aggressively. You don't even know me! I was doing my best to clean up my salad, because it was thirteen dollars and money's been tight for me lately and you should really mind your own business!"

Because she shouldn't get away with something like that. She should know the results of her psychopathic actions. But then she didn't say anything, just looked kind of guilty actually, and instead of feeling vindicated, my heart started racing from the confrontation. I needed a minute to collect myself, and that's how I ended up standing in an ATM vestibule between Fifth and Sixth Avenues, trying to breathe slowly and get my heart to stop fluttering like a butterfly that's high on crack cocaine. I was there because it was the most peaceful place that I could find, and that in and of itself seemed like a problem.

It was quiet in the ATM vestibule, this paradise that I carved out for myself. I sat on a ledge where they kept the deposit slips and pens and decided that maybe I'd never leave. I wondered, *Do you think they'd let me live here?* No, of course not. Those grumblers outside would make sure that I paid the price. No square inch of this city was free. And yet, somehow, despite the expense, there were too many fucking people here. The island was not big enough. We were all just kidding ourselves. *Look at this place.* I looked out the window at all the miserable fucking people in their black coats with their giant black umbrellas, looking down at the ground, maneuvering swiftly through the streets like they were getting away with something as the rain soaked their backs.

Fucking hell. That was midtown. Or at least that was how I felt about it, and I went there each day for work, once *Outdoor World* folded and I couldn't survive in the city on my Nobu salary alone. This job had a decent salary and health benefits. Sorting documents in a small room in a giant building in midtown with only the Xerox machine to keep me company? Yes, I could do that. Will xerox for food. But each day I was becoming more and more hostile. Midtown made you feel like an ant trapped amid a towering maze of buildings, waiting for a giant shoe to crush you to death. The sky was barely visible, only in small patches, and you had to strain yourself to catch it. When you did catch it, it was not at all the relief you'd imagined it would be. *Where's the rest of it? Where is the rest of everything?* There was an unsettling amount of movement on the ground—people covering every piece of the sidewalks, lines from the door at Starbucks, a drill puncturing the pavement and creating a ruckus, two taxis swerving and blowing their horns, one driver sticking his head out the window and saying to the other, "What's the matter with you? You want to kill someone just to get a fucking fare?"

Sirens started going off, and police vehicles were zipping by. Police vans filled with officers holding guns, policemen on horses. Tell me, please, what situation in New York City requires a cavalry? I needed to know. We were probably about to get blown up. I had to assume that whenever I saw more than ten police cars zooming by. I just wished that I could get some fucking lunch before getting blown up by terrorists. Dear terrorists: I'd like to get blown up on a full stomach, if possible. More sirens. More police vehicles. Whistles. Car horns. Endless car horns. *What was going on?* Should I ask someone? Should I google it? Wouldn't that be something new? It's not like I google "NYC disaster" or "NYC fireworks" at least once per day. Nooooo, that never happens. What an extremely irrational and unproductive thing to do. You'd think I'd have gotten used to this by now. Bryant Park was nothing if not a bastion of emergency preparedness. This time, I was not going to care. I was tired of it. I'd reached that glorious point of ambivalence. I no longer wanted to know. And what was the difference anyway? It wasn't like I had a salad to get back to.

Well, while sitting in this ATM vestibule as the sky spit rain out onto the pavement like it had been holding it in for months, I started to realize what I'd been holding in for months. I started to get some good thinking done, in my infuriated state, and I finally realized it: New York was the reason for all my problems. This. Fucking. City. And I didn't have to live here. Nobody forced anyone to live in New York. It was not mandatory. You know what I could do? I could really help myself and move. I could take that job at the newspaper in Colorado that I applied to on a whim after the breakup with Jesse. It was writing about the music scene in a small town, previewing the concerts that took place at a somewhat well-known venue there. I never thought I'd hear back. But then they called and asked if I'd be willing to move to Colorado, a question I'd never before considered, and a response flew out of my mouth.

"Yes," I said, startling myself. "Yes, I would."

It now dawned on me that perhaps that escape route was also an ingenious plan. In Colorado, I'd be able to write about music. Wasn't that the goal, even if it did take me away from home? I wouldn't have to work at this place, copying and binding documents and going to somebody's birthday in the conference room at three o'clock, eating overly sweet cake and making awkward conversation and feeling sick afterward, but sadly, that was the thing I'd been looking forward to all day.

So far, in New York, I'd written about hunting and fishing, dog-breeding manuals, articles about the best office supplies in a magazine that caters exclusively to office supply managers, all freelance jobs I'd taken on, practically for free, in addition to my regular day job. FYI: there are two magazines about office supplies. The other is the *American Journal of Office Supplies*, which was considering paying me five cents a word to review office supplies (!), but I had to submit a one-thousand-word writing sample and a page of literary criticism, and I hadn't heard back yet.

The city didn't care. I wouldn't win any awards for sticking it out in this world where I was panicking inside and my heart was always racing because of all these strangers down my throat from the second I got onto the subway each morning, the homeless guy in the Superman shirt who harassed me on my way to work, telling me I'd be so pretty if only I would just *smile*.

Sometimes, the fact that my mother disappeared into this

city—was very literally swallowed up by it—instilled in me a certain amount of horror. The irrational side of me took over, in a packed subway car, or on the street with sirens blaring. The irrational side of me said: *The city took her. It could take me too.* I still didn't understand why she had to be there, in that part of the city, at that moment. Intellectually, I understood—that was her job; it was a weekday. But I still didn't understand, on some primitive level, why she had to be *there,* of all places that she could have been.

I had to drag myself toward the light, but I had no idea where to find it. Any solace I'd found with Jesse was now gone. I'd tried to move on. Had gone on all these dates, these glorified job interviews at this mediocre Italian restaurant on Twenty-Third Street. It was possible that I was going out on dates for the sole purpose of avoiding the rising dread that happened when I came home to my empty apartment, the sound of the tumblers in the locks, my landlord raising the rent and then recommending I get a loan from my father. Side note: Do you think they would let me live at the mediocre Italian restaurant on Twenty-Third Street?

A few days earlier, I was walking in Union Square and there was a *thirty-foot-tall* poster of Jesse's band in the window of the Virgin Megastore because *there is no justice in this town.* His band's debut album turned out to be a huge hit, hailed as one of the best of the year, with its innovative homage to African music. Three guys, the Empire State Building in the background. I won't sugarcoat this: the city was not big enough for this poster and me to coexist.

And yeah, I had Arthur. It was true—I had Arthur, with his ruddy cheeks and big stomach and jokes that made me slightly queasy. He had made my mother happy. He had accompanied her to all the museum exhibitions and Broadway shows that she wanted to see. Living with him had fulfilled her lifelong dream of a glamorous existence in Manhattan. He offered me his guest room, whenever I needed it. That should have been enough to keep him in my good graces forever. And yet . . . I vented to Emma, who often stayed over at his place for a few days. I thought that one day she might talk to me about his habits. He had *such habits*. But she never did. Not only did she not express her annoyance, she actually didn't seem annoyed. She responded to Arthur's endless jokes with a smile that was not quite genuine but rather faithful. *Emma had the ability to fake it? Who knew?* I followed her directions and closed my eyes and took deep breaths and pictured myself on the beach, the waves crashing, the warm sand between my toes. The problem was that I still pictured myself tackling Arthur to the ground, but in a more coastal setting.

I went to his apartment sometimes, looking for some semblance of home when I believed that my windowless apartment was the source of my sadness. But being at his place didn't feel right either. Not anymore. Last week I was on his computer and accidentally came upon the logged-out screen from a dating website for people over sixty and felt instantly the sinking feeling of being no longer welcome in his home. *He was dating again?* Of course. What did I expect? I froze when I saw the website. I sat facing the wall that night as he watched television, imagining what Arthur's dating life might look like, sinking lower and lower into despair. I thought: *Do I feel better here or at my own apartment?* I sat there in a daze, trying to plan how I'd get through tomorrow, and the next day, the dread of more and more tomorrows in this town. All this running around, frantic, never stopping to land, never finding the right place to land, all of it with crushing urgency, and *for what?*

In Colorado, I saw nothing but pure relief. The volume on

my thoughts would come down a few notches. The change of scenery would take me out of my own head. From the neck up, I would be free. I would notice the difference. For the first time, I would discover other parts of myself, like someone suddenly aware that she has legs. In Colorado, I'd be able to write without also working at an asset management firm, or a restaurant, without dog walking or pretending to like cats because some guy at Two Cats Productions likes cats and maybe he'll hire me to write about a band or maybe I'll watch his cat sometime.

Sitting there, escaping the rain, in a moment of solitude before heading back to work, I felt better than I had in a while, even just to start thinking about leaving. I didn't want to suffer anymore. I knew this place, but I was starting to see it differently, from that window on Forty-Second Street. Now, I wanted nothing more than to get out. Because New York was dirty and gray and noisy and claustrophobic and I think that New York of all places would appreciate it when I say:

Fuck this.

part three

WINTER 2010

EVE

A JAPANESE CIRCUS ON SAINT MARKS

I walked through the door and was faced with a poster of a woman being either tortured or pleasured by red octopuses. The ceiling was low. The room was narrow but stretched far back. As I continued on through the restaurant, this dark tunnel of oddities, I scanned the crowd for a familiar face. There was a Japanese flag with graffiti covering it, naked mannequins wearing gas masks, a sculpture of Godzilla destroying the Tokyo Tower. *Did it have to be so creepy?* I guess I'd been out of town for too long.

I hate to admit this but, in those first few months back in the city, I was kind of a menace to society. I was wearing ripped jeans and a bad attitude. I was stomping around the East Village thinking, *You just try to mess with me again, New York! I dare you!* I wanted everyone to know that even though I was "back," I wasn't going to run the whole New York race. There was more out there than just this city, and I knew about it now. I'd hiked mountains. I'd gone *camping*. I'd made myself into a music reporter. I'd gone to hundreds of concerts and interviewed famous musicians on the phone while they ate lunch in their tour buses. I'd dated guys who jumped out of helicopters without a second thought. Basically: I had *lived*. I had seen things. I had an *edge*.

But when I wasn't paying attention, New York was seeping back into me. How else can I explain it? The damn city fit like a glove. Why else would I feel so at home, so *finally* back at home, even on Saint Marks Place, which was the intersection of punk and Japan and drug paraphernalia? I looked up at the building that matched the address in my hands. The minute I'd heard 25 Saint Marks Place, it sounded familiar. I'd researched it for one of my music columns on electronic music. 19-25 Saint Marks Place used to be the home of the Electric Circus, a nightclub that embodied the bohemianism and club culture of the sixties. Experimental bands like the Grateful Dead and the Velvet Underground played there, with jugglers, mimes, flamethrowers and trapeze artists performing during breaks in the music. It was the epitome of that drug-fueled psychedelic time, with black lights and strobe lights and the pervasive smell of smoke everywhere. Over the years, 19-25 Saint Marks Place went from nightclub to German music society to community hall to Polish organization to a "dry disco" for Alcoholics Anonymous. Then, the building was split up into apartment buildings. And now, on the ground floor of 25 Saint Marks Place, there was a very strange Japanese restaurant where I was meeting my friends for the first time in a long while.

When I first got to Colorado, the new backdrop, new people, new food, new *everything* felt like some version of therapy. All my old rhythms were gone. It was like I had fallen into a maze with different intricacies and I was moving within it, a bit lost, but like a person who had been lit up from the inside. There was a fair degree of stumbling. I often felt like an outsider. There were nights when I would have killed to hear the sound of my phone ring. But all that felt like part of the experience, and it went away eventually, once I'd made a few friends at the newspaper.

But nearly three years later, I must admit, it was equally exquisite to return to New York. The city—yes, even the old, crummy, loud, chaotic city—had become new, especially the parts of it that I hadn't experienced much before. Saint Marks was like being transported to another world, to a smattering of weirdness that looked like it belonged in Tokyo. It was a strip of neon lights, the awnings cluttered next to one another, the colorful signs selling psychic readings, comics, socks, records, piercings, wigs, foot massages. And yet, I was walking through it with such euphoria. Escaping the city is easy, but there is no known cure for how good it feels to come back.

Outside the restaurant, there were a number of people standing around, waiting to get in. There was a slightly demonic statue in the entranceway, and an electronic cat's arm was moving up and down. It was the type of place where you felt like you had to be in the know to go inside, and I certainly wasn't. As I stood in front of the sliding door, I felt a strange rush of excitement. *I was going to see my friends again!* Yes: the friends who I'd snubbed, who I'd so desperately needed a break from, moved across the country from, the friends who I'd decided were no good, too difficult, too "New York." I was now thrilled with the knowledge that they were inside.

"My friends are here already," I was prepared to say to anyone who asked, but nobody did. There didn't appear to be a single person in charge. There were only hurried waiters and platters of steaming food and bedlam.

Then I saw Kate and Maya, sitting at a long, rectangular table against the back wall. Behind them, there was a picture of two feet crushing a line of delicately drawn plants and flowers. Some of the people at the table I recognized, some were strangers. Kate was leaning against Maya. They were cracking up at something on her phone. Kate gripped Maya's arm and fell into her, laughing. The girl next to Kate, who I didn't recognize, was looking at them, probably wondering what all the fuss was about, but I knew. They could throw themselves into laughter as much as they could despair or paranoia. It was just the way they were—open and honest and volatile.

The sight of Kate and Maya made me hopeful. There'd been some time apart, but we'd grown up together, in a way. Or at least, we'd spent some important years together. Scarlett had drifted from the group, ever since heading to Los Angeles for medical school. We hardly heard from her, except for an occasional update about the weather, for instance, "Heard it's snowing there. It's seventy-five in LA!" or "Hey, guys! I think I'm officially a Californian. It's fifty degrees outside and I'm freezing! I'm wearing boots!" Maya would forward the e-mail to Kate and me and write, "I'd like to tell her where she can put her boots. Has she always been this self-righteous?" Maya was upset because while she was spending her days at Elmhurst Hospital in Queens cleaning vomit off the floor in a packed waiting room, Scarlett appeared to be studying on the beach.

As I walked toward them, some changes to Maya and Kate were immediately noticeable. Maya wasn't wearing those big glasses anymore. She'd opted for a more conventional, less cartoonish pair. She was also wearing a black sweater she'd worn occasionally in college, but back then it was for job interviews and other proper occasions only. Now, the sweater appeared to be part of her everyday rotation. Kate's clothes were more formal too. Instead of her usual T-shirt or tank top, worn in college as an homage to her California roots, she was wearing an off-white silk shirt, and a black blazer was slung over the chair behind her.

"EVE!" Kate yelled, above the noise. I leaned across the table to hug them and they pulled my arm and tried to drag me over the table completely. I felt my shirt coming up, a fork graze against my stomach. A few, more sensible people got up to allow me to shuffle inside. I scanned the table, waving hello to the few guys I recognized from college who had all been buddies on the hockey team—Glick, Ben, another guy they called Danza.

They're still hanging out with these guys? I thought to myself. *On purpose?*

"Oooooo, she's so *Colorado* now," I could hear Glick say to the others. I had no clue why he was saying that. All right. I had some clue. It was the jeans.

"These guys? Still?" I said, turning to Kate and Maya, cocking my head to the right and eyeing them.

"We've become drinking buddies!" Maya said proudly. "They're very easy to deal with, as it turns out."

"They're always available on a random Thursday," Kate said, listing off the benefits on her fingers. "They're punctual. They often pay for drinks. They didn't abandon us for Colorado."

I smiled. "Ohhhh, I see."

"Why are you back?" Glick shouted. "Please explain in three sentences or less." He pointed at my mouth with his chopsticks, as if offering me a microphone.

"I got a better job here," I said into the chopsticks. I didn't think he'd be interested in the details of how I'd managed to translate three years of music reporting in Colorado into a job as an assistant at Voice, a music-sharing program that published original content on its website. Career talk wasn't really his specialty.

"I can't believe we got you out of your apartment!" Kate said.

"Yeah, what have you been *doing*?" Maya wanted to know.

"Working," I said.

Kate nodded. Maya rolled her eyes. "Yeah, right," she said. "You've been on your couch eating frozen yogurt and you know it."

"Like I can't be doing both?" I replied.

Maya laughed. "Oh, that's all right," she said, hugging me. I felt the warmth of her. *Finally, somebody who actually knew me, who I actually knew.* The smell of her sweater brought me right back to college. When I first met Maya, it was two weeks into freshman year, and she was standing in front of her closet and telling me about this club downtown in the Meatpacking District that had space-themed dance parties every Monday night. "Deep Space Mondays!" she had explained, while throwing clothes across the room. I went with her downtown to the club that night, wearing one of her short, sparkly skirts, and we danced for hours to electronic, deep space–y, futuristic music and then went where all broke girls in college go at the end of the night for sustenance—Duane Reade. We sat on the staircase of someone's town house, bleary-eyed and eating Entenmann's cookies, unable to stop laughing, laughing so hard that it hurt. We discovered that we were different but the same, and in one glorious moment, I saw my future, and it was friendship with a girl named Maya. I just couldn't believe that I wouldn't get to tell my mother, the woman who had sat across from me at that little round kitchen table throughout middle school and high school, analyzing the state of my friendships. I remember from the second that I became friends with Maya, I couldn't believe that I wouldn't get to tell my mother all about her. *How could I not tell her? How could I never get to tell her that I'd made my first friend in college?*

As Maya pulled away from me, she grabbed hold of my earlobe and inspected it, her eyes about an inch away from my face.

"Is this an extra piercing? Are you in the midst of a Goth phase?" She gave Kate an urgent look, pulled my ear toward her. "What is going on?" she demanded.

"Um, *no*," I answered, with a smile. "I'm not sixteen."

"Have you heard anything from Jesse?" Maya asked.

"No," I said, shaking my head and looking down at my plate. "Thank God."

The truth was I spent most of my time wandering music stores, after work and on the weekends, and I had to deliberately avoid anything related to Jesse's band. It seemed like everywhere I looked, there he was. Lately, the band was receiving some backlash. They were repeatedly called a group of upper-class Ivy League graduates staking improper claim to foreign music. But the bad press only enhanced their popularity. I tried not to look, but late at night I read articles where Jesse was quoted defending the band, saying that they all had part-time jobs in college, that to this day they were paying off student loans.

I didn't tell anyone at Voice that I knew him, even though it would have helped me there. Voice was a place where I felt entirely out of my league. I went to parties at the office in SoHo—this beautiful loft with signed album covers on the walls, "listening" rooms filled with silk pillows—seriously, each room contained no fewer than twenty brightly colored pillows scattered on the floor. The owner was a billionaire who made his money doing something else before this that nobody really understood, so there was no shortage of funds.

I went to the shows that I was assigned to, and didn't think twice about going alone. I didn't feel scared, didn't feel *so very alone* in the city. As I walked the streets of the East Village, I looked down at myself and realized that something in Colorado made this person happen. It must have been the journey, the being taken out of my element, the new friends who disregarded me every time I said, "But I'm a little bit afraid of heights!" I'd gotten so full on my independence.

"Have you guys ordered yet?" I asked, staring down at the menu of "food challenges"— turkey testicles and maggot-fried noodles and a giant plate of rice that was free but only if you could eat it in less than twenty minutes. There was a "Russian roulette" appetizer, which involved a ball of dough, filled with wasabi, hidden among other identical-looking dumplings that contained octopus. The menu was enormous and an organizational disaster. There was nothing recognizable on it. I flipped through pages and pages of Japanese words next to English words that were just as foreign.

"Who picked this place anyway?" I said.

"Who do you think?" Kate looked at Maya. I should have known. Maya loved restaurants with a theme, or anything kitschy. In college, she used to drag me to Ninja New York because she liked the waiters dressed as ninjas, the magic tricks that they performed between courses. I tried to be a good sport about it, to take the "secret passageway" into the restaurant instead of the standard elevator. But then, one time, a ninja jumped out from behind our table and startled me to the point where the piece of sushi that had been in my chopsticks went flying into the air. "Never again," I vowed after, and she agreed that it had been a bit too much that time.

"*People*," said Glick. "Let's make some decisions. What are we drinking tonight?"

I looked around at the table. There were pitchers of beer everywhere. Apparently, that wasn't enough. Maya insisted that we order a round of sake bombs. She gave directions to the waiter. "We need eight shots of hot sake." The guys ordered chicken wings, platters of them, so many that the waiter asked if they wanted the platinum level of chicken wing situations. They turned him down in favor of the bronze, which showed a lot of restraint on their part.

"So," I said, turning to Maya. "How's residency treating you?"

"Ohhhh, fine," Maya said. "If you don't count the fact that every time I have to take a test, I lose feeling in my hands."

"What?"

"Eve. I want to be a *surgeon*. My hands are very important to me."

"Well, my hands are very important to me too, but . . ."

She acted like there was no further explanation necessary, and then, when I gave her a blank stare, said slowly as though she were explaining something obvious to a child, *"And sooooo* that would be the worst thing, for something to happen to my hands. Stress can do some crazy shit to you. Do you remember when I took acid a week before my MCATs because I thought it would get rid of my anxiety?"

"Yeah, and it actually just made things much worse," Kate said. *"Obviously."*

"I went to Grant's Tomb! I felt the need to visit some sort of memorial, but I thought that everyone I saw was a *ghost*."

"So now you're imagining that you're losing feeling in your hands?" I asked.

"Of course. It makes perfect sense."

"Well, I'm a writer, so . . ." I put my hands out in front of me, looked down at them. They were feeling tingly, all of a sudden.

"Stop it!" Kate yelled, pushing my hands against the table. "Don't listen to her. She's insane." She gave Maya a look of warning. "Don't encourage her."

"On the plus side, I get to wear black scrubs now! *Black!*" she said, thrilled by the notion. "So much better than blue, in terms of the potential for accessorizing. Do you know how hard it is to accessorize with light blue?"

I shook my head.

"It's very limiting," she insisted. "Especially with my skin tone. Black will be so much better."

"Sounds like a very positive development," I said. I looked across the table at Kate, who was giving Maya an annoyed look. "And how's the world of finance?" I asked her.

She sighed. "It's good, but intense. I'm trying to deal." She closed her eyes slightly, took a deep breath, and touched her index finger to her thumb. "Charlie keeps trying to get me to see a life coach, but I don't like the idea of being told what to do by someone who willingly became a life coach."

I laughed. Charlie was Kate's fiancé, who I'd seen pictures of on Facebook but had never actually met. He was from Arkansas and worked as a photographer's assistant at a studio in Chelsea. Strange how much had happened since I left, that Kate had a fiancé who I didn't even know.

"Where is Charlie tonight?" I asked.

"On a shoot in Istanbul. He's so annoyingly good at his job." She sighed. "All these famous photographers like Annie Leibovitz and Mark Seliger are constantly requesting his presence. I'm just hoping he doesn't sleep with one of the models." She said this breezily, but there was a slight discomfort in her eyes, something too close to real fear. I knew Kate well enough to know not to press further, to just laugh and ask more about it when it was just the two of us, in a quieter setting.

"And how's it going with . . . Erol?" I asked Maya. She was dating a lawyer whose family was originally from Turkey. He grew up on Long Island. That was all I knew.

"Ugh I am *done* with him. Last night . . . we were watching a movie on the couch and I fell asleep and woke up at four a.m. on the couch and he was *in my bed*! Not okay. I hate him now. Aaaaaaannd I'm single again."

Kate winced.

"He was in your bed?" I said.

"He says that he *tried* to wake me. He said that he *tried* to carry me but he, and I quote, 'couldn't get a good grip.' I told him that the way out of this fight was not to call me obese."

Kate and I burst out in laughter.

"Oh come on," I said, once I'd recovered. "It sounds like it was pretty harmless."

"I don't know," she said, with a smile peeking through. "I may stop being mad. I'm considering it. He's a sweet guy and makes me laugh and he has a *perfect* face. But he's on probation."

"Fair enough."

"Also do you think I can really marry someone whose name is so close to *egg roll*? I don't want to confuse my Chinese delivery man."

I smiled. "Is that really an issue?"

"Eve. I order Chinese all the time. It's important that my delivery guy understand me." She sighed. "It's Turkish. Erol. I guess it could be worse," she said. "His name could be Ishebog."

We laughed. She took a sip of her drink. "Ooo! Whatever happened to that . . . reporter? That you were dating? Tell us about the men in Colorado."

"So cute," I said. My instinct was to tell them every detail, but I decided not to get so absorbed in their world again, to just give brief answers and move on. *Maturity!*

"What kind of answer is that? Is this a test?" Maya demanded. I shrugged, and kept my mouth shut.

"How's your new apartment?" Kate asked.

"It is the most beautiful place I've ever lived," I said truthfully.

I'd found a studio in the East Village that was smaller than my bedroom in Arthur's apartment but had immeasurable value, in terms of my self-esteem. I had to dip into my savings from Colorado to pay the first month's rent. I didn't care. The girl living there told me that there were a hundred other girls just like me waiting for a place like this, and that was all she had to say. I bit the line.

"Although I did have a bit of a mice problem," I added, wincing. Maya backed her chair away from me and then stood up on it.

"MICE?" she yelled, from way up there.

"I didn't bring them here with me!" I said, looking up at her. She sat back down. "That's right. What I meant is that I *had* a mouse problem, but it's not an issue anymore because we became friends and casually socialize."

"Like Cinderella?" Maya replied.

I nodded. "It's exactly like that."

About a week in, I discovered that the apartment that a hundred girls dreamed of living in had mice. I bought some poison that the guy at the store claimed was more humane than the traps. But when that seemed to be exacerbating the problem, I broke down and paid for an exterminator, who told me that the poison that I spread throughout the perimeter of my apartment was basically the equivalent of feeding the mice cereal. *More humane, indeed!* I couldn't vacuum it up quickly enough. But, inevitably, when the influx of mice slowed down, it all turned into a funny story. I began to talk fondly of it, my cute little East Village apartment with its adorable mouse infestation. Only in New York!

When the shots of sake arrived, Maya explained to everyone

exactly what to do. She showed us how to set the chopsticks on top of the glass, place the shot between the chopsticks, slam the table, wait for the shot to fall into the beer, and then gulp it all down.

"Wait. Why can't we just drop the shot into the glass?" Glick's friend Ben, who was sitting next to him, asked. It was a wonder I didn't know two things about Ben, after all these years of running into him. The main reason was probably that he didn't talk much. Almost never, actually, whereas Glick was loud and had a way of picking at people's vulnerabilities.

"It's more fun this way!" she insisted.

"Aren't we going to cause a scene?" I looked around the restaurant.

"No! It's fine," she said confidently, like a pro.

On the count of three, everyone slammed the table and then downed their glasses of fizzy beer containing just a hint of something sharper. I stopped halfway through mine. I couldn't do it. I'd had enough. The whole thing in one gulp? Impossible. I tried to hide the evidence. Maya and Kate would kill me if they knew.

"Another round," Glick said to a waitress, running his hand across his mouth. "That was delicious. And extra shots." Kate squealed in protest. As the two of them fought about whether to order more, I sat there looking at my half-empty glass, pushing it to the far corner of the table, attempting to mix it in with the other glasses.

When I looked up, Ben was staring directly at me.

– – – –

"Hey," he protested quietly. He'd seen the whole thing. I gave him a look as if to say, *Please don't rat me out*, and then our eyes locked into this bizarre moment of familiarity, something bordering on affection.

What the fuck? Because of my subpar drinking skills?

After a few seconds, I looked away. I started lining up the silverware on the table. *What was that?* I guess it was obvious. It was a connection of some kind. I recognized it. I just didn't see it coming, with some guy I'd run into a thousand times before and thought, *Ugh, do I have to say hi to him or can I keep walking?* Plus, we were in this brightly lit, completely unromantic place, and by unromantic, I mean: there were at least thirty chicken wing bones lying on the table between us.

After that, there was the second round of sake bombs, this one I downed completely to avoid another moment with Ben. I tried to talk Maya out of her latest theory that if a guy she was dating didn't know how she took her burger, he didn't have the right to continue living. I ate a few dumplings, and cubes of something that looked like chicken but tasted like shrimp. When the waitress started pouring free wine into our glasses, I got pretty drunk, along with everyone else at the table. I sighed and cracked open a fortune cookie.

"You know what, you guys," I said, exhaling. "I know that I said Colorado was great and everything but . . . it wasn't that great, not always."

What I didn't tell my friends was that despite my outward attempts to become so very Colorado, on the inside I remained myself. When I listened to my friends in Colorado describe the adrenaline rush of hiking to the top of a mountain whenever a full moon occurred, the awesome feeling of being one with nature, there was a tiny piece of me that tallied up a list of safety concerns. I had to force myself not to feign an illness whenever I was asked to participate. Mountain biking the "nastiest" trail in Utah? *Too hungover.* A three-day hiking trip? *Recovering from a bad cold.* Rock climbing Independence Pass? *Would love to but . . . cough cough . . . I'm feeling a resurgence of a latent bronchial disease.* In the end, I went most of the time, but only because I was faced with a decision between going with them and spending the entire weekend as a social outcast.

"We figured," Maya said, not even pretending to be surprised. "Otherwise, why would you come back?"

"I really missed you guys!" Wow, so the wine had done a number on me. I felt like I was about to cry. "Well, I mean, the writing part *was* good, to get to write about music and everything. Plus, to get away from New York for a little bit."

"And the same old people," Kate said, her eyes rolling toward Glick, who was putting chopsticks in his nose.

"But the guys out there were dangerous," I said.

"What does that mean?" Kate asked. I held up my glass and eyed it suspiciously. "It means I almost died in an avalanche, several times, trying to be a *fun* girl."

"They were *that* cute?" Maya reached for her drink.

"Yes. I told you. I almost died. No, but reeeeeeaaaallllllyyyy, even with Jesse, it was the same way . . . between the charm and the bad moods . . . I'm always trying to keep up, always changing myself to be what I think I'm supposed to be. I'm always the sad victim going after the same dysfunctional guy. I'll tell you one thing: I am not sitting around in my pink pajamas anymore waiting for some guy to call. It's too cliché and *unfair,* you know?"

"You do that?" Kate said.

"Metaphorically speaking, yes."

"I've missed you, Eve," she said. "You're the only one I know who wears metaphorical pajamas."

"It's unfair compared to who? *Men?*" Maya exclaimed. "If you compare yourself to men, you're going to feel like an insane lunatic."

"I'm telling you, guys! It is hard work to be a wide-eyed romantic," I insisted.

"Is that what you think you are?" Kate started to laugh. "You take pretty much a doomsday approach to every relationship that you ever get involved in."

"So don't be such a romantic. Come visit me at the hospital one day," Maya said. "People are dying everywhere."

"I'm serious! I think I'm ready for a grown-up relationship with someone normal."

Kate gasped. Maya stared at me. *"Someone normal?"*

I nodded.

"But that really flies in the face of your whole policy," Maya said, horrified.

"Congratulations!" Kate shook my hand, her grip strong and sure, much like I imagined it was in her business meetings. "Welcome to adulthood. Let's find your first victim."

Before I could stop myself, I glanced guiltily at Ben, who was watching Glick shove chopsticks up his nose and unsuccessfully try to keep them there, and then looked down at my plate quickly.

But not quickly enough.

"BEN?" Kate shrieked.

"Shhh! No! Shut up! Shut up!" I paused. "But what do you think of him? Do you think he's *too* quiet and maybe *too* nice?"

"Eve. He was on the hockey team. How nice can he be?" Maya said.

"Yeah, I'm sure he's thrown a few punches, if that makes you feel better," Kate added. I thought about the slight dent at the bridge of Ben's nose, which made it look a little broken, and was the only flaw on his face.

"It does!" I said.

"You can take the girl out of the insane asylum. . . ." Maya looked at me and shook her head slowly.

The restaurant emptied out until we were the only table left, along with a few teenaged girls in the corner, the sushi chefs plying them with drinks. Glick got up and then came back to tell us that there was a bar upstairs and that he was in love with the bartender. He told us this as if he was dead serious. "I asked her what time she was getting off," he said in a daze. "And then I asked her to fix me a gin and tonic. And then I gave her all the money in my wallet." He took out his wallet, as if to verify the story, and opened it up for us and shook it over the table. It was, in fact, empty.

When the check arrived, it came with plastic cups of colored sugar, which we were meant to take over to a vintage cotton candy maker. I fought for a pink cup. Ben stood up, and the first thing I noticed was that his hooded sweatshirt went down to his knees. He was a good-looking guy, but it was hard to tell, with the baggy clothes, the orange T-shirt with a series of holes at the neck.

I pranced over to the corner and dumped the sugar inside the machine, then watched the colored cotton whirl onto my chopstick. I took a few bites and then gave it to Maya, who took one look at it and threw it into the garbage. "I feel sick enough already," she said, as if I'd insulted her. We all trooped upstairs to the bar on the second story. It was crowded, with deafening electronic music and a balcony overlooking Saint Marks, where people were smoking cigarettes. The walls were red, with gold Japanese letters painted on them. There was a small chandelier in the center of the room. We were standing at the bar, shouting at the top of our lungs. Maya was talking to us about her birthday, which was a week away.

"Maybe we should just go to Dave and Buster's!" She started laughing. "It's a pretty trashy crowd and the food is disgusting but they have some salads. . . . Should we do that? Do you think you could stomach it?" She looked at me. "It's so fun! They have skeeball!"

"May . . . be. Where is it?"

"It's in Times Square," she replied.

Kate groaned. "Of course it is."

"Or we could go to O Ya?" Maya said. "But it's *omakase* only, and it's three hundred dollars."

Kate stared her down. "So our choices are Dave and Buster's or a three-hundred-dollar-per-person *omakase*?"

Suddenly, Ben tapped me on the shoulder.

"Do you want to go out to the balcony?" he asked.

The music had become a throbbing bass loop of the same four notes, on repeat, shaking the floors. I was dying to escape it.

"Sure," I said.

Once we were out there, I leaned over the railing and looked down at the people on the street below. In my new apartment, my preferred spot was right next to the window, sitting on the ledge, watching everyone on the street walk by. Since it was on the second floor, I was close enough to see faces, to hear words, to feel like I had company. It was the city equivalent of hiking a mountain—a way to get lost in something outside of yourself. Except in New York, there was the added advantage of glimpsing into another person's existence. When observing, I always started from the ground and scanned up. I watched their feet pound the pavement; catching the urgency of their stride, then examined how they had dressed for the day, their facial expressions. Then, I waited for some piece of conversation. The juicier bits usually came from someone on the phone. People on the phone tended to forget that they were not in their own private universe.

I got into the hypnotic rhythm of watching people, until I heard Ben clear his throat behind me.

"So, what was that downstairs?" he asked.

I smiled and said, "I think it was a moment." He moved to stand next to me.

"What should we do now?"

I saw, out of the corner of my eye, a flash of yellow. Inside the room, a Japanese man was blowing fire through a hoop.

"Okay, seriously where are we?" I said.

He looked inside. "Isn't it obvious? We're at a Japanese circus."

I laughed.

"I feel like I should say something right now though . . . regarding the moment?" He looked at me for approval.

"You should." I nodded.

"Should I say something about your eyes?"

"Blech. No."

"Well, what's your preference then?"

I slowly shook my head. "No way, man. I'm not going to help you out."

"Oh come on. Give me some topics. Should we talk about college? Your job? Oh! Your cuteness?"

"My cuteness?" I gave him a threatening look.

The longer the silence lasted, the more nervous he looked, and the more confidence I gained. I'd never made someone nervous before. Everyone made *me* nervous. Didn't he know?

I looked over at my friends back inside. More people started coming out onto the balcony. We were jammed into a corner.

He put his hand on my back, and the contact gave me a little rush. Even once his hand left, I could still feel his thumb there. I felt myself falling for just a few seconds as we stood there quietly, that feeling like I had no base, like I wasn't safe. *Look down. Look down.* The alcohol and the balcony were making it worse.

"I feel like this thing is about to collapse," I said, staring at my feet.

He shook his head. "All the balconies in this neighborhood are over a hundred years old," he said. "This is no less safe than the ground."

"Why do you sound like an expert?"

He smiled. "I know a lot of random facts about the city. It's part of my job."

"Where do you work?" I said, trying to focus. *There's that anxious feeling in my stomach. It's happening again.*

"Skidmore, Owings and Merrill. It's an architectural firm. I work in their structural engineering department. We're building the Freedom Tower," he said proudly.

"Really? That's pretty cool."

"Yeah, except it's a mess." He straightened his back and looked less like the hunched-over, hands-in-pockets, hooded-sweatshirt guy I'd vaguely registered in college. I had a flash of looking out the window of my dorm room, sophomore year, and seeing Ben with his baseball cap and hood on, walking to the bookstore.

"Why?"

"It's a nonstop back-and-forth between the architects and the engineers in terms of what's possible. But there's been a lot of frustration on both sides. Plus, it's an emotionally loaded project, politically charged. But," he said, with a sigh, "there is a certain satisfaction in bringing order to the ideas, I guess."

He started telling me about the history of Saint Marks and the buildings that surrounded us. "They were built in 1831," he said. "Look at the divisions of the building, the contradictory shades of red and brown. It's four buildings now, but it used to be one very large ballroom with a balcony." He pointed to the ceiling inside. "They plastered the walls and got rid of the right angles so that people would feel like they were in a big cavern."

"Saint Marks is such a weird mash of cultures," I said.

"It feels like it's on its last breath though, doesn't it? I mean, all the music venues have closed down. Punks don't hang out here anymore. There's nothing dangerous. There are no muggings. The drug dealers have all moved to Avenue D. It doesn't have an edge. It's like the ghost of a bygone era."

"Sure," I said, with a laugh. "Once the drug dealers go . . ."

"The Seven-Eleven," he said, shaking his head.

"What's wrong with a Seven-Eleven?"

"It depends on the location, but once that gets built in a place like this, it is the end. The East Village has a deep distrust of any chain stores, doesn't matter what kind, upscale or not. There's a lot of pride here. The local residents are invested. The community board is active. Which is why this neighborhood has been slower to change than any other part of the city."

I looked up at the awning on the store above us. SEARCH AND DESTROY was printed on it. There were various doll parts stacked in the window with menacing faces, a plastic pig, Mickey Mouse dressed in an Uncle Sam costume, a gas mask, a sign that read NOBODY INNOCENT.

"I came down here a lot when I was sixteen," he continued. "I used to hang out on the street with my friends before and after shows." His voice was low, steady, solid, matter-of-fact. I felt like I was meeting Ben for the first time. Our entire interaction before this, in college and throughout New York, at a party, standing around in a group of people, faded from memory.

"But you look so clean!"

"What do you mean?" he asked, confused.

"Oh, I just meant, um . . . nothing. Never mind. So you hung out here after the shows?" I was about to be all *This guy just does not get me*, but I stopped myself. *Grown-up relationship. Grown-up!*

"Yup, and I got pretty beat up right over"—he extended his arm and pointed down the street—"there."

"What's that mean?" I was beginning to see some rebellion in Ben, and that right there got me, a little bit. He had some edge, I thought, hidden under there, beneath the spotless exterior. Thank God.

He shook his head. "There were all these groups. Everyone was very specific about which bands they liked. And they took it seriously."

"Why?"

"Why were there groups, or why did they take it seriously?"

"Umm . . . both?" The wheels in my head were turning with a possible headline, first sentence. But then I realized that even if this was an interesting topic to write about, I was about ten years too late.

"I don't know. I went to a show at CBGB and I guess I bumped into the wrong guy. Then we came to Saint Marks and his friend punched me. Actually, he didn't just punch me. He broke an orbital bone next to my eye."

I cringed.

"I have to say, it's funny to be here talking to a cute girl in the exact location where ten years ago I got smacked in the face," he said, concentrating on me. "See. I managed to say something about your cuteness after all."

"Phew!" I said. He laughed. I couldn't help but notice how happy he seemed. *What am I doing that is pleasing him so much?*

Oh, I can see where all this is going. How can I resist? There isn't the faintest chance I am going to miss this. I am cured now! Ben's orbital bone had recovered and I am no longer worried about being left. This is my chance to break through. Ben is smart and sweet and haven't I been through the wringer already with guys who I couldn't trust? They leave too. Maybe this one will fix something inside of me.

"Do you ever feel like you experience the city differently? Because of your job?" I said, with searching eyes, *playing with my hair, doing my best.*

"Definitely," he said. "Like when I'm in the subway and I'm staring at a column or a beam. I don't even realize it, but I'm tracing the load path, trying to figure out how the loads are transferred." I gave him a confused look. He started to get more enthusiastic. "So in the subway station, you have the street traffic above, which is supported by a series of beams running across the street, and the columns that you see support the beams. If you look at them closely though, you can see the connections in the beams and that's interesting to me. Like, you can see whether they used rivets or bolts. Rivets were used until the sixties, and after that, technology advanced and bolts were developed and could be installed easily in the field. Whether you see rivets or bolts or some combination tells you when something was built. It suggests what has been refurbished and what is really old. So in the subway you might see riveted connections next to bolt connections, and then you know that someone in the eighties made a change, which tells you the history of the station."

I nodded, unsure of how to respond. I didn't know anything

about rivets or bolts, but I did know about the larger situation at hand. A boy liked a girl.

The nice ones never come to you.

"Ben." My eyes narrowed on him.

"Yeah?"

"Do you want to make out?"

He looked at me as if I'd asked him the dumbest question imaginable.

"Umm." He made a sweeping gesture with his hand. "Yes."

BEN

I woke up at her apartment and my first thought was: *Oh shit*. Because that was my general reaction whenever I woke up in bed with someone familiar. In my experience, it is far less scary to wake up with a borderline stranger. As I lay next to her, staring at an amalgam of her arm and pillow and hair, I gave myself the third degree.

Did I just do something wrong?

Did I just get into something I . . . didn't want to get into?

But then I told myself that I had no reason to worry. I went from *oh shit* to *oh, wait a minute, that was fine*. My arm was sore. I moved it from under her. I regained feeling in my forearm first, but my shoulder had been shifted so badly all night that it took longer.

One of Eve's legs was visible at the other end of the bed. Her hair was strewn across her back, below her shoulders. It was an even shade of brown, although a few strands were catching the sun peeking through her window shades and looked lighter. Last night, she'd kept it half tied in this clip at the back of her head. The clip was now lying on the night table, flat and small and with three red stones in a line. I looked over at the table, which also had a pair of blue earrings in the shape of triangles lying next to a tissue box and a black alarm clock.

I examined the sliver of her face that was showing. She was pretty, the kind of pretty where you could stare at her face for a while. I'm not one for making a big deal out of eye contact or anything like that, but last night across the table we'd definitely had something. Jesus, what was that? I made fun of her and all of a sudden she was smiling. It was definitely a moment. How to describe it I'm not sure. But it was interesting. It caught my attention. Even though I'd been around her before, that was the first time we'd actually smiled at each other. It was enough to spark something. Enough that it led to this. I made the decision that when she woke up, I would ask her to go for breakfast. If it had been a one-night, zero-strings, sort-of-anonymous thing, I would have gotten the hell out of there, no questions asked. But Eve and I had gone to college together. We had an overlapping friend circle. We could share a meal. I was tired of those one-night things anyway. I wanted to give this a shot.

I looked around at her place. The paint on the walls, which looked to have been recently rehabilitated, revealed a few irregularities near the ceiling. To the right of the bed, there was a dresser with a rectangular mirror over it. There was no clutter, no superfluous objects of any kind. From the bed, I could see the outline of a colored carpet, the top of a pile of scarves, all folded in a basket. Its nicest feature was that from the window next to the bed, you could see Fifth Street and the bare branches of a tree. It was quiet out there. It was unlike lying in my own bed in

Hoboken, where I heard every truck barreling by all night long. But that apartment had its advantages—my roommate and I got to keep some of the furniture and porcelain egg collection from the two ninety-year-old women who lived and died in the apartment before us. Stuff that screamed bachelor's paradise.

As I waited for Eve to wake up, I thought back on whether I did anything embarrassing during the night, if I was snoring, the sexual experience. I pieced together the sequence of events that led to me falling asleep there. We were hooking up at the bar, and next thing I knew I was walking her home and when we got to her door, instead of saying good-bye, she just kept talking and walking into the building, up to her apartment. I wasn't sure whether I was supposed to follow her, but she wasn't telling me *not* to follow her and I didn't need a whole lot more than that to boost my confidence. She showed me around her apartment. The only part I remembered was how she stopped in front of a bookshelf and drunkenly explained her whole organizational system. She had four of the books isolated, alone on a shelf, and told me that those were her favorites, that they'd earned their position above the masses. "Don't worry. They don't get lonely. They have each other," she had said reassuringly. After that statement, I remember grabbing her for no reason I could understand, other than instinct. Why? Because she was a voracious reader? Never did it for me before. But okay, in this scenario, somehow it was working for me, and we ended up in her bed and neither she nor I were making too much of the whole deal. We were acting like this was just something that we did.

When she started to rustle under the covers, I turned my eyes toward her, though not my whole body, and I tried not to smile. I didn't want her to think I was making fun of her, but it was a funny situation. Two people who have known each other peripherally for years waking up in bed together is pretty odd, if you think about it. She turned to me and said hi in that way that girls say hi, like there's so much more that they are saying, and you'd better get it, buddy. And then she pulled the thick comforter up over her head, tucking herself into a ball, and groaned.

"It's too much pressure," I could hear her say.

"What is?"

"What if I don't look adorably sleepy right now? I feel like I'm supposed to look adorably sleepy."

I smiled. "Well, there's no way to tell, with you under there."

She reemerged, so that only the top of her head and eyes were visible.

"You look just okay," I said, and then shrugged.

She went into hiding. I laughed, started to sit up and then decided against it, and put my head back down against the pillow. After a minute or so, she came out, presumably for air, and I turned to face her. I couldn't even look at her for too long because if I did, it was that moment at the restaurant all over again. Good, but too much, too soon.

"Did you have fun last night?" I asked.

"I did." Her voice was flat but agreeable.

"What was your favorite part?"

"The cotton candy," she said.

"Jerk."

She started to laugh pretty hard, and I could see the inside of her mouth.

I don't know why but watching this girl laugh in bed was the most instinctually appealing thing I'd seen in a long time. "Do you want to get breakfast or something?" I said.

She appeared to think it over. Usually, I did the walk of shame as soon as possible. The great thing about New York was that there was usually a whole parade of people also doing the walk of shame. Every time I passed a girl who was still in her all-black and heels, I smiled. I was sure there were a few guys too, but their nightwear was harder to spot. Then I usually showered, got food and coffee, and decided whether to text her. My A game was to make conversation, to find out what she had planned for the rest of the weekend, then later in the day (much later), send a text like *You better not have missed your toothpick convention!* Or whatever it was.

After she thought about breakfast for a while, she didn't say anything. She just got out of bed, grabbed a T-shirt from a drawer and slipped it on, like her apartment was on fire, and left me there. She skipped out of sight and then next thing I heard was the water running in the bathroom.

When she came back from the bathroom, with a toothbrush hanging out of her mouth, she said some words that were all mangled because of the brush, but I think it was: "Okay, we can get breakfast." I started to get dressed.

It was completely still outside, on our walk. The cold stung my ears, and I pulled my hood up to cover them. The streets were empty and the sky was white. Everything appeared to be frozen. There were a few snowflakes coming down, dotting the sidewalk. My theory was that neighborhoods with an active nightlife were always vacant in the mornings. It was as if the neighborhood itself had to recover from all the activity the night before and it hadn't woken up yet. Unfortunately, this peaceful setting only emphasized the sudden weighted, nearing-uncomfortable silence between us. I could think of something to say, but I didn't want to be overly chatty first thing in the morning, especially with a girl who didn't seem to like that sort of thing.

Eve was looking down at her feet as she walked. She mumbled

something about a bagel place on Sixth Avenue, but we had to walk from the East Village to the West Village in order to get there.

"That's fine," I said. "I'm in no rush."

We passed Cooper Union and Astor Place, and then walked on Macdougal Street, past all the NYU bars and comedy clubs. We started to talk, to make simple conversation about how this or that compared to Columbia. She pointed out the places that she frequented on a daily basis. She seemed to wake up, a little more, as blocks went by.

"This place serves exclusively peanut butter sandwiches. Can you believe that? Who goes out and buys a peanut butter sandwich? Make it at home! It's so easy!" she said.

"I know," I said. "How lazy can you be?"

"Maybe there's something special about them." She shrugged, getting oddly contemplative about it. "I don't know. I've never had them. I shouldn't talk."

We walked under the arch of Washington Square, passed a man wearing at least eight jackets, one on top of the other, and mumbling to himself about loyalty. We continued up Fifth Avenue, through the residential area with elegant apartment buildings and doormen in gray uniforms. From the street, you could glimpse into the marble lobbies. When we got to Sixth Avenue, she pointed out the bagel place, a navy awning and two benches outside it. When we got closer, I noticed that the windows were foggy. We opened the door to about twenty people lined up, almost to the door. Apparently, this was where everyone was. It smelled like freshly baked bread and coffee and everything I wanted at that moment to get myself feeling right again. We stood at the end of the line.

"What are you gonna get?" I said, to break the silence that had set in, again.

"Umm . . ." She looked up at the menu, written on a chalkboard, and then at the bins of bagels. Each one had a small sign on it, POPPY, SESAME, WHOLE WHEAT, EVERYTHING. Eve looked at each sign like she was studying the metaphysical differences between them.

As we stood there inching along, taking small steps that felt like progress, we got closer and closer to the bins of bagels, but it wasn't easy between us. We talked a lot about Glick, his cagey trips to Atlantic City, whether he had a gambling problem. The atmosphere in the bagel place didn't help, with the chaos of people ordering and paying, everyone trying to get their bagels and then get out as quickly as possible. People were shouting at the employees behind the counter, who listened and then ducked between and behind one another. The whole situation required some strategic maneuvering or you'd get bulldozed by the person behind you. It wasn't the ideal atmosphere for holding down a conversation, but we did our best.

When we finally got our bagels, coffee, and an orange juice, we got a table that was wedged in a row of six other tables, all too close together. The guy next to us was sitting by himself and had his nose in the newspaper, which seemed promising. At least we wouldn't have to listen to him yammering away, which was more than we could say about the guy on the other side of us, who was pontificating to a girl who looked half his age about the best seafood he ever ate, which was "surprisingly!" in Albuquerque, New Mexico. But then, even the guy with the newspaper betrayed us. Every few minutes, we would hear a sucking sound coming from his direction. He was smacking his lips as he ate. Eve and I took turns looking over at him. At first, it was no big deal, but after his eighth or ninth smack, we paused, fed up.

She mouthed: *Should we kill him?*

I laughed, and it melted some of the tension between us. I decided that as soon as we got out of there, I was going to ask for her phone number.

Unfortunately, it was at this exact point when she started to leave. She said she had to go and apologized. She got up, riffled through her bag, got out her wallet, threw a few dollars down onto the table, even though I'd already paid. *Hadn't she seen me pay? Doesn't she know I'm the type of guy who pays for bagels?*

Then, she crumpled up her mostly uneaten bagel in its wrapper and tossed the ball into the garbage and, with a hand gesture that was a cross between a wave and a salute, left. I sat there for a few seconds, trying to register what had just happened.

I stood and caught up with her outside on the street, halfway down the block, as confused as I can say I've ever been, with one or two poppy seeds stuck between my teeth.

"What's going on?" I said. She turned.

"You're a nice guy and all!" she said. "But I can tell from your breakfast suggestion . . ." Her eyes wandered off.

"You can tell what from my breakfast suggestion?" I smiled. "That I wanted . . . breakfast?"

"I can just tell that you're looking for someone . . . to date. Maybe even seriously. But you don't want me."

"Huh?"

"Trust me," she said. And then, on Twelfth Street and Sixth Avenue, in front of a closed-down Village Wine & Spirit Shop, she gave me an awkward hug. It was so bad that I would forever think of this spot as the Site of the Awkward Hug. I remember thinking that it was the *worst* in the history of hugs, her body a safe distance from mine, her hands barely touching my shoulders. We went toward each other at different moments. I was going in as she was going out. Half of her was already running off.

"Don't tell anyone what happened," she said, rustling through her bag, looking for something.

"I couldn't even tell you," I answered.

When she left, I went back inside. I'd never seen someone pull something like that. I glanced at our table, the empty chairs pushed away from it. There was only a sad piece of my bagel left in its parchment paper. From the evidence, it looked like I'd been eating alone.

Underneath the chair that she'd been sitting in, I noticed a small, white rectangular card and what appeared to be a folded-up receipt. The two slips of paper stood out against the wood floor. I went to pick them up. They must have fallen out of her wallet. She'd gone through her bag so quickly, in such a rush to get away from me, *but why?* I took them from the floor. I unfolded the receipt. It was from a music store. Well, that made sense.

I flipped over the card. It was an old card. I could tell because the grain of the paper was worn and soft, the print was faded:

JOSEPHINE PORTER
Executive Assistant
Callahan & Gibbs, LLP
Two World Trade Center

The font was red and familiar. It was a business card from the law firm where my father was a partner. And it had a woman's name on it, that, with a sinking feeling, I knew I recognized. It was coming to me, in an immense rush of clarity. I felt light-headed, like the blood had run out of my face, like my feet were the only things connected to the floor.

The foundation beneath me had cracked wide-open and nothing mattered anymore.

- - - -

My father went into work that day like it was any other day. He did his usual routine—the sound of his alarm clock once, twice, three times. He always did push-ups and sit-ups in the living room, in his boxers and a white T-shirt, his hair sticking straight up. He showered while my mother cut up some fruit for him in the kitchen. He emerged twenty minutes later and devoured it all. Then, he opened up a carton of yogurt that stunk up the entire kitchen. He went at it with a big spoon. I hated the smell, and told him that, often.

I imagined him in his car, sitting in traffic, listening to the Eagles or one of his "coffeehouse" or "light music" radio stations that he reserved for his morning commute. I pictured him getting to his building, always careful not to touch any doors or other people, opening the doors with his foot, touching the elevator button with his knuckles. He was afraid of germs and, as far as I knew, not much else.

He was at his desk for ten minutes, he said, when he heard something hit the other tower. So I pictured him, sitting there with his coffee, his eyes lazy and scanning his in-box, getting disrupted by something from the outside world. The news came that it was a plane. Nobody said anything about terrorism. They thought it was just some accident, some terrible freak thing. But then it quickly turned more horrific, as they saw a gaping hole in the building, the violent flames inside of it, papers flying everywhere, and people jumping to their deaths. They could see only the silhouettes of human forms moving, earthbound and freeing themselves, dropping down against the setting of 22,000 eighteen-inch-wide windows. I learned about the construction of the towers in school. The windows were meant to be narrow, so that people who were afraid of heights would feel secure inside the building. They had to be built to bear the weight of the interior floors, but also to withstand the pressure of the wind.

My dad said that anyone who went toward the window to look out at the other tower quickly recoiled or shrieked at the dreadfulness. "It just got so, so hot," he said. "I could feel the heat on my face, like I was standing next to an open oven." At this point in the story, I usually interrupted him, because I knew what he was about to say, and I yelled, "How could you not leave right when you saw that? How could you not get the fuck out of there? Why would you even think about staying?" I told him that I would have been *gone*. Out of there. As fast as my legs could take me. He always said a variation on the same thing: *Yes, you say that now, but we had no idea another plane was coming. No idea! Who could have imagined? We thought we were the lucky ones. Lightning didn't strike twice.* He decided to stay. He said most of the partners were staying. That also *killed* me, when he said that. As if any kind of law firm structure mattered, in a situation like that. They told their secretaries to stay.

But after a few minutes, his secretary started packing up to leave. She said, "If they're going to stay, then that's their choice to make. *We* have to get out of here. I have two daughters at home. They already don't have a father. They're not going to lose their mother too." She convinced him to leave with her. He thought she was being kind of dramatic. She was a bit of a worrier, to begin with. But he went with her, if only to keep her company. She was very fragile, always. And at that moment she seemed particularly unhinged. When they got down to the lobby, he said, "I'm just going to get my car out of the garage. I'll drive you home." She lived on the Upper East Side. He figured he'd do her a favor.

LESLIE COHEN

"Get your car? *Are you crazy?*" She practically dragged him out of the building.

The world was ending, and my dad was going to get his car. But that was how he was. Calm under pressure. Growing up, my dad was the only relaxed presence in our house. My brother was always going at it with my mom. My mom fought with my dad. She didn't believe in going to sleep angry, so she had a cracker-jack strategy of just screaming like hell at him before they went to bed. She'd do strange things sometimes, like rearrange all the furniture in the middle of the night. But my dad knew how to calm her down. He knew how to grab her by the shoulders and speak in a solid voice and generally stop the madness. That was how their relationship worked.

That's why I am 100 percent certain that, left to his own devices, he would not have left his office. Thus, it wasn't his wisdom—it never would have been his wisdom—but hers, this woman who I'd never even met, who saved his life. And that was why he made it safely out of the building. That was why, when the elevator made its final trip down, from among the one hundred and ten floors to the lobby, my dad was on it.

But he was one of the lucky ones. On Vesey Street, they heard a loud noise, a blast, like those heard in thousands of movies, going off above them. A plane had hit the second tower. The ground trembled beneath their feet, and they could see the building sway. His secretary ran in one direction, and my father ran in the other. And that split-second decision that they both made on Vesey Street—or what was once Vesey Street but then a haze of smoke and fire—was the difference between life and death. He never saw her again. Falling debris, everyone said.

Her funeral was later, and I remember how in the weeks following September Eleventh, guilt literally enveloped him. He felt this crushing sense of regret that he'd told her to stay. I walked in on him once watching television with his head in his hands. I heard him say to my mother, who was sitting next to him with her hand on his back, "Why didn't we leave right away? Why did I tell her to stay?" He felt so responsible. And in a way, in this one dreadful way, he was.

I remember feeling guilty about it too, like my own relaxed nature, inherited from him, was somehow at fault. I had some stupid reason I didn't go to the funeral, some school-related thing that I was behind on, but really I just didn't want to face it. This woman had a daughter who was my age. *Fuck.* I didn't want to see that. I had just nearly lost my father. It was "okay" for me not to go. My parents accepted my excuse. And that was kind of it. But I knew the plain truth. I didn't want to face it, and there was a word for people like that, for eighteen-year-old me. *Gutless.*

Now, as I turned the card over and over in my palm, I felt like that same eighteen-year-old kid. I put the card in my wallet and left the bagel place, my mind unwilling to comprehend what this would mean to Eve when—if—she found out. When—if— I ever told her.

Like I said, *gutless.*

I'd probably never see her again anyway.

BEN

-----

93 SECOND AVENUE, BETWEEN FIFTH AND SIXTH STREETS,
EAST VILLAGE

Three weeks later, I was on Second Avenue and Fourth Street at around eleven at night, trying to decide where to get pizza. I was pretty drunk and hungry and had the wherewithal to know that I should probably sober up a little before getting on the train. I was debating between East Village Pizza on Ninth and First and Stromboli Pizza on Saint Marks and First. I was about to turn right on Fifth Street to go to Stromboli when I changed my mind. Stromboli, though commonly thought of as the best pizza in the East Village, was a tourist trap. East Village Pizza was better. More of a locals' spot. So I kept going straight on Second Avenue instead of turning right, and that was when I ran into Eve. She was standing between two restaurants, underneath a black, unmarked door.

"Hi," I said cautiously, as if approaching a small animal in the woods that could get freaked out by sudden movements.

"Oh! Hi!" She seemed happy to see me. I guess because she was alone.

"What are you doing here?"

"I'm about to go to some concert. What are *you* doing here?" She was different from how she was at the bagel place. More like the girl she was the night before that, on Saint Marks. Fun. In the mood to play.

"I'm about to go get some pizza."

She smiled. "Interesting . . . do you want to come with me instead?"

I looked at her for an extra second, because my brain hadn't quite caught up. It felt like a trick. And then I said all right, despite our less-than-stellar breakfast, because *all right,* I'd play. Game on. Also, she was wearing this short-sleeved dress, striped, blue and white, that hugged her closely on top and scooped down in the front, not so low that you could see anything but just almost; and hanging out with her, compared to whatever other options I had for the end of the night, still sounded better. As I said, I was drunk and hungry.

I stood inside Lit Lounge with her, and everything that I'd been thinking before just kind of flew out of my head. Whatever happened in the past was so far away. There was something exciting about her. And I had short-term memory. Should I ask her about the card? Her mother? Maybe later. Things were going well, and I had a feeling that the revelation I needed to make had the potential to blow it all up, especially with someone like Eve.

I decided to talk around it, first.

"So what was the deal?" I said, while we waited at the bar for the show to start. "Why did you leave like that?"

"Oh, I'm so sorry," she said, turning toward me. "It was stupid of me. I just freaked out!"

"Why?"

"I don't know!" she said, covering her face with her hands.

Every now and then, a dark bra strap appeared at one shoulder, and she'd adjust and tuck it away. It was an innocent-looking dress, girlish, which contrasted sharply with her black nail polish, the faint impression of rebellion.

"You don't know why you freaked out?"

Her dark hair was parted on the side and tied back. Her lips were pink, but she wasn't wearing any makeup.

"Yeah, but I do that a lot. So don't flatter yourself!"

Flatter myself?

"I don't know . . . I guess it wasn't just 'breakfast,' it was just the whole *idea* of breakfast. Nobody has ever asked me to get breakfast before, after, you know, sleeping over. It seemed so serious."

"Breakfast?"

"Yes! After a first hookup? I almost called the police."

"Oh yeah? What would you have said?"

She smiled. "Oh, they would have understood. I would have asked for a female cop."

I had no idea she would interpret it that way. I shrugged. "Okay."

"Let me make it up to you?" Her smile got bigger. "We'll have fun now."

She looked at me excitedly and then took my hand.

"C'mon! C'mon!" She dragged me across the room by the arm. "The music is downstairs, in the basement. They call it the Lit Dungeon." She raised her eyebrows. I followed her down a spiraling staircase. "Between noise complaints, underage drinking, and drugs, this place has gotten into trouble, like, a thousand times, but they've somehow managed to stay open, and you have to respect that, you know? At one point, the owner even had this crazy policy where the staff would steal your belongings when you weren't looking, wait for you to report it stolen, then give it back to you, and that's how they would warn you about leaving your things unattended."

"That is exceedingly stupid."

"Oh, I agree."

"Are you going to write about this show?" I asked her, as we made our way down into the darkness.

"Yeah," she replied. "I think I might. Another one of my famous articles!" She looked down and laughed a little self-deprecatingly. I wasn't sure I liked it.

"What?"

"Oh, nothing. It's just that, you know, people don't go to Voice for the articles. They go there to steal music."

"That's not true," I said. "They're putting the articles there for a reason."

The basement was lit up by a red light. The space was small, dark, and grimy, with a low ceiling. The stage had red Christmas lights above it, strewn across the ceiling in a line that wasn't straight. A guitarist and a drummer came out onstage and started to set up. A few in the crowd whistled. The drummer wiped his face with a towel and straightened his baseball cap. The guitarist took a sip from the drink that he'd brought out with him. He was dressed in black and had his back toward us. We were standing in front of the drummer, who kept fidgeting in his seat.

"Is there anything I should know about this band?" I said.

She shook her head.

"I don't know much about music," I admitted.

"Neither do I," she said.

I looked at her curiously. "You work at Voice!"

"Yeah, but I don't really *know* about music, not the way that some people do. Some people have this encyclopedic knowledge of music history and albums and bands." She scanned the crowd. "I just know when I like something and I feel really strongly about it. And when I like it, I let it take over. I let it trigger feelings, memories, whatever emotions come up. That's the key. Just see if you like it," she said. "See if it affects you. And then let yourself be affected."

I looked at her bra strap. She twirled around at the sound of the drummer cracking his drumsticks together, his elbows waving in the air, and then he started, his whole body propelling forward. Eve was in front of me and started to move to the beat. We kept getting pressed up against each other, because of the crowd, which was good because we were in that weird in-between period when you've hooked up once or twice but you don't want to hold hands or even make bodily contact in real life because everything is very unclear. But being at the concert made it easier, because we were forced to touch each other and it broke the ice without either of us really realizing it.

At first, I touched her hips accidentally, and then it wasn't long before I did it on purpose because it seemed like I could get away with it. Her body looked great and it took a lot out of me to be restrained, but I knew I had to be. She rested back into me every now and then. I was buzzing and she was smiling, really trying to be nice to me. I could tell. It was just like the night we hooked up, the night she'd cast her weird Eve spell on me and made me follow her home like a puppy. She was the same way tonight, like something had cracked open inside of her. I didn't know what to do, but I knew I didn't want to ruin it, to send her back into her other mode of being—the Eve I knew in college who said hello and kept walking, the Eve who sat at a bagel place without talking. She had this shell around her sometimes, but not now. I let her dance, the skirt of her dress sweeping back and forth in front of me. Every so often, I put my hands on her sides, in borderline innocent places, always borderline.

After a few songs, she leaned into me and whispered, "Do you like them?"

"What?" My eyes drifted down from her eyes slightly, and then I thought, *Shit,* and yanked them back up.

"The band?"

I shrugged. "Oh. Yeah. It's good."

She waited, moving a bracelet up and down on her wrist. "That's it?"

I was at a loss. "I like it. It's good."

"Yeah, but how does it make you feel?"

I really was at a loss. *Was there music playing?* I had no idea. I couldn't think of anything at all except touching her.

"I *feel* like I want to kiss you, and the fact that there's a drumbeat in the background doesn't really matter to me."

"But you want to kiss me more here than you would if we were outside on the street," she said.

"I don't think so." I stared at her mouth. "I think it's about even."

She squinted the way she did when she was suspicious of something. "You've been slammed too many times against the boards," she said. "You've sustained emotional brain damage. It's a good thing I'm here. Oh! You know what we should do after this?"

"What?" I said, still thinking through what she'd said, piecing it together. I was stuck on *emotional brain damage.*

"We should try to sneak backstage with my credentials!" She grabbed hold of my elbows until she was fully against me.

"Okay," I said.

"Okay? That's it?" She smiled. "Not big on words, huh?"

I shrugged. "Yeah, but when I say *okay*, I mean it in the *grandest* sense of the word." She laughed, moved away, and widened her eyes at the sound of the first few notes of a song that she liked. She turned back around.

"You're going to think I'm so much less cool once I get us sent to Lit Lounge jail!" She pulled away and then came toward me again. "They probably have a jail for assistants and interns who try to pass themselves off as legitimate people, right?"

I studied the crowd—it was a mix of young people standing up and older people sitting at the bar. The people in front of us kept yelling for some song, worried they weren't going to play it.

I just kept watching Eve.

- - - -

Once the concert was over, we walked to the far end of the space and Eve opened the door to some back room, like it was something she did all the time. "I just want to try to ask the band a few questions! One or two quotes for my article would be a game changer!"

I followed her and we waited for a bouncer to consult a list that Eve and I weren't on.

"Could you check with Kim?" she said, when he failed to let us in. "She said that it would be okay for me ask the band a few questions after the show."

The bouncer looked confused but then left to consult with someone.

"Who is Kim?" I asked, once he'd left.

"I have no idea!" She leaned into me to say. "It sounds like it could be someone though, right? Kim?"

I gave her a puzzled look.

"I just thought that if I dropped a name, it would add an air of authenticity to our story."

"Ah."

It was freezing in this room. It had a window open. As we waited, Eve started snapping her fingers, tapping her shoes against the ground, which echoed throughout the stairwell.

"Oh, by the way, you left this behind," I said, taking the business card out of my wallet and handing it to her, testing the waters.

She closed her eyes and took the card and held it against her chest. "Thank you," she said, and then put it in her wallet. "I was so afraid I'd lost it."

"Is that . . . was that . . . your mother?" I stuttered out. Feigning ignorance felt like the safest approach. But I also knew that by handing her that card, by asking her that question, I was officially hiding something from her.

"Yep," she said, and there it was. Simple as that. *Thud.* She was confirming what I already knew, but it didn't seem real until this moment. The woman on the card was my father's secretary, and she had two daughters and one of those daughters was Eve. She continued talking, but I could only half hear what she was saying. It was all fuzzy, like someone had lowered the volume without my permission.

"I was afraid I'd lost it, and I don't like to lose things," she said. "I lost a glove once and I was devastated."

"Over a glove?" I managed to say, though I still hadn't come back to reality. And then I remembered something else, once she said the word *glove.* It was a story that my father told me when I was younger. Every now and then, his secretary, Eve's mother, would come up in conversation. It was a snow day and my brother and I were fighting over who got to use the car, and he wanted us to realize just how stupid our fight was. He told us this story of how his secretary came into work on a cold winter morning and her hands were all red and she was blowing on them. He asked her why she didn't wear her gloves and she said, "I gave them to my daughter this morning." Well, he shut us up right then and there. There were families out there that didn't have enough gloves to go around. It stopped us dead in our tracks.

Eve laughed. "I wrote a song about my gloves. Not these," she said, looking down at her hands. "A glove that I lost once. Do you want to hear it?"

"The song?" I didn't know what she or I were really saying. I was too busy feeling half exhilarated that I'd gotten away with giving her back the card without explaining my connection to it, and half guilty as fuck.

"I'm not going to sing it, but I'll tell you the words." She semi-sang it to me in a more high-pitched voice than was natural, holding a glove with each of her hands and moving them in unison, as if they were doing a coordinated dance number, which, apparently, they were.

"Why?" I asked, when she was finished.

"It's how they feel about each other!" she said. "It was the saddest day. They've been together for so long! They've gone everywhere together! Imagine the life that it's living now, one without the other. . . ."

I thought about the gloves and her mother and how it all made Eve seem "good" but not in a moral sense. I could tell that she was caring and kind but not necessarily in a maternal way. *What was it?* Okay, she was cute. I couldn't help the fact that she was cute. I had nothing in common with her, in terms of interests or profession or ways of interpreting the world, but she was just so graceful; even the way her eyes wandered a room had a certain grace or charm or *something*. I felt like I could have watched this girl make ramen soup and she would have done it with this kind of naturally caring disposition.

"I have to say, I've never imagined the life that my gloves would be living, if they didn't have me."

"Never?" She couldn't believe it.

"Nope."

She shrugged. "I think about what my possessions would do without me all the time."

"That's pretty odd."

We were quiet for a minute. As we stood there waiting for the bouncer to return, I took a stab at a few different topics, none of which really worked. I felt something like panic coming over me. *This is the bagel place all over again! It's bagel-con 1! The highest level of emergency bagel preparedness!* But then, I had a sudden idea. It was like a challenge, dealing with Eve. It was a game where we were down two goals in the third period. It was a building concept with an undetermined support system. I would tell her about my father, about this random connection between us. Maybe it would bring us closer. Or maybe it would ruin the entire night. I wasn't ready to find out.

So instead, I reached into my coat pockets and took out my gloves. I put them next to hers.

"Do you think they like each other?" I said, looking down at my crummy brown gloves next to her green ones.

She smiled. *Ah-ha. Got her.*

"It is *way* too soon to tell," she said.

- - - -

After finally getting turned down, we made our way back upstairs. We took two seats at the end of the bar and ordered drinks. There was a guy sitting there with long hair and tattoos all over his arms, talking to the guy next to him, who had a scruffy beard and a leather vest, about the "Disneyfication" of the East Village.

"Like, look at him," one said to the other, pointing to a young guy walking toward us wearing a polo shirt and khakis. "His outfit is *classic*. This place used to be Studio Fifty-Four and bathroom coke parties, and now it's garbage Top Forty and NYU kids."

The other man nodded. "I guess the word got out that Lit girls were easy! There are sharks in the water, man!"

"I'm telling you. The prices have gone up. There's a freaking *cover*. This gentrification has gotten out of hand ever since the yuppie community board declared war on meaningful nightlife."

Eve smiled at me. "I think we're part of the problem," she whispered conspiratorially. "We should remain inconspicuous."

"All right, I'll cancel the Shirley Temples," I said, turning toward the bartender.

"Shhhhhh!" she said, covering my hand with her hand. "Don't even joke! What's the most hard-core thing we could order? Tequila? Order us tequila!"

I kept her hand there, running my fingertips along her fingertips. She took a breath. She didn't lift her head. "What?" I asked, trying to hide how happy I was with where all this was going, but she didn't reply, and that was okay. If she was feeling what I was feeling, it was okay. I could tell that she was close to leaving with me. My knees were tapping against her knees. I drained my beer and then paid the check, with either money or a dry-cleaning receipt. No idea.

Outside, there were people lined up on the street behind a rope, waiting to get into the next show, which started after midnight. They were all wearing big, shapeless coats and constantly moving to keep warm, bouncing up and down against the cracked pavement.

"All right, so come home with me," I said. I could see my breath in the air. Her cheeks were chilled pink. I looked to reach for her hands, but they were covered in gloves already.

"Oh, I don't know." She looked away, settled her eyes on the ATM that was next to her and covered in black-and-white stickers and dark red graffiti, signs that read things like: GBGB WAS HERE, LOVE ME, and THE DARKNESS. We were standing in front of a Thai restaurant, our legs next to a sandwich board advertising today's specials—crabmeat fried rice, *kai kua* noodle, drunken noodle. The specials were written in pink chalk, in haste. I looked down at them, not wanting to stare directly at Eve, as her face turned confused and then to considering.

I had her thinking about it. I had this girl's attention. But who knew for how much longer?

I looked up. I went and kissed her, and it was a damn good kiss. It was actually perfect. When I moved away from her, I saw that she was about to change her mind. She squinted at me.

"I don't want to go to New Jersey." She smiled.

"Nobody does," I said, and then lifted her up and carried her to the Ninth Street PATH station.

EVE

FIFTH STREET, MY APARTMENT, A ROOM OF MY OWN

The trail of rose petals began at my door and led to the bed. I looked down at my feet, at the faded yellow petals strewn across the wood floor. My initial thought, honestly, was: *I am about to get murdered by a very creative serial killer.* But then I realized that the petals were familiar. There had been roses of that exact color, in a vase on my kitchen counter, for about a week.

"You used *old* rose petals?" I went into the kitchen, where Ben was standing in his boxers.

He turned around and looked at me. "Yeah? So?"

"You're not supposed to use *old* rose petals!" I started to smile. "You're supposed to use new ones, assuming this is the romantic gesture that I think it's supposed to be."

"But we had roses already." He looked perplexed.

"*We* didn't have anything. *I* had roses that were about to die."

"Exactly! They were dying, so I gave them a new purpose. People use *new* rose petals?"

"Yes!"

"But that's such a waste."

I stared at him. "What are you still doing here anyway?"

He shrugged. "Well, after you left, I fell back asleep. And then I decided to be romantic, with the rose petals, so that you'd have something nice to see when you got home. And then I made myself a sandwich, which was delicious, by the way."

I went at him with a book I grabbed off the table. "Get out!" I swatted him on the shoulder, as if he were a fly. "Get out! Get out! Get out!"

"But . . ." He turned and looked helplessly at the kitchen counter, where every single one of my condiment jars was open and had a knife sticking out of it. He took a deep breath, like he was about to say something profound, and used a concerned voice. "But I haven't even told you about the sandwich yet."

He started to remove each knife from its appropriated jar and ran them under the tap water. When he was finished, he dried them all off with a towel.

"I'm not trying to be mean," I said, watching him. "I'm just worried that you're going to confuse our relationship with a proper one. No rose petals, okay?"

"So you aren't really my girlfriend?" He smirked, waiting for me to take the bait.

My eyes narrowed on him. "You know that we're just sleeping together."

He grinned and interlocked his fingers, stretched them over his head, yawning.

"It's weird how you keep kicking me out and then the next weekend texting me, *I misssssss you, where arrrrre you? What are you up to?* Some people might think that you don't know what you want."

"Funny. I don't feel confused."

He was right, and I was wrong. But that all seemed like much less of a concern if he was no longer in my apartment.

"I'm just not sure why you're asking me what my plans are on any given Saturday night, when you know that it's the same answer every time."

"What?" I said quietly.

"If you go, I'll go." He reached for me.

I walked over to the bed, picked up his T-shirt from the floor.

"That's pathetic," I said, throwing the shirt at him. He caught it and laughed.

Ben tried to explain, as I was pushing him out the door, that it was the result of serendipity that led him to me, over and over again. In the field of engineering, he said that it could be a measure of great progress to figure something out by chance, something that was not sought after deliberately. It was to stumble upon something much better than what was originally desired.

"It was a fluke," I said, and then walked away from him, started to clean up my apartment, to gather a few glasses scattered about, collecting them in the sink.

"Synchronicity," he insisted.

"I don't know what that means!" I yelled behind me.

Ben took on a professor-like tone. "It's the idea that just as events may be connected by causality, they may also be connected by meaning. Rather than being 'meant to be' or a result of fate, some things just fall together in time. It's a principle of explanation, a hypothetical factor equal in rank to causality. So I didn't seek you out. X didn't cause Y. But I think the fact that we kept running into each other punctured a hole in rationalism. It broke intellectual resistance. We've come into each other's lives over and over again, and that's fine. No big deal. But because we have, we begin to feel a destiny with each other that tests whether we actually have one, and then we do, because we thought that we might."

"*You* thought that we might." *I* had no idea what he was talking about.

"Oh come on. It's a meaningful coincidence. Look. Think about how easy it would have been for this not to have happened, or for some variation to have taken place instead. That's the phenomenon of parallel universes, the theory of quantum physics that we are all somehow navigating through alternate worlds that are correlated to our past histories, among the myriad possible other worlds that are not as correlated."

"I don't believe in parallel universes."

"How would you know? Maybe *this version* of you doesn't believe, but others might. All I can tell you is that I think back on all those times that we ran into each other and I think, *Thank God you were there*, you know? You could have been anywhere, in any number of places, and you were there."

"So this is destiny? Is that your little theory? I don't think so, Ben."

"C'mon," he said. "What are the chances that we'd ever even interact with each other, let alone have the best sex of your life?" He smiled.

"GET OUT!" I shouted.

I watched him get dressed. I didn't stop him through the T-shirt and pants and belt, but then once he started lacing up his shoes, the guilt came on. I examined the floor around his feet, the brown suede shoes, his hands fiddling with the laces. I thought, *What are you doing?* I didn't want him to leave. I went over to him and put my head against his shoulder. He stopped moving.

"I don't think we should have any more sleepovers," I said. He laughed and put his arm around my waist.

"No more cuddling then," he said, his mouth close to my ear, his arms wrapped around me tightly. "Your loss."

- - - -

After he left, I picked up the rose petals from the floor and threw them into the garbage. I put everything back in order—dishes and glasses into the dishwasher, the comforter smoothed evenly over the bed, clothes folded into piles. The sun was creating a big block of warm light in the middle of the apartment. I decided to go out for a walk, to get rid of some of the energy inside of me, the chaotic thoughts. I was ready to make the city work for me, as it always did, when I felt this way. I'd walk for a while, stomp the pavement. I'd lose myself in the activity around me, in the strange faces and hodgepodge of stores and restaurants, and then I'd come home, feeling restored. I grabbed a jacket from my closet and bounced down the single flight of stairs, past the double doors, the entrance hallway with its pink tiles lining the walls.

Once outside, my preference was always to go left, toward Astor Square. Fifth Street was a row of walk-ups and townhouses, with trees planted every so often, which made it charming and picturesque. All the buildings on the block were around five stories high. There was very little traffic, few pedestrians walking by. Fifth Street was always my savior. Whenever I turned onto it, I felt an immediate sense of relief. My building was a pink walk-up with a mint-green door and a steep white staircase leading up to it. It was less authentic-looking than the other dark red and brown walk-ups on the block, and more like the cartoon version, but I loved the fact that I could see it from down the street. I told people who came over to look for the "cutest" walk-up on the block, and they always found it easily, the walk-up that looked like it was frosted pink for somebody's birthday.

As I walked, thoughts about my mother were turning every which way. I hadn't told Ben yet about her, or about my father. I kept telling myself that it wasn't worth it, that my relationship with Ben wasn't important enough. We didn't talk about our parents. And from what I could tell, his family life was perfect, which would only make me, even more so, the damaged girl. *She'll be so dependent on me*, he'll think. *Her father left, and she'll never trust another man.* When Ben returned my mother's card to me, I could have told him then. I was so relieved to put it back into its rightful place in my wallet. It had felt so empty, with the card gone. I'd kept it there ever since the day she gave it to me. There was nothing extraordinary about the card itself, or about the fact that she gave it to me. At the time, it was a mostly practical measure. She was giving me a way to contact her at work, in case her cell phone wasn't working. It was actually sort of annoying. "Just don't turn off your cell," I had said. "Nobody shuts off their cell phone these days, Mom, like ever." She had the habit of turning it off when she wasn't using it, which my sister and I found infuriating.

Looking back on it though, I think she was actually sort of proud of that card. It symbolized something larger—how she'd managed to move on from what happened with my father. She had a new husband and a new job—both located in Manhattan. When she first got the card, she pointed out to us how the letters were raised slightly, explained that that was a sign that they weren't cheaply made, that the letters were embossed and not simply printed. "Only fancy companies do that," she'd said. Then she showed us the address, that ever so important address—"downtown *Manhattan*," she'd declared, in case we hadn't noticed.

I had rolled my eyes, took the card, planned to plug the number into my phone and then forget about it, toss it. But then, after a few days had gone by, I found that I rather liked having it in there, tucked away, a small white rectangle that was visible whenever I opened my wallet. It was a reminder of how well she was doing now, and *thank God,* after all she'd been through. I didn't have to worry about her anymore. It also served as a kind of connection to her, something that I could feel. And then once she was gone, really gone, I was certainly not removing it then. I guess I liked to think back on that time when she gave it to me, of her desire to protect me.

It was just a small, reassuring object. It wasn't sentimental, really, but it was her, present. I pictured her outstretched hand, handing it to me, with no idea of the wrenching moments that would come later. I literally could not remove it from my wallet. It was silly, no rhyme or reason to keep it there. I had more sentimental things, so many objects that meant more, but the card reminded me, each time I saw it, of the first time I saw it, a time before, when my life was intact, not perfect of course, but intact. Back when I had more of a grip on things, a safety net beneath me. Don't get me wrong. There were a few holes in the net. I'd discovered them over the years, one cavernous hole for my father, but I knew where the holes were, and I was grateful for the part that was strung together. At least I had that. Actually, you know what, I wasn't grateful for it. It was just there. I lived my life, dealt with whatever small problems came up, and it was just there, in case I needed it. But then when it was gone, I so missed that time. I missed life with that hole-filled but somewhat solid object beneath me, life before it all became untethered, before I found myself not tied to anything. The funny thing was I kept looking around for a replacement—left, right, up, down—

scanning for something to ground me. I didn't care. Just tie me to something! It wasn't like I was alone, really. I had my sister and friends and various certified adults who cared, my mother's friends, my stepfather. But it wasn't enough. It felt profoundly like not enough. Losing my mother, the biggest adjustment was to a life untethered. I had this feeling like I could do anything and go anywhere and it wouldn't matter, like nobody was keeping track of me. I had this freedom that I hated.

- - - -

It was dark outside by the time I got home. Emma was sitting on the steps in front of my building, bags piled next to her.

"Learn to answer your phone," she said, and then gave me her signature look of hostility.

"I couldn't hear it on the street," I replied, coming up the stairs. "I thought you were coming later."

"My friends are already out," she said. "I need to eat before I meet up with them, and Arthur says I have to spend time with you first."

"That's very generous of you." I unlocked the door, and she walked ahead of me.

"Look at this place," she said. "Everything is so ordered and immaculate. It's so unrepresentative of who you are."

She was wearing jeans and a sweater, but she had long blond hair and long legs, so everything that she wore made her look statuesque. Her hair had gotten blonder lately, which made her look more like our mother. "Where's a good place to get food?" She got on her phone and started typing. "Are you hungry? Do you want anything?" she asked.

An hour later, she was lying on my floor with a salad and a

container of french fries. Emma drifted between my apartment and Arthur's, while she saved up to afford her own place. Arthur and I didn't mesh, didn't have any chemistry. Basically: if life were a sitcom, Arthur and I would never have been given our own subplot. We were okay, as two parts of a larger group, but the writers would never have put us alone together. Emma was better with him. They talked a lot about sports. Even went to a few games together, a James Taylor concert. But whenever Arthur and I were alone together, silence blanketed the room.

"I can't believe he's not driving you bonkers," I said to her. "When I lived there, he annoyed the hell out of me. So many jokes."

Arthur couldn't pick out a tomato at the grocery store without making conversation with those around him, without doing a little comedy routine in the produce aisle. When waitresses at restaurants asked him for his drink order, he said, "Hmmm, hmmm, hmmm," with great joy, as if there was such *great joy* in being asked, and then declared his choice with gusto, as if he were giving them the thrill of the century.

"I don't get annoyed," Emma said plainly. And I thought, *Right.* Emma behaved as if everything didn't affect her, whereas I always felt like I was wrenched out from underneath.

"Have you heard his latest ringtone?" I asked.

"I think so."

"'Stayin' Alive'?"

"Yeah, I think it went off when we were at dinner once."

"I never thought I would hear that song so many times in my life."

"Yeah," she said distantly. "It's an odd choice."

I sat there in silence as Emma got up to use my computer. I lay on my bed. She barely regarded me, or looked up from her typing. She eyed the notepad that was next to the computer, and then picked it up, held it in front of my face. I looked closer. At the bottom of the page, it read, "Remind me to tell you something about LES Jewels."

I took it from her, ripped the sheet from the pad, and crumpled the paper into a ball. The note was from Ben. LES Jewels, a.k.a. Lower East Side Jewels, was a homeless person known throughout the East Village. Ben and I had seen him the night before, asking for spare change outside of Tompkins Square Park, and then again by Ray's Candy Store. LES Jewels knew everybody. He was what one might call a lovable neighborhood eccentric. He talked to people. But he was also mentally ill and kind of a problem. He would stop cars in the middle of the street and refuse to move. Ben and I often discussed him, along with the other characters who frequented the East Village, but Ben was the one who drifted into full-on research mode about it, always coming up with new tidbits to tell me.

"Who is this from?" Emma asked. "And why are you smiling so much?" I forced my face into a frown and studied her. She stood up, looked at my closet with a thin layer of mistrust. She rifled through the T-shirts that were folded near the foot of the bed.

"What is going on?" she demanded, holding up a COLUMBIA ENGINEERING T-shirt.

I gave her a wide-eyed look. "What if I were dating someone? Would that be so crazy?"

She made a face as if she were sucking on something sour. "Who would date you?"

She smiled and sat down in my desk chair. "I'm just kidding," she said. "Sort of." She grabbed the paper and pen and started writing.

"It's nothing," I said. "It's just some guy."

"What guy?"

"This guy, Ben."

"Who is he? Do you have a secret boyfriend?" Every now and then, Emma still fell into the role of the younger sister who didn't want to be left out. The one screaming "Welcome to the family!" to my childhood crush.

"He's not my boyfriend," I said quickly. "Last night, we went to this stupid Christmas party in the community gardens on Ninth Street. There was this potluck and they built a fire in a wheelbarrow and . . ." I started to talk about the party, getting increasingly animated. "There was this guy there, Biker Bill. He's one of the Hells Angels. You know the Hells Angels? He has a ponytail and a goatee and he's this huge guy. Everyone calls him Biker Bill. Anyway, Biker Bill was like . . . not moving from in front of this fire and the cops started coming by. There was this man claiming to be a veteran paratrooper with a gun collection. It was a bunch of weirdos. Anyway, Lower East Side Jewels tried to put out the fire with his shoe and . . ."

"Why'd you go to that?"

I shrugged. "I thought I'd get a story out of it."

She looked confused. "Why?"

"I thought I'd find out more about C-squat, that abandoned building on Avenue C that squatters live in."

She stared at me blankly.

"Ben told me about it. I had no idea it even existed, but then I started reading. Basically, in the nineties, all these squatters got evicted from this building on Avenue C but some managed to stay. There are apartments, and in the basement they put on punk shows. And, like, *good* shows sometimes. Some of the members of this really influential turn-of-the-century punk band still live there. Oh! I met this girl at the party who is in mortuary school." I raised my eyebrows. "She actually climbed to the top of the Williamsburg Bridge. She also broke into a building in Times Square and showed me a picture of her looking down on this big crowd from up above. She told me an insane story about her boyfriend and how she accused him of killing her dog and they had to get an autopsy because she didn't believe that he didn't kill the dog. . . . Who has a situation like that? Anyway, the whole C-squat thing fascinated me, because so many musicians lived there and some still do. There's also a lot of drug use and people stealing from one another but I just wanted to find out more about this weird housing situation."

"Why? So that you could go there and look for dates?"

"No!" I yelled, and then glared at her. "Because I thought it might make for a good story for Voice."

"I wouldn't put it past you," she spat. "Is that where Ben lives?"

I tilted my head to the side. "Ben is a structural engineer who lives in Hoboken."

"So why don't you like him?" she said. "Is he actually nice?"

"Yeah . . ." I thought about it for a second. "He is pretty nice. And what's sort of cool about him is that you *think* he's this normal engineer guy but then he knows everything about all these *random* things. But I can tell that he doesn't have any real *issues*. And that's kind of what I don't like about him, you know?"

She tried to absorb this. "You are fucking psycho," she said, looking at me with not the slightest smile and tugging at the frayed edges of her sweater.

"I know," I told her. "I sound crazy."

She rolled her eyes. "You don't *sound* crazy, you actually *are* crazy."

Since I was the older sibling and a very mature adult, I would refrain from reminding her that she too had her own issues.

Emma was famous for having nine hundred male *friends*, and zero boyfriends. When we were growing up, they would come over to our house, act like they virtually worshipped the ground she walked on, and she would carry on framing photographs they had taken for her and setting up the television with some show to watch together. Many of them even confided in me, looking to me for some insight. I merely sympathized and explained that Emma was different. I think the whole idea of a relationship terrified her. It was too illogical.

But I wouldn't say any of this to Emma. We weren't sisters who were best friends. We were sisters who were sisters. We had the same natural tendencies. Our voices were impossible to distinguish. Certain small gestures were identical. But in other ways, we were complete opposites. The way that we reacted to what happened with our parents was different. We both felt the losses, but we managed them separately. I tried to shield myself from future pain by studying everyone around me. Emma watched horror movies before she went to sleep at night. When she got older, she went out. A lot. One morning when she was seventeen, I found her passed out in the kitchen of Arthur's apartment. She claimed that she had inhaled too many helium balloons at a party, which seemed totally plausible to Arthur but *not* to me. I found out later that she'd slept with someone's boyfriend and got herself banned from a graduation party.

Then there was one time that she got high with her friends in our shared bathroom in Arthur's apartment and left a candle burning overnight and caused a small fire. Even months later, the incident didn't leave her so easily. She'd feel anxious over something and then say: "I think it's also the fire." She asked questions about it. *How fast can fire spread? Do you think I could have burned down the whole apartment? Is it because this apart-*

ment is old? What happens to a fire in a new apartment? Is it true that doorknobs get hot the fastest? She passed her hand over the candles at restaurants and tried to put them out with her fingertips. She had nightmares about explosions and the apartment burning down. Arthur took her to see a psychiatrist, who told her that it wasn't about the fire but what she associated with the fire. The doctor said that the shock of the fire was causing Emma to reexperience the trauma of our father leaving. She explained that shock could remain in people's systems for a long time, and it could manifest itself in a variety of ways.

When our mother died, I thought it would all go to hell, but Emma went away to school in North Carolina and actually came back more grounded. It was as if she'd gone through a tunnel and come out the other side. She decided that she wanted to be a CEO. "Of what kind of company?" I asked. Apparently, it didn't matter. "I don't care. I just want to be the boss," she said. She came up with ideas. I was a bad judge of them. I couldn't imagine anyone taking her seriously. In my mind, she was frozen at age twelve. Who would listen to her? Even sitting in my room now, when she said, "I have to jump on a conference call quickly," my first thought was: *That's hysterical.*

She went back to the computer but remained astonished, even as her eyes focused on the screen. She got up.

"Eve." She sighed. "You want to be disturbed, be disturbed. I can't stop you."

"I'm not being disturbed. I like Ben. He's nice, but he's also kind of boring to me for some reason."

"Because he's not addicted to heroin?"

"No . . . we just aren't . . . the same person."

"So?"

"So . . . he isn't my type."

"Because he's not addicted to heroin."

"Stop."

"Go to C-squat. Shoot heroin. Live there among your people."

"What are you talking about?"

"You know exactly what I'm talking about," she said. Her anger arrived without notice. "We had some bad things happen to us. And I'm sure some psychologist somewhere could have a field day with the connection between our dad leaving and our future relationships with men, or the loss of our mother and how that somehow echoed the loss of our father years earlier. But you're *choosing* to hang on to this."

"I don't think that—"

"It was like that time when we were younger and we went to the grocery store and you picked out a loaf of bread and then you decided later that you didn't actually want the loaf of bread so you put it back with the olives, and you felt *so bad* that it wasn't with the other breads that you made me go back to the store with you 'to put it back with its bread friends,' so that it would have a greater chance of being purchased. And then, even after we put it back, that night, you were all 'What do you think happened with the bread? Do you think someone bought it? Do you think some nice couple took it home with them?' You named it and gave it a whole personality and kept talking about it like we *abandoned* it. And it was kind of funny, of course. But it was also kind of like you projected all your own psychological issues onto this loaf of bread, instead of realizing, like a normal person, that bread doesn't have feelings. It was like you wanted to have this big *abandonment* issue. Well, fine. It's there for you if you need it, that's for sure. And nobody is going to take it away from you. Except for you."

I was watching her like she was sharpening a knife in front

of me. She kept going. She controlled the conversation with authority, an "I'm an adult now" voice that only came out on certain occasions, when our mother used to tell her what size sweater to buy or what to eat for breakfast.

"You feel an obligation to be this way," she went on. "And honestly, I understand why you *were* like this. But now? Still? I think you're just scared of what would happen if you didn't have this to fall back on. It's been in your system for so long and you've become awfully good at accommodating it. It's like, a long time ago, you decided you'd never be happy."

"Listen," I interrupted her, not sure how she'd gotten me so riled up. "I'm not going to sit here and have you psychoanalyze me. Everyone has issues. You have yours."

Why couldn't Emma just tell me that she felt the same way? That would actually help. I would think, *See? We are all just humans trying to get by! Life! We are all just a little bit overwhelmed.* I wanted to explain about Ben, in a way that would make sense to her. I almost told her about his lame attempt at fate or "meant to be" as a reason why I could never date him. She would have found this to be utterly preposterous. I wanted to scream: *I might disappoint him.* Yes, I could envision a time when I would disappoint him. It was like an invisible wall that I couldn't break through. Or wouldn't break through. I didn't know which anymore. That was the most frightening part, that Emma was right. *I was the one who was keeping this problem around.*

When she finished changing her clothes into "going out" attire, a black sweater with holes and red lipstick, she stepped back from the mirror and surveyed me.

"It doesn't necessarily have to be like that," she said. "If you don't like this guy, then fine. But don't be one of those *damaged* people, because that's what happened to us, but it isn't *who you are*. Do you have any candy?"

For a split second, her face looked just like the little girl she used to be, who wouldn't leave me alone, who doted on me and followed me around until I let her in on my games. It was a time before—before she had her own friends, before red lipstick and thrift-store jeans and road trips to San Francisco with some guy with angular features who I worried would kick her out of the car by Vegas.

"You always wanted to understand everything," she said, banging around in my kitchen. She came back with a fistful of jelly beans. "Like, take Dad for example. You wanted to understand what he did, but I always felt like he was like a turtle." She crossed my bedroom and shoved all her clothes into a bag.

"What?"

"He was an unknowable mystery. Who knows why a turtle does what it does? I have no idea. Would you even try to understand? Do you ever watch a turtle roaming around and think, *Hmmm, I wonder why it went that way? I wonder why it ate that plant? I wonder why it likes that rock?*"

"No," I said, with a smile.

"Exactly. You have to think of Dad as a turtle. And we as a civilization just don't understand the psychological motivations of turtles that well."

"You can't yell at me for personifying bread and then compare Dad to a turtle."

"We are sisters after all!" she replied, and then came over to me. I opened my hand instinctually. She dropped a few jelly beans into my open palm, the flavors that she didn't like but that I did.

When she was ready to leave, I walked her down the stairs and out the door. As I watched her moving along Fifth Street and farther away, I felt an unexpected pang. She must have been feeling it too, because after she'd walked about halfway down the block, she turned to look back at me and I thought, *We are sisters after all. This is what it's like to have a sister. You're not having a great time together. You sit across from each other and you talk about the issues of the day—whether some guy she's texting with is really busy at work, how busy can a person be? Or is he blowing her off? You give her advice that she half takes. You say variations of what your mother used to tell you both. You say, Focus on work; make a date with someone else; stop worrying about things you can't control; a watched pot never boils! It is almost always the case that one of you is single and the other is not. The one who is not gives the advice, careful not to seem too smug or condescending. The one who is single tries not to seem hostile, to just take the advice because, really, she can't afford to create any enemies right now and she knows that you have the best intentions but she also can't be bothered to mask her annoyance. If you were her friend and not her sister, she would pep up a little bit more, she would be more upbeat, more receptive, and more outwardly grateful. She would say things like "Thanks!" and "That's really helpful!" But she's your sister, so she sits there with a frown on her face, as if your advice is some kind of imposition. But she's not* not *listening. She's not* not *paying attention. So you can feel free to keep speaking, if that suits you, if that thrills you. And then you both sit there in semicomfortable silence, secretly wishing you were with a friend and wondering why it's awkward and then consoling yourself with the fact that at least you're not alone. You think:* Why does she have to be in such a bad mood? Couldn't she put on the slightest bit of an act for me? I'm a person too. Doesn't she realize that? *You glance at the clock and think it'll be a relief to part ways, to have only one of you in the room to deal with. Sometimes it's a little bit too much, having two people together with such similarities. So you part ways. And at first it is a relief. But then you realize it's a little bit harder than you thought it would be. You hadn't anticipated that the separation would make you feel anything. But it's only apparent during the process of separating. It only hurts when she walks away. You smile widely, you wave at each other in an overly enthusiastic way that makes you both laugh, because, yeah right, like this is such a big deal? You give each other strange exaggerated looks of being frightened for no reason, because you're not actually frightened. But you both know. It's a "good luck out there!" kind of look. It's not about anything specific. It's about life. It's an acknowledgment that you're moving through it separately and hoping the best for each other. She keeps walking, and eventually you can't see her anymore. It's official. You're apart. But she's not abandoning you. She's back to her life and you're back to yours. And that's fine. You still think, you still feel, on some visceral level, like you could almost cry, but then it passes. A few minutes pass and it's okay. It's really okay.*

After she left, I went back inside and called Ben. "All right," I said, when he picked up. "Tell me about the sandwich."

BEN

218 EAST FIFTH STREET, BETWEEN SECOND AVENUE AND BOWERY,
APARTMENT 2W, EAST VILLAGE

A woman grabbed hold of my arm.

"I know you," she said. "I know you, exactly!" She took my hand.

I was on Christopher Street. I had just left a store that sold tea and coffee, a place that had been around since the 1920s, so read the sign. You could smell the store from the sidewalk, the sweet and bitter aroma of spices. Inside, the shop was crammed with burlap sacks of coffee beans labeled TURKISH, CHINA, BRAZIL, and bins of tea leaves marked ORANGE and JASMINE. Behind the counter there were jars of spices, coffee grinders, and brass scales.

I was hanging around the Village for research. The plans for the Freedom Tower had come to a halt, yet again, because of the advisory committee, which was embroiled in a heated debate over whether to include retail space in the plans. This time it was the Take Back the Memorial advocates causing problems, this one woman whose brother was the pilot of the hijacked plane that crashed into the Pentagon. She was against any retail development in the area, wanted to rid the memorial of those tenants and to expand the plans for a memorial museum. She said that to even think about retail establishments was to turn yet another part of Manhattan into a shopping mall. Another board member, whose husband worked in the South Tower, said that it was outrageous to plan for shops without first sitting down with the families, for the Port Authority to sign leases with any retail entity without first having asked for public input. We kept going over the parts of Manhattan that had retail establishments but weren't ruined by them. We kept referencing the East Village. And so that was where I was spending my Saturday, on Christopher Street, trying to figure out what was different about these shops versus the ones in any other neighborhood. It wasn't like the establishments in the East Village weren't selling things. They were. They were just old, and some of them were one-of-a-kind, but not all.

I also chose the East Village to walk around because it had the advantage of being Eve's neighborhood. She had become important to me. After I left the coffee place, I went to a bakery on Commerce Street and picked up a few things for her. I didn't know for sure whether I would see her at the end of the day. I didn't even know if she was home or busy or what, but I was suddenly counting on it.

Over on Tenth Street, between First and Avenue A, I had come across a shop covered in plants. The sign read, EXOTIC PLANTS • GEMS & CRYSTALS • BONSAI • ORCHIDS • FLOWERS FOR ALL OCCASIONS. There were flowers out in front, positioned in rows along the sidewalk, cactuses, and potted herbs of all kinds. Hanging plants and dream catchers covered the store windows. The smell coming from inside this place . . . It was incense and burning wood, but to the extreme. I couldn't imagine how anyone stayed inside there for longer than five minutes without going crazy.

Which might explain the woman who currently had my arm in a death vise.

I paused. "I don't think so," I said slowly.

"Yes, I *know* you!" she insisted. "You have been so busy with friends, relationships, your job, your family, that you haven't had time for *magic!*" Her blue-polished nails dug into my skin. "Am I right?"

"You got me!" I said, trying to move away from her.

She nodded knowingly. "You need a witch in your life, don't you?"

"Umm." I shook my head. "I don't think so." I tried to walk away. If by witch she meant a woman with mysterious powers over me, then yeah, I already had one of those.

"No. No. I can tell. You need one. Come inside for a few minutes, won't you?" I squinted as I looked in. It was white inside. A cloud of smoke occupied the whole store.

"You're busy? What are you doing? Where are you going?" she asked.

I didn't think to say the truth, which was "Wandering around but eventually going to see a girl I can't stop thinking about and I'd rather not show up smelling like a poisonous garden."

"Crystals have healing powers. Did you know that? Let me show you some of them. Aren't you interested in healing? Well-being? Neutralizing negativity? Becoming an integrated, whole being?"

She turned over my hand and looked at my palm. A grave expression appeared on her face.

"Oh, you *definitely* need to come in here," she said.

I looked down at my hand and started to laugh. "What? See something you don't like?"

"Oh *yes*. Are you a scientist?"

"No, I'm an engineer."

"I knew it! I knew you were a scientist!"

"I'm not a . . . Are your crystals this accurate? Anyway, I really gotta run."

"Don't you want to establish your life's purpose?"

"Those are some powerful rocks."

She looked taken aback. "Oh, they're not *rocks*."

"Really?" I said, staring in between the plants, through the window. "Because they look a whole lot like rocks."

She frowned.

"I'll tell you what," I said. "You give me one scientific fact, and I'll come inside and take a look."

She held her hands together in front of her chest. "Crystal healing is ancient, dating back at least six thousand years to ancient Mesopotamia. It is centuries . . ." She seemed to lose her train of thought.

"So these crystals are from Mesopotamia?"

"No, they're from Arkansas."

I laughed.

"Okay, my dear," she said, ready to level with me. "Let's say you don't believe in the healing powers, don't you want to see something of beauty? We have some truly beautiful items. Just trust me, okay? *Trust me.* It is worth seeing. You go to museums, don't you? Why miss a thing of beauty?"

"All right, all right," I said, to get her to stop harassing me. I walked through the hall of plants and pulled open the door. I felt bad for that poor woman. She had a tough job. Or so I thought.

Once I went inside, I realized that within the cloud of smoke, the store was packed with people. As it turned out, there was a decent market in this city for objects that alleviated tension and unblocked emotional distress. Because she was following me around the store, I bought a stone for four dollars that was meant to "enhance clarity and levelheaded decisions." Really, I just wanted to get the hell out of there. The smell was giving me a headache.

I had the stone in my pocket, and I was headed toward Eve's, grateful for the non-incense-scented air. You never really appreciate your standard, smog-filled, city-polluted oxygen until it's taken away from you. From my apartment in Hoboken, I could see the Manhattan skyline, the skyscrapers in midtown and how the city dipped down in the Village and then, in the financial district, went back up. Skyscrapers were clustered downtown and in midtown for a reason. Geology controlled the skyline. The gray rock below the streets of Manhattan dictated that the higher buildings be found where the rock was closer to the surface, so that it could support that weight. Underneath the Village, the rock was not as strong, which is why the Village used to be all marshes. The rock was lower, and it took a lot more work to dig down.

I texted Eve, when I got close to her place. The text needed to be something casual, something that didn't scream *relationship*. Small animal in the woods.

I typed: *Going out tonight?*

Her response came right away.

Nope! Sorry. Sick. Have the flu I think.

I felt the sting of disappointment, texted back.

Can I bring you something?

I stood on the street waiting, a block away from her apartment.

No, it's okay. But if you're going out downtown, I wouldn't mind

*if you stopped by and kept me company for a bit. I lost my job yes-
terday. Voice was shut down by a federal court. Did you know that
it's against the law to steal music?*

I typed quickly into my phone. *Seriously?*

Eve was pretty keen on daily life at Voice. She made fun of
herself, said that it was assumed at the office that anything she
had to say about music was lame, but I knew that underneath it
all, she had a good idea of what she was doing. She loved her job
like I loved mine, which was a great thing about her. So many
people complained about work. My phone vibrated in my hand.

Yeah . . . I wouldn't mind it if you stopped by.

I circled the block a few times, to give her the impression
that I wasn't a lunatic standing outside her door. When I showed
up there, she didn't question it. She answered with a blanket
wrapped around her like a burrito.

"Excuse me," I said. "Have you seen Eve?"

She looked at me and then sneezed, pulling the blanket
across her face to cover her nose. "Very funny," she said, her
voice nasal and different.

I dug into my pockets, handed her the stone from the crystal
shop.

"I brought you a healing crystal," I said. She gazed down at it
quizzically, a tiny blue dot in the palm of her hand. The expression on her face was just enough amusement for me.

"I'm kidding," I said, and then took it back, presented her
with a white paper bag. "I brought you cookies." She perked up.
"I thought you'd kick me out if I brought soup. You'd say it was
too cliché or something irritating like that."

She took the bag and peeked inside it.

"Fiiiiine, you can stay," she said, and brought the bag into
the kitchen.

"Oh, thank you very much. Because it's so pleasant in here."
I looked around her apartment, which had piles of tissues everywhere, cough drops spilled over the bed; nose spray, a bottle of NyQuil, and a thermometer were on the night table.

She looked up at the ceiling, like she was about to sneeze again, and then she sneezed. Four times. "How did you get so sick?" I asked.

"I don't know," she said, frustrated, like she'd been contemplating this very question for weeks. "I think just lack of sleep and everything caught up to me. I've been going to five concerts a week."

"Five?"

"I was actually proud of myself." She pursed her lips together and smiled. "Until yesterday."

"What happened with your job?"

She shrugged. "It sucks. But I'll find something else. It'll probably involve fewer pillows though."

"Yeah . . . but that was weird anyway."

"Yeah."

I tried to think of a consoling thing to say but came up with nothing. I could tell her some version of "I'm sorry" or "Everything's going to be okay," except she'd hate that. She'd start all over again, with the cocoon that she was always building around herself. Or she'd bludgeon me to death with the nearest sharp object. Hard to tell with Eve.

She got into bed and pulled the comforter up until it reached her chin. There was a mountain of crumpled tissues next to her. She was alternating between grabbing for a mug with a tea bag dangling in it from her night table, and picking at a few crackers on a napkin.

"Sit by me," she said. I went over to the radiator and put

my hand over it. Little heat was emanating out. It was warming nothing but the radiator itself.

"Aren't you cold?"

"Yeah, but if you sit by me, I'll feel better," she said, looking up at me, her eyes wide, her hair messy against a white pillow.

"What about the rules?" I said, mocking her. I was still fixated on the cold. *How was she supposed to get better like this?*

She sighed. "You're here already. What's it matter?"

I touched the wall behind her pillow. It was freezing. I touched her head. Her head and hair were cold too, which made sense. She was basically outside. The problem with radiators in old apartments was that you had no control over them. The building controlled the boiler. There was steam heat and water heat, gravity systems and pipe systems—*what was this?* I looked around. There was one square window in the wall and I went over to it. It wasn't properly sealed. As a temporary solution, I wondered if there was a way to make a headboard, to create a barrier between her head and the outside world. I searched the room for a slab of wood.

"What are you looking for?" she asked.

"Do you have any large chunks of wood lying around?"

She smiled. "Are you kidding?"

"Never mind."

I went over to her and got into bed. I crawled over her to reach the side closest to the window. I sat up, felt my back against the cold wall, and put one arm around her. I looked down at the side of her face. The tip of her nose was red. Her eyes were closed.

"I always want to sit right next to you," I said. "Even when there are other, more germ-free options."

"I know."

"Seriously, you look like one big germ right now," I said. "Like one of those big green germs from the commercials for cold medicine."

"Why am I *big*?"

"That's your issue? Fine. You're a cute little germ."

"Better."

"Eve. I'm telling you this in your weakened state because I think you'll be more susceptible to reason when your body isn't strong enough to be totally irrational."

She looked up at me.

"What is it?"

"I want to take you out on a real date. On Tuesday."

"Tuesday? Why Tuesday?"

"Because Monday sounded too eager in my head on the way over here."

She groaned. "You don't understand. I've had a few . . . blows, which I haven't really told you about. It could have been worse, I guess. But it was pretty bad and I'm scared that it won't work out between us because you and I are so . . . different . . . and I don't know if I could ever explain it to you in a way that would really make sense . . . to someone who's never experienced . . ."

This felt like the moment to tell her everything. About my father. The card. But I looked at her and I just instinctually did not want to do anything that would hurt her further. I wanted to make her feel better, not worse. I had this plan in my head to just get her to more solid ground, and then, once I had her there, I could tell her whatever I wanted. I just had to book that date, get us on track for a real relationship, and in order to do that, I had to defuse her fear, not send her running scared. Fortunately, that was something that I knew how to do.

"Can I tell you something about my job?" I said.

"What?"

"When you're designing a building, you have to think about all the possible things that can happen to that building—hurricanes, snowstorms, insane traffic. . . . No one knows what's going to happen exactly, but we need to be able to predict with a certain level of probability what is likely to occur. We boil things down to mathematics, even though it really doesn't lend itself to such an exact science. There are so many unknowns, but you have to think to yourself, *What's most likely?* You do the calculations that will give you a high level of certainty that it will work, and then you move forward. And it's such a satisfying feeling, to be able to let go of the what-ifs and finally move forward."

She didn't say anything, but I could tell that she was listening. Her eyes were open and she looked peaceful. For once, she wasn't furrowing her brow.

"Anyway, I can't predict the future, but I can tell you that based on the evidence at my disposal, I feel fairly certain that this will work. And that's all anyone can give you. That's all you'll ever get. It's *the best* that you can ask for."

Her eyes widened for one last protest. "But what about . . ."

I shook my head. "No. No amount of imaginary potential hypothetical factors is going to scare me away, because those are constants in everything. We're going out on Tuesday. And if you say no, I'll take away the cookies."

She crossed her arms on top of the sheets and exhaled. "I can't believe you're telling me this while I have malaria."

That was it. *I'd won.*

I lifted the comforter to put it over my jeans. "You don't have malaria."

"I think it could be a parasite. I have no appetite. I'm usually very hungry. How else do you explain it?"

"It's not a parasite," I said, with a sigh. "You have to feed them. You'd be extra hungry."

She laughed and gave me a warm look. I smiled and then closed my eyes, nudged her foot against mine.

"Tuesday."

"Maybe."

"Tuesday."

"You'll regret it," she mumbled.

"Let's just see."

I pulled her in closer to me. After a few minutes, she was quiet. With Eve that meant one thing: she was falling asleep.

"Don't try to lull me into a false sense of security," she said.

I laughed. "Why is it false?"

I reached over her head and turned off the light so that the only thing illuminating the room was a streetlamp on Fifth Street.

EVE

A CUBAN RESTAURANT ON CHRISTOPHER STREET

Ben met me outside my building and stood waiting for me at the bottom of the steps, rubbing his hands together in the cold.

"Nice place," he said, looking up at the pink facade.

"Very funny," I said. "You could have come inside." I zipped up my jacket and fixed my scarf so that it protected my nose and chin as we started walking.

"I wanted you to have the *real date* experience."

"Well, if you had come inside, you would have seen me agonizing over which turtleneck to put on." I smiled at him.

He concentrated on the ground for a few seconds. "Oh. Because it's the least appealing thing you could wear?"

"Exactly!"

"You're insane."

"Ah, you know me so well, considering it's our first date."

"Yeah, well, unlucky for me." He put his hands in his pockets and ducked his chin into the collar of his jacket.

"You wanted this!" I pointed at him.

"I know. I know." He held his arm out in front of me so that I couldn't cross against the light and into oncoming traffic. I bumped up against it. "It's just . . . I forgot what happens when you talk," he said.

Ben, impressively, surprisingly, chose a restaurant with a nice vibe—the walls covered in murals, warm lighting from hanging lanterns, a tiny votive candle on each table, and the sweet smell of plantains, mixed with garlic and onions, drifting from the kitchen. There was a man with a beard sitting at a large round table and rolling cigars, the flecks of brown in two piles next to him.

"Very authentic," I commented, pointing at the man as we sat at our table.

"I wouldn't know," Ben said, glancing back with a smile.

We sat in chairs covered in white leather. Ben gave the menu a serious look, as if trying to solve some complex mathematical equation that was written on it. I, on the other hand, looked at the menu for two seconds and then decided on something that felt safe involving rice and chicken. It didn't matter. When I was nervous, I tasted no food.

We closed our menus and drank water. Ben told me a story about a Russian lady who incorrectly dialed his cell phone several times that day. It was hands down one of the worst stories I had ever heard him tell. The story went on through our drink orders and went absolutely nowhere of any interest. In an accidental declaration of boredom, I knocked over my water glass with my elbow. Our date was officially off to an awkward start.

The waiter arrived with a steaming plate of fajitas for Ben. He then hesitantly placed a gigantic mound of yellow rice, with tiny specks of chicken, in front of me. Ben eyed my dish.

"That's . . . a lot of rice," he said. I brushed him off and started to take my fork to it. Pretended it was nothing. *I eat this amount of rice all the time!* But he was right. It was a lot of rice. I could barely see him over it. *Note to self: next time don't be such a crazy person, and take an extra minute or two with the menu, okay?* To save face, I launched into another topic, anything other than the fact that I was so nervous that I'd accidentally ordered a side dish.

We talked about our friends from college, which felt easy, harmless. That drifted into conversation about our families. Ben told me about his brother, who had just moved to Costa Rica, which upset their mother.

"When she's around my brother, they fight all the time. They're literally at each other's throats. But she doesn't want him to be so far away either. It makes zero sense."

"If by zero you mean total, then yes, you are correct."

"I don't get it!"

"What's not to get?"

"Explain it to me then."

"It's like they love each other too much to actually love each other. The fighting is easier sometimes. But it means the same thing. It's just a different way of expressing it."

"A more violent way."

"Yeah, well, sometimes, violence *is* the answer."

"How do you know all this?"

I smiled. "It's basic human psychology."

"Oh, you're full of baloney."

"Rice. I'm full of rice."

By the time the *tres leches* cake arrived, it seemed as if the first-date jitters had somehow lifted, and Ben and I started to have a pretty good time.

"I'd like to visit him there, sometime. Have you ever gone surfing?" Apparently, Ben wanted to learn to surf. *Yes, I imagined with some adjustments we could go to Costa Rica together and be one of those couples that surfs.* It reminded me, for a brief second, of the guys I dated in Colorado. It wouldn't be too hard to drift into that pseudo-outdoorsy girl again, for him. But instead, I let it all go.

"No. I haven't. And I don't really want to."

"Why not?"

"I'm scared of the ocean," I said firmly, as if it was the most obvious thing imaginable. I needed Ben to know this. I needed him to know everything, as it really was. That was how things had always been between us, and I didn't see any reason to alter that now.

He laughed. "What's to be scared of?"

"Um. Hello? Sharks? Ever heard of them?"

– – – –

We left the restaurant and walked across Washington Square Park. There was an ice-cream truck pulled up next to the entrance to the park. The lights weren't on. No music. The guy inside was leaning out the window, looking for customers, wearing a red Santa hat.

"It's a hard day to be selling ice cream," I said to Ben. "We should get something."

"It's freezing!"

"Yeah but maybe the ice cream will be so cold that it'll make us warmer."

"That's not how temperature works."

"Tell you what. You buy me an ice cream, and I'll let you spend the rest of the walk telling me how temperature works."

Ben perked up. "Deal."

We walked up to the truck. I asked for a small vanilla cone with colored sprinkles.

"Colored sprinkles?" Ben's eyes widened. "How old are you?"

"What toppings do you get? Butterscotch?"

"I don't get toppings."

"Why not?"

"Because I'm an adult," he said proudly.

"That's a mistake," I said. "Adulthood is highly overrated."

As we walked, I felt my teeth chattering. I took a few last licks and then tossed the remains of the cone into a nearby garbage can and tried to wipe my hands with a crumpled napkin. Then, I put my gloves back on as fast as possible.

"Told you," Ben said, shaking his head and interrupting his own lecture on thermodynamics. He put his arm around me.

"Look at that magnificent fountain," I said, pointing to the facade of NYU's library, as if referring to something majestic and not just a small stream of running water down the side of the building. "It was built in the eighteenth century, which you can tell from the pattern of the bricks and the . . ." I tried to feign as much structural engineering knowledge as I could, doing my best Ben impression. "You see . . . the Pilgrims came here in 1734, and they wanted to build something that would reflect their old way of life so . . ."

"That's not a fountain," Ben said, rolling his eyes. "That's a leak."

"Oh." I stopped walking. "Should we call someone?"

– – – –

Ben reached for my hand to hold as we walked. It was a clear night, the sky had been dark for hours, and we seemed to be the only ones on the street. We got to my building and stood there.

"You know, I don't sleep with guys after the first date."

He laughed. "Ohhh, only *before* the first date, huh?"

"That's right. That is my policy."

"You know I've been up there several times before."

"Yeah, but . . ."

"What's the matter? Don't think I know how to take off a turtleneck?"

I pretended to be frustrated and kept my eyes on the sidewalk, and maybe I was a little frustrated because I couldn't think of what to say or how to stop him from coming upstairs and couldn't stop smiling and was almost embarrassed by how happy I felt. And then he came closer and kissed me and sort of knocked all the thoughts out of my head. After the kiss was over, I couldn't move, couldn't think, definitely was *not* going to tell him not to come upstairs.

Everything quieted down after that, like the city after a big snowstorm. I don't remember deciding to go upstairs, but we did. All that I can remember clearly is that kissing him suddenly felt like the only thing I'd ever done of any importance. I remember reality slipping away. I remember letting go of everything. I remember that it somehow became seven o'clock in the morning, that we were still up talking, yes—even Ben was talking, a little bit, that the sun was coming up, threatening to end it all, to usher us on to the next activity, but we didn't care. We just kept doing whatever it was that we were doing, and laughed at the daylight.

EVE

BROOKLYN

The first birthday card I got from my father after he left us was postmarked from February, but I didn't get it until May because that was when I decided to finally check my student mailbox, which nobody checked, since they were usually filled with junk. I wasn't wrong, but this particular piece of junk was loaded. When my mother died, I'd half expected him to reappear. But where had he been? He must have known. He was capable of finding out, from someone, somewhere, what had happened. But apparently, all he'd done was send this card to a mailbox that I never checked. I remembered squinting when I looked at the return address, not wanting to know exactly, or to look too closely. Just to think of him living somewhere stirred up something within me, to know that he was so close and yet didn't see the need to find us. The fact that he dared to call someplace home, the little hollow gestures that he must have made to have it seem that way, while leaving my sister and me so unattended.

From then on, a birthday card arrived every year from the

same address in Brooklyn. The cards barely touched my fingers. Each year I opened it, glanced at the words there on the white page, written with a thick marker, and then shoved it down into the trash, as far as it could go, getting my hands dirty. At first, when he left, I imagined that he must have gone somewhere far away—a remote fishing village in Alaska, an island off the coast of Indonesia. Boston. Once I saw that address, I decided, so that I could live in New York without fear, that the chances of running into him in Manhattan were slim to none. I decided that I would never go to Brooklyn and that he wasn't likely to leave it. Therefore, our universes were kept separate. If, for some reason, I had to go for work, I went and left as quickly as possible. I kept my head down the whole time, limiting my peripheral vision, but it didn't really work. My heart raced each time I saw a man with similar eyes or hair, of a similar height, with his head shape.

I didn't respond to the cards. A response wasn't required or requested. But this year, when the card arrived, Ben was there.

"You should call him," Ben had said, watching me that night, sitting on the floor, all teary-eyed and looking at old photos. "I'll stay here with you while you call. Don't you want to find out more about what happened?"

"No. Not really," I said, in a soft voice, not looking up at him. I reached for my headphones and plugged them into my ears. "I just want to listen to music and forget about it," I said.

"*Okay*, fourteen-year-old version of my girlfriend." Ben removed the earbuds with one gentle yank of the cord.

"Hey!" I snapped.

"Eve. You have to be an adult sometimes. Eat a vegetable. Both literally and figuratively." He sat down on the floor next to me. I glared at him.

"Let's just say, years from now, you change your mind," he said calmly. "You might not be able to anymore. He's not going to be around forever. Maybe it's time you talk to him."

I had followed his logic and somehow ended up calling an old family friend and asking for my father's number. A few weeks later, after downing half a glass of wine, and under Ben's watchful eye, I called.

"Eve. Hi. Thanks for calling," he said.

He invited me to lunch in Brooklyn, as if it were nothing. I didn't add anything to the conversation. I listened to his familiar voice on the phone and said I'd go to lunch and then hung up, relieved, like I had gotten off a bad ride just in time. Apparently, Ben's naiveté and kindness were trickling into me. He had a sensible and even-tempered opinion about everything. It was infuriating.

I told Emma about the call, the possibility of a lunch, but then assured her that she wouldn't have to go, that only one of us should have to be subjected to this nonsense and, since I was the older sibling, I would take the hit. She didn't protest. As usual, she wasn't too bothered by the whole situation.

All of which had brought me here, to a café on Seventh Street, waiting to go see my dad, feeling very bothered indeed. I sat in a daze, at a table by the window, next to a bouquet of flowers inside a watering can, tracing the lines of the wooden table with my finger. I couldn't stop holding on to things. My body felt like it was on high alert. A waitress asked if I wanted anything and scared the shit out of me. I kept looking at the elderly couple sitting two tables over.

"So you see? Raisins," the woman said to the man, affectionately, pointing to her pound cake.

"Today, they have raisins," he replied. "Yesterday was a different story. What do you think? I'm going to get you the wrong cake on purpose?"

She smiled at him and then looked over at me, perhaps noticing that I'd been staring, speculating, *Do they still like each other? Are they happy?* I gave her a quick smile and then looked away. A woman came over and put down two cups of coffee on their table. "Ah-ha," the man said, eyeballing the backside of the waitress. *There it is. The flaws are never visible right away.*

"Here, fuel up." Ben stood over me and handed me a doughnut wrapped in cellophane and a small glass of apple juice. "The only thing worse than you in the throes of an emotional episode is you in the throes of an emotional episode on an empty stomach."

"I thought I was supposed to be an adult today?" I said, turning away from the lecherous old guy and looking up at the doughnut and apple juice.

"Best not to shock your system."

He'd thought of everything. So I nodded, sipped, chewed, couldn't really taste. *The main thing is to control my anger.* That was the biggest obstacle, to keep it in a ball and crumple it up inside of me and not release it, not even slightly. I kept imagining what would happen, if for just one second, I let it go. That would be so much worse than acting as if nothing had ever happened. So that's what I would do. I would *act.* I decided that in order to see him again, I couldn't go down the wrong road, even a little bit, of *how could you* or *what were you.* . . . No way. But would it be written all over my face? My face usually betrayed me in situations like this. But then again, he didn't know me very well. I decided that I would stay silent and concealing, but every now and then, when I thought of the whole situation, my mind went to a dark, truthful place and I had to chase it down quickly, to bring it back.

Ben and I sat in the Eighth Street subway station. I caught his attention and mouthed, *I'm nervous.* He ignored me, and I sat there with my hands in my lap. A few months of officially dating me had taught him not to indulge me too much. When the Stillwell Avenue–Coney Island R train arrived, we stood up. He embraced me and kissed my cheek and said, "Don't even think about it," with the breeze from the train whipping by us.

"What's that supposed to mean?" I said back, and he laughed. The past two months with Ben had been a lot of sex and talking, sex and talking. It was like we were trying to catch each other up on everything that had happened in our lives up until this point. Most of that "catching up" happened in bed, as a matter of convenience. This trip to Brooklyn was one of our rare public appearances.

We were on the train for about thirty minutes—Prince, Canal, City Hall, South Ferry, Court Street, Jay Street—long enough to get into the rhythm of the darkness and then the blink of white lights, the slowing down and speeding up, the incoming and outgoing passengers, getting closer and closer to a place where I had no desire to go. I kept reminding myself that I could turn back at any point. I said to myself, *Yeah, you're going this way, but that doesn't mean you have to keep going. You are just going to see how far you can go, to test yourself, and then, once you get there, you will simply turn back around and that's all.*

But I kept going. And when we got out of the subway, we walked on Flatbush Avenue for a few minutes, until we got to Nevins. We made a left. "Three-block warning," said Ben, because I had no idea where we were. My stomach lurched.

It was a modern building on a block filled with commercial establishments—dental and law offices, an African braiding salon, an urgent-care medical facility, a wash center, a liquor store.

It looked out of place, the only gray facade among a series of redbrick numbers. The building had four stories, with three rows of windows painted black. Next to it, there was a Salvation Army store, where the lights were on, the door open, and I could see a long row of T-shirts organized by color. A sign above the store read, HELP US HELP OTHERS.

A woman held the door open for us at my father's building and I wanted to ask her if we could hang out in her apartment for a while instead. After we got out of the elevator, I stood in the middle of the hallway and took off my jacket, folded it over my arm. Suddenly, I was very warm and wondering why I hadn't fought this more. *Why am I here?*

The click of a door opening disrupted my thoughts. When I saw him at the door, I was struck by how old he looked. Maybe that was obvious, but I really expected him to look the same. He was still thin. His face had the same angular features, cheeks slightly sunken in, a full head of straight gray hair. But I remembered him being taller, or bigger somehow. How harmless he seemed, in person, no longer a fading image in my head. He had a warm expression on his face, as he hugged me and shook Ben's hand. And then he actually started to look a little uncomfortable. My heart was beating erratically, out of rhythm. I ran my hand over my chest in a soft circle, discreetly massaging the place where my heart was, trying to calm it down. *It's okay. It's okay. Nothing's happening.* I studied Ben's face, the outline of his body, latched on to his arm as if I could absorb all the quietness inside of him by osmosis. *Look how calm he looks! He looks like he does on any other day!*

My father turned to lead us into his apartment. He pointed out various things and then sat down in a chair, awkwardly. All the chairs and couches in the apartment looked like the type of

brightly colored and modernistic furniture that would be purchased by a college student without a budget. Against one wall,
there was a large cabinet that stood out. It had an array of objects
inside it, behind a barrier of glass—a clock shaped like a lemon
and small Russian dolls, a tray with Chinese lettering on it. They
looked like the souvenirs of travel. I wondered, my insides rising,
*Is this what he's been doing this whole time? Collecting these ob-
jects from around the world?*

Along another wall, there were pictures of him with some
woman, in front of various backdrops—wearing matching red
sweaters on a mountain, sitting on lawn chairs on the beach,
dressed up and kissing at somebody's wedding. I didn't know how
long this woman had been in my father's life, but all the photos
appeared to have been taken during the same time period.

"Nicole!" he said, and the woman from the pictures appeared
in person, with a drink in her hand. She greeted me with a hug
but didn't quite pull me toward her. I only felt her fingertips on
my back.

Great, I thought, and plastered a smile on my face. I felt another wave of fear melting over me.

"This is my daughter Eve and her boyfriend, Ben."

She smiled sincerely.

"Get the children some drinks, would you?" he said. The
word *children* stuck with me. It made it sound like we belonged
to him, but did she know?

Nicole sipped her drink and looked us over. "Of course! What
can I get you?"

Who is this person? I know. I know. *"Nicole." But seriously,
who is this person?*

"Nothing," I said, and then Ben raised his eyebrows at me.
"Actually, wine works," I said. "Thanks."

"What do you have?" Ben said, and then appeared to think over his options as Nicole listed them. Only Ben would be in this kind of a situation and carefully consider his drink options, as if we were on a cruise in the Mediterranean.

"White is fine," Ben said, looking at her glass. "Whatever is open."

"You found the place okay?" my father said. "I know all these streets are confusing when you're used to Manhattan."

Nicole emerged with our drinks and a small plate of candy fruit slices. They were the kind that I used to love as a kid. I couldn't tell whether this was done on purpose. *Is he trying to remind me of my childhood?* I took one, slowly, hesitantly, deciding that it was a coincidence.

Nicole's hair was long reddish waves that she kept playing with, twirling and twirling strands around her finger and then gathering it all up and releasing it. Her clothes were dark and loose-fitting. She wore a large black silk shirt with buttons down the side like a sofa cushion. The clothes masked a body that I couldn't determine. I wondered if she had a family of her own, how much younger she was than he, how they met, where she grew up, what they fought about, if they kept anything from each other, whether she was behaving sweetly just for show. *Is this her apartment or his?* I looked for signs to see if she felt like she belonged.

We took seats on the couch. Nicole put the plate of fruit slices on the coffee table. There was silence. I looked at the view of Manhattan from their window. When the questions started, my father let Nicole ask them, which was fine, less weird than having my own father ask me basic facts about my life.

"I used to write about music for a newspaper in Colorado, and then I moved back to New York and wrote for a website in SoHo, and now I write for a magazine," I said.

"Very cool!" she said, her eyes studying me. "What kind of magazine?"

"It's a music magazine. . . ." I said, thinking it over, how much to tell. "It's called *Interview*. I interview musicians—"

Ben interrupted me. "Yeah, and she gets to go to some pretty cool concerts for free." It was unusual for Ben to speak without being spoken to directly, but it was the result of my having proffered some big threats on the way here. "You *have* to talk. You got me into this. Now you have to take the pressure off me," I had said, with a pointed finger in his face.

"You're making it sound *way* cooler than it is," I interjected. "It's mostly me moving around the words of famous people until it sounds like they said something interesting."

"A true journalist!" Ben said. I gave him a strange look. *A true journalist? Who is this person?*

My father laughed, a hint of surprise still lingering on his face.

"They're very good," Ben added. "Her articles. I, for one, never miss them."

My father gave me a look of admiration. I flinched and then darted my eyes away, like I'd been staring directly into the sun.

"Tell them about the article you're working on now," Ben said.

"It's stupid," I said, shaking my head.

"No it's not. It's good."

"It's about one of the original members of a band that was big back in the nineties. . . ." I stared at Ben as I talked. "He's in this new band now that he formed with members of other bands that have broken up and . . . I talked to him about detaching songs from their emotional significance."

"Tell them the headline," he said.

I shot him a look. Nicole and my dad looked extremely curious. It all felt so stupid, that we were even talking about this, but it was too late now. "'A Better Place,'" I said. "It's cheesy."

"It's great," Ben said.

I sighed and then replied, "Ben's an engineer," which incited a raucous response from everyone. "No music there!" my father exclaimed. The way he said it brought me right back to childhood, how he'd repeat a good line that he saw on television and thought was funny.

At least Ben could always be counted on for a twenty-minute soliloquy on his work. He started talking about the sixteen acres of ground in Lower Manhattan that consumed his life. At first, when Ben mentioned the Freedom Tower, my father looked over at me, but I ignored him completely, kept my eyes on Ben as he talked. *Don't you dare,* I thought. *You are way too late.*

"It's different than her world," he said. "To say the least. We just unveiled the final design, but we have to address some security concerns raised by the police department," he explained. "They want us to add an eighty-seven-foot concrete base to the design, which originally was supposed to be glass prisms. The architect is worried that the building will look too much like a concrete bunker. We're trying to decide now whether the glass prisms without the concrete are even workable. Some testing has revealed that the prismatic glass shatters easily. We may have to add stainless steel panels and blast-resistant glass. So you see, Eve's interested in how the world feels. I'm interested in how it works. Together, we might know everything."

I gave him a funny look. Okay, *now* he was going overboard with the talking.

Nicole started telling us about herself. I listened but was only vaguely aware of what she was saying. She was a professor at a college in Brooklyn and had a studio in their apartment somewhere. What kind of professor and what form of art? I had no idea because I couldn't bring myself to ask, couldn't hold on to the details anyway. My mind took in all the information about her and then promptly spit it back out. Maybe it was some kind of self-protective measure.

We moved to the dining room. In front of us on the table were clear noodles in a wooden bowl, a salad with chicken and mandarin oranges, a dish filled with soy sauce. I took a bit of everything but really couldn't process much of what I was eating. It was vaguely Asian, and the whole thing seemed rather exotic for my father. The last time I saw him, he thought that grilled cheese dunked into ketchup was his own personal culinary invention.

Nicole went back and forth from the kitchen, and we waited for her before we started eating. I remained friendly and upbeat throughout the two courses. I actually sounded genuine. There was no sign at all of the veritable shit storm occurring inside of me as I forked mouthfuls of greens and swallowed tender bites of noodles. I sat and ate and was vacantly compliant. Inside, I was straining to put that face forward, that passive persona. They talked about a recent trip to Tokyo. I couldn't remember my parents ever leaving the country. And whenever we did go somewhere, my father was always pretty grumpy about it. He said once, after a bumpy flight, that he would never again get into a plane that he wasn't flying himself. So if my father was interested in traveling and other cultures, it was this newish version of him steering the ship.

He never mentioned what had occurred, and I didn't blame him. I wouldn't have known how to either. Every now and then, my eyes locked with his across the table for a few uncomfortable seconds. But that was it. I looked down at my plate and kept eating, each piece of lettuce individually, for fear of running out of tasks to occupy myself with. I must have chewed each piece a hundred times, until it was a tiny pulp. I chewed until the lettuce liquefied.

It was an altogether tolerable lunch, until he mentioned Disney World.

"We're going to Orlando next," he said, rolling his eyes at Nicole. "Her niece's wedding. Anyway, it's not exactly a trip to Disney World, but we'll manage."

The forty dollars. The forty dollars that went missing, right after my father took off. My mind started spinning. *How could he have taken it? How does someone do something like that? And it wasn't just someone. It was my father. My chin looked like his. My hands looked like his. Was I capable of something like that? Did I have it in me, hidden somewhere deep inside? Would it come out someday?*

I had to talk to him. I had to understand. Otherwise, this whole trip would be pointless. But I couldn't say anything at this table, with this perfectly pleasant woman and her noodles.

"Can I interest anyone in some dessert?" Nicole chimed in. "Carrot cake and whipped cream?"

"No, thanks," I said. I kicked Ben under the table. He looked up and said, "What?"

My father appeared insulted. Nicole stared off. It seemed to be not the answer they'd expected.

"We should really get going," I said. Ben seemed confused.

"Okay!" Nicole said, although I could tell that she didn't quite mean it.

"Didn't you . . . make the cake?" my dad said to Nicole.

"It's okay! No problem!" She perked up. "It'll be breakfast tomorrow." She curled her fingers around a napkin.

I helped clear a few plates. Nicole began to stack the dishwasher. Lunch had ended and it was fine. Civil. But it wasn't right. None of this was right. I looked at my dad, and said, almost involuntarily, "Can I talk to you?" I pointed to the hallway, which led to other rooms.

"We'll just be a few minutes!" he called to Ben and Nicole. I paused and then followed him.

From the bedroom, I could see the open door to the bathroom, clothing hanging from the towel bar, a package of toilet paper on the floor. Something inside of me was about to snap. Every object brought me deeper into despair. I tried to focus on the space between things so as not to look at any one thing directly.

"I'm not sure I'm capable of this level of acting," I said, meeting his eyes. I could hear the wind blowing outside, rattling the bedroom window slightly. "It's not in my repertoire."

"I don't understand," he said.

"Why didn't *you* call? Didn't you ever want to see me? There were so many times when it would have really helped. . . ." My voice cracked. "For you to want to see me."

"I'm sorry." He looked at the ceiling. He seemed like he was biding his time. He went over to the desk and sat down in the chair next to it. "Believe me. I know. But I was in such a bad place, back then. It wouldn't have helped you to have me around. It would have only hurt you. And then, once I was finally in a better place, it became so hard to go back. . . . And tell you what? That I was selfish but that I needed to be?"

I stared at him, unsure of how to fill the silence that followed. I waited for him to go on. I shook my head. I felt a ringing in my temples. All my thoughts were fixed on a single principle: do not cry.

"That doesn't feel like enough of a reason," I said. "Didn't you care about us? Didn't you worry about us when Mom died?"

He paused. "Of course," he said, and then started rubbing his face. He was no longer trying to control his expression. "But I didn't know how to solve the problem of worrying about you. I didn't know how to connect with you again, after I did . . . what I did." He sat there looking disappointed, like he'd screwed up whatever small idea he had about how this day would go. "It was easier to block it all out. But things in my life are better. I feel happy. I'm with Nicole now. She's such a good, decent person. She doesn't have a bad bone in her body. You'd really like her."

That was *so* not the point. I wanted to scream at him, "That is *so* not the point!" And then, I did.

"The point is that you left us, and we still needed you! Do you have any idea how that feels? You were our father. We were supposed to *mean something* to you. It defies logic in EVERY way, for you to stop caring, and just *leave* like that. No explanation. No nothing. And way to take the forty dollars on your way out, Dad. Way to really seal the deal of us hating you forever. Did you think that we wouldn't notice? Guess what? I notice everything now. EVERYTHING. You taught me that lesson, not to take my eyes off anyone, not to trust a soul, not even the people closest to me."

I realized, as I was saying it, that I was starting to lie. It wasn't quite true, what I was saying. At least not anymore.

"I don't know what to say," he replied. That was his big answer, the words I'd been waiting nearly fifteen years to hear. "Do you want to go to the wedding in Orlando with us? We can go to Disney World. . . ."

I looked at him like he was insane, which, at this point, could not be ruled out. I could feel my heartbeat in my throat. Out of the corner of my eye, I saw a porcelain turtle on the dresser, climbing up a sculpture of a wooden tree. *Emma,* I thought, *and her stupid turtle analogy.* She was right. He was 0 percent human and 100 percent turtle. But I wasn't like him. No matter what my chin or hands looked like. I would never have done what he did. I knew better. Way better. My mother had made sure of that. I could get angry at him. I could ask a ton of questions. None of that would help me.

"Clearly," I said, "we aren't going to resolve this now, or maybe ever. I have to get out of here."

"Okay," he said. And then, I saw a familiar look in his eyes. *Suffering.* I saw an image of myself, from years ago, in the dark reflection of a bank, an ATM vestibule in midtown. *He is suffering.* No matter what happened in the past, when I thought of what it really meant to suffer, I did not want that for another human being, especially not for my father, who, at one point in time, had done a lot for me. Acceptance was the only way out for me.

"But . . . listen . . . maybe we'll have lunch again sometime," I said, as if this one had been a great success.

He looked at me again, the suffering gone, replaced by a mixture of pleasure and surprise.

"That'd be great," he said. "Anytime."

- - - -

Once Ben and I were outside and walking, I was going fast. He was trailing behind me. The cars on Atlantic Avenue were whizzing by. Two homeless people were fighting over a shoe. Now that I was out of that apartment, I was feeling the full weight of what had happened there.

"Where are we going now?" Ben said. "Home?" His voice

sounded distant, as if it were coming from far away. I turned back to him.

"Take me to the nearest place that's peaceful," I said.

"Okay," he said, catching up. "But you're going in the wrong direction."

He took me by the shoulders and pointed me the other way. I didn't know where we were going, but I trusted him to know. We walked, for a few minutes, in total silence.

"I thought it went well," he said. The worst part was that he was being totally sincere.

"Are you kidding?" I turned around.

"No? I thought it went okay. Did it not?"

"Oh, sure. It was okay. On the plus side, he wants to take us to Disney World!"

"What?"

"Don't ask."

"But I mean, nothing happened? Aren't you relieved? I thought that went pretty well. It was all fine."

I told him what my father said to me. "He had zero answers. Do you know how fucked up that is? I can't believe I actually thought that seeing him would be worth something. I actually fell for it."

"All right."

"That's it? That's all you have to say?"

"What am I supposed to say?"

"I'm not going to tell you what you're supposed to say. You're supposed to just *understand*."

"But I don't understand."

"Exactly. I just want to have an intellectual discussion about what has taken place."

"No, you don't. You want to have an emotional discussion."

"Yeah, so that I don't have to feel like such an *alien* in the world."

He looked at me with a smile, and I started to smile too, despite everything.

He shook his head. "You *are* an alien," he said. "Unfortunately, you're my alien and I have to deal with you . . . at least until you go back to whatever planet you came from."

"I'm from *here*," I said, stomping one foot against the ground.

"So you say." He put his arm around my shoulders and we kept walking.

"That place made no sense," Ben said, after a few blocks of quiet. "The layout just made no sense. Every room was open to the other room. There wasn't a single room with privacy from the rest of the house. They had this big center room, which was fine, but then the rest of the house seemed like an afterthought. All the other rooms were odd shapes and sizes, and it was unclear what they were meant for. . . . Very odd."

"*That's* what you're thinking about?"

"Yeah. What's on your mind, Aristotle? You're probably thinking about what snack you're going to get next, so don't get all high-and-mighty with me."

"No I'm not. And *by the way*, when someone kicks you under the table, you're not supposed to say 'What?' You're supposed to silently acknowledge it and then act based on what you think that person is trying to tell you."

"I had no idea why you were kicking me," he said.

"Because I wanted you to say no to dessert."

"And I was supposed to infer that from a kick?"

"Yes!"

"But you always want dessert."

I sighed. "Not in this situation."

He shrugged and said in a low voice, almost to himself, "A kick means no dessert. Who would have thought?"

It took a while for me to adjust back into the outside world. I was waiting for something to wear off but it was still sitting with me. We reached Prospect Park, where we sat for a while under a tree, on the grass. I could see the windows of all the nice town houses around the park from where I was sitting. I pictured cozy scenes inside those town houses, imagined curtains and fireplaces and families cuddled under blankets. The people inside those houses could have been miserable, for all I knew, but somehow I was convinced that they weren't. I had a certain perception of it, looking through the windows and the panes of glass alongside the doors. I felt like those bright family scenes inside were something I was watching from a dark room. *What separated us? What was more real? Why did it have to feel like a vision of what I would never have? Why did I feel like Ben belonged there and I didn't?*

I started watching this family in the park. I couldn't take my eyes off them. Honestly, the whole scene was ordinary. There was a man, a woman, a child, and a dog. They were having a picnic. It was the first day of winter that felt a little bit like spring. On top of a grassy mound, a blanket was spread out beneath the picture of a perfect young family—the parents both still attractive and slim, the dad with his hair tousled in the breeze, his jeans hanging just right, his T-shirt worn, soft, sexy. The mom had her long blond hair pulled back in a ponytail. She wore shorts and a striped sweater. Her clothes were comfortable, but not unfashionable. The little boy was around a year old. He was just barely strong enough to stand on his own, and that seemed to be the momentary focus—he was learning how to walk, and the dad was holding him up by his hands, as he attempted to take a few unstable steps. The mom was filming it all, smiling behind her phone. Their fluffy dog had, up until this point, been observing from a slight distance. Suddenly, the little white fluff ball came soaring into the scene, galloping as fast as its legs could take it. It went right for the child, knocking him down, deterring whatever progress had been made. Luckily, the dad was holding the kid up anyway. The child didn't absorb the full impact of the collision. It was just enough to jostle him slightly, for his knees to buckle under, and for him to plop back down onto the grass. Basically, it was enough for comic effect, but not enough to cause any fear or damage. The dad leaned back in laughter, the mom smiled widely, happy she'd managed to capture the whole thing on video. *One for the bloopers reel!* I imagined one saying to the other later, at home, exhausted from their day of activities. They would theorize that the dog was just vying for attention, that he'd lost his place in the spotlight, since the baby was born. I didn't understand it. I should have seen all this and thought: *THIS is it. This is what a person sees and takes the plunge. This is what a person sees and thinks:* I want this.

But instead, I waited. I waited and thought, *No, no, this can't be right.* It couldn't be. It was too cute, too perfect. I didn't believe. I kept watching, waiting, hoping. And then, sure enough, when some time had passed, the baby started to cry, the father took him in his arms and back onto the blanket. The dog started sniffing at other passing dogs. The mom walked a few feet away from all of them, lit up a cigarette, and started tapping on her phone. I imagined that she was composing a message to an ex-boyfriend, but that was probably overkill. The father tried to get her to come back over, back toward the blanket, but she shot him a nasty look. My eyes felt heavy. I started to fall asleep in Ben's arms, thinking, *This I understand. This, I believe.*

"There are too many families here," I mumbled to Ben. "Take me back to the land of Lower East Side Jewels and Biker Bill. They make me feel like I have my shit together."

He started to untangle from me, brushed grass from his legs, then stopped moving.

"Actually, I have to tell you something."

"What?" My stomach lurched. *I felt another blow coming on. That rising dread. A familiar feeling. Everything becoming moving parts.*

BEN

PROSPECT PARK

Sitting there with Eve, I finally realized the depth of my mistake. I was going to be with this girl for a while, maybe forever. She needed to know who my father was. Where was my sense of foresight? Seeing her with her father, the strain that it caused her beforehand and even after it was over, I realized how disordered life can be. You can't just permanently shut up about things to avoid them. That doesn't create order. It was a matter of engineering. You had to take into account the past and the future, the situation as is, not as you wanted it to be. For some reason, this whole thing with Eve reminded me of the George Washington Bridge.

Growing up, I was always sitting in the back of my parents' car, looking out the window at that bridge, sleek and relatively flat, with no peak or apex in the middle. Driving one way, you had a view of downtown Manhattan. The other way, you could see the palisades, the rugged cliffs covered with trees. The towers were actually more compact than they needed to be. When the engineers were planning it, they decided on steel because the towers were meant to support a masonry facade. It was supposed to look more like the Brooklyn Bridge, but it was built in the thirties, in the height of the Depression, and they ran out of money. They decided that it looked just as well without the masonry, and it ended up with a more modern look to it. The bridge was initially built with a single upper level, but it was also built with the ability to add a second level. They didn't see a need for it back then, because there wasn't enough traffic, but they recognized that there would be that need one day. It was such incredible foresight, to give the towers that capacity.

So I needed to tell her. Because *there would be that need one day.*

"My father actually knew your mother," I said. "She was his secretary. At the law firm? He was with her right before . . . and I didn't tell you because he always felt guilty, and I guess I did too, that they didn't leave the building right away. And maybe they would have both survived, if they had. He told her to stay. He thought that it was safer to stay, for whatever stupid reason. Eventually, they left together because she insisted. But there was a slight delay, because he told her to stay."

"Wait. What?" she said. I paused, started pulling at the grass.

"I know," I said. "I should have told you. I put it together back when I saw that business card. The one that I returned to you?" I realized how bad this sounded as I was saying it. And I started to panic. There had to be more. There had to be more that I could say. "But . . . maybe . . . your mom saved my dad's life, and now it's my job to save yours?"

"So you figured this out . . . when?"

"At the bagel place."

"What bagel place?"

"You know, after the first night."

"All the way back then?"

"Yeah," I said, looking down. "And so, they got out . . . that morning . . . in the first place, because of your mom. He would have stayed otherwise. . . . I'm sure. . . . He can be sort of dense and too calm sometimes, and I'm telling you because you should know everything that's true, of course, but also because I really don't want to be like him."

Her eyes looked different all of a sudden. Glassy. Oh *fuck*. I'd really fucked up. There is something about a girl on the verge of tears that is absolutely terrifying. No. Not just a girl. Eve. That was much, much worse.

"Why didn't you tell me this sooner?"

"I didn't know how you'd react."

"So you said nothing?"

"I just kept putting it off. But now I see how messy things can get and I don't want us to be like you and your dad."

"Oh, well, that's good. High standards."

"I felt responsible."

"So you're dating me because you feel sorry for me?"

I paused, searching for the right words. "I do feel sorry for you sometimes, yeah. But that's not why I'm with you. I'm with you because . . ." I looked away from her and around at the park. "Because you have not a single pair of socks that doesn't have a hole in them . . . and you can't throw out a sock because you're too afraid that one sock might feel bad because it lost its other, companion sock. And even though that's mildly deranged, I love you for it. And I can't say that this sock quality was ever something I was looking for in a girl, but here it is, and that's how I feel, and there's not a damn thing that I can do about it."

She looked at me with wet eyes and a tear running down one cheek. She stayed silent. I stared at the grass for a few minutes, got the feeling that I couldn't touch her, or that I shouldn't touch her. And then she stood up and brushed herself off, with an unreadable look on her face.

EVE

A SYNAGOGUE ON THE LOWER EAST SIDE

Kate and her fiancé, Charlie, chose a Gothic synagogue for their wedding that looked like nothing special from the street—just a simple, decaying facade of red stone. But it was deceiving, for all the grandeur that was inside. It was built to resemble the Cathedral of Notre Dame in Paris, with its pointed arch windows, doorways crowned by triangular molding, and fifty-foot-high ceilings, cathedral blue and dotted with painted gold stars. That night, there were enough candles inside to make a bonfire of the entire structure, with just one false move. The candles were in glass vases along the floor, scattered across the steps of the main hall, along the bar next to liquor bottles, garnishing trays of hors d'oeuvres. Every table had bunches of white orchids, white roses, pink lilies.

I was on my way to getting tipsy when I noticed a golden spotlight coming from the dance floor. I went toward it and watched as the newlyweds sashayed to Louis Armstrong; her nose nestled against his cheek, bashfully hiding her face from the world of onlookers, as if this were all a bit much for her, this which she meticulously planned for herself.

I see trees of green, red roses, too,
I see them bloom, for me and you

It didn't seem to matter to anyone that this wedding was kind of a charade. Well, not a *charade* exactly, but let's say this: it didn't tell the whole story. But that was forgotten now. *Gone* were all those lunches with Kate where she discussed problems with Charlie, some of those lunches ending in tears. *Gone* were the nights when she texted me that she'd had enough, promised she'd be over at my apartment in an hour, once she'd broken up with him. I waited for her text. Heard nothing. I didn't hear from her again that night. I wouldn't hear from her again until a few days later, with some generic message like, *Everything's okay!* But all that was in the past, and reflecting on it now was just bad for business.

Despite my hesitations about Charlie, when Kate got engaged to him, I promised myself that I'd be a good friend. I'd hit all the checkpoints. So I attended two engagement parties, a bachelorette party in Miami that wiped out my checking account, a bridal shower, a second bridal shower that she deemed nonmandatory for bridesmaids but I went anyway (secretly, because I was hungry that morning and thought there'd be sandwiches and maybe a gift bag). As it turned out, there was only a platter of fruit, and we were all immediately whisked away from it, instructed to take a coat hanger and start sticking sequins to it. Sometimes, life is just like a bridal shower. You show up expecting breakfast and a gift and you end up doing a demeaning arts-and-crafts project.

Before the ceremony, I examined Kate in the big white dress, looking terrified, and I gave her a look like, *Are you okay?* She certainly didn't look okay. I kept watching her. But by the time she walked down the aisle, she had put on her game face. She focused in on the other end of the synagogue, where the doors were opening wider and wider, letting a flood of sunlight in through the stained glass windows.

And now, an hour later, the deed had been done, and I was gaping at them, along with the crowd, at this supposedly perfect couple, as they took their first official spin around the dance floor. I was one among five bridesmaids in matching dresses and loose side ponytails. We were all a bit weepy, but we allowed this kind of thing at weddings. We embraced it, the elaborate, surreal distraction that a wedding provided. We were huddled together in the corner, trying to keep a few misty tears from falling.

Except for Maya, who was legitimately crying her eyes out.

"Are you okay?" I whispered, when her sobbing became audible.

"I am just so, so . . ." We were all expecting her to say "happy," but instead she said, *"tired."* Lately, Maya had been working long, late shifts at the hospital. Thus, her tears were not so much a sign of emotion as they were an indication that she was physically breaking down. I looked at the other girls, who were all giggling and handing Maya tissues from their purses.

After the song was over, we made our way to our respective tables. We knew the drill. Lately, our lives had become one wedding after another. It was a well-worn routine that started with that thick, creamy envelope at the doorstep, that bomb of script and websites and middle names of old friends that suddenly appeared as if discovered overnight. And the last stop on the journey was right here, at the main event. Soon, the salads would be placed down in unison. The champagne glasses would be raised into the air too many times to count. The best man would reference the groom's rowdier days; a bridesmaid would read a poem that she wrote; "The bride's childhood friend had quite the sense of humor!" some elderly person would comment. Then, the official crepe-colored bride-tested bride's-mother-approved cake would be cut. The more risqué groom's cake (shaped like a football helmet, maybe, such whimsy!) would be devoured. There was a rhythm to these events.

"Why are you dreading this so much?" Ben had asked me before I left. He was in Chicago for a work trip he'd tried to get out of, but couldn't. This was the first wedding I would go to without him. It was actually the first time that we'd spent a few days apart in a while.

"Because one of my closest friends is marrying a guy who has been making her miserable for the past year," I said. "I just *don't trust him*. I don't like him and I don't trust him."

"Duly noted. But can't you just have fun anyway?" Getting Ben to understand wasn't easy. To him, a wedding was *food + dance = fun*. In my mind, there were variables.

"I will try, obviously!" I said, because he sounded distant, maybe annoyed. Since that day in Brooklyn, something was off between us. The truth was, I still hadn't worked out how I felt about Ben withholding what he did from me for so long. At first, I was hurt. Then, secretly, a little bit relieved. Ben was flawed. The other shoe had dropped. I could breathe again. But with those breaths came the realization that our relationship might not be what I thought it was. It made us into something familiar. But it also made us into something sad.

"Hey," he said. "Maybe they'll live happily ever after."

"If they live happily ever after, then my whole logic system comes crashing down."

"*Your whole logic system?* You have one of those?"

Now that I was standing at this place of flower-filled, candle-lit, alcohol-induced merriment, I found myself wishing that Ben were there, despite whatever tension I'd been feeling between us lately. The night had a nostalgic feel to it, with Kate's friends and other people from college I'd known years ago. I looked over at Kate: her lips a sultry red, her hair smooth waves and clipped on one side with a single diamond pin. *Maybe I am wrong. Maybe everything will be okay.* She seemed present, busy, moving from table to table, hugging cousins and friends of hers I'd never met before.

She really was a beautiful bride. I feel like I have no choice but to describe her that way because in all the thousands of toasts at all the hundreds of events that had taken place before this, that was how Kate had been described—by Charlie, by Charlie's friends—that was always the focus—how *beautiful* she was, what a *beautiful couple* they made. Major score, Charlie. Major score. But the Kate I knew was so much more than that.

The seven-person band began a series of familiar numbers, pleasant background music, not exciting enough to dance to but perfect for cocktail conversation under the golden lights. Since Ben wasn't there, I was seated next to a stranger. All the bridesmaids had come with their boyfriends or husbands, and I'd thrown off the seating arrangement. I asked Kate ahead of time if I could be seated next to one of the other girls, but she politely explained that it had to be boy-girl-boy-girl. Actually, I believe her exact words were something more like: "You're dead to me."

I turned left and right, subtly scanning to see whom she'd put next to me. The guys on both sides of me were people I vaguely knew from college but whom I hadn't seen since then. All three of us were awkwardly staring about the room. My friends were across the table, oohing and aahing over the table setting. I decided to break the ice and mingle. There were strangers on both sides of me who I would never see again but who I now had to pretend to be utterly fascinated by. For the next two hours, I would ask where they were from, how they got to work in the morning, what they ate for breakfast, how many times they brushed their teeth per day, what kind of hope for promotion they had at their jobs, their travel plans for the next year, as if it were all adding up to something. We would go our separate ways in a few hours and none of this information would matter ever again, but I still had to ask. God help me if I didn't ask. They'd take away my filet mignon as punishment.

"Hi, I'm Eve," I said to the guy to the left of me.

"Steven," he said, shaking my hand and seeming relieved. "My wife, Rebecca." I reached across the table to a woman wearing glasses and a turquoise dress. "Did we go to college together?" he asked.

"I think so, yeah!" I responded.

"So, what are you up to now?" he turned to me and asked. The question-and-answer portion of the evening was officially under way.

"I'm a writer, for a magazine," I said.

"What kind of magazine?" he asked.

"It's about music."

"Is it anything I might have heard of?"

I must have paused for too long, because, at this, his wife gave him a light shove and laughed.

"What kind of question is that? Do you read music magazines?" She rolled her eyes. She hadn't really been paying attention up until now, just letting him conduct the affairs. She had her own problems, pushing leaves of radicchio around her plate and dealing with nonsense conversation from the guy next to her.

"It's called *Interview*," I said.

He nodded. He said that he didn't listen to music because he was too busy with work, which seemed like a perfectly acceptable thing to say except for *it wasn't*. I asked him about his job, and then eventually, we reached a dead end.

"So . . . what do you do for fun?" I said.

"Fun?" He laughed. "What's that?"

I'm sure I was being dramatic. In my mind I was all, *What is happening to the world?* But really, I'd just been given an unfortunate seating assignment. I heard a song that I liked and got up. I leaned down next to Maya.

"We have to dance," I said. "The guy sitting next to me doesn't know what fun is." She looked over at her fiancé, Erol, who was currently transfixed with his salad. She considered the possibility, stabbing a piece of avocado with her fork.

"Okay, let's do it."

We made our way to the center of the dance floor, started moving to the beat of the deafeningly loud music, loosening up more and more as time passed. We knew every word to every song, and sung them without fear, our eyes locked on each other as though we were alone in the room. There'd been so many dance parties in our history. We knew what to do. We danced and lost touch with reality, made a clean break with it, just like we had back in college, so giddy and following the song with our bodies until nothing else mattered. At some point, Maya took off her heels, disappeared to throw them by our table, and then came back, with one hand in the air, another holding a champagne flute, a resurgence of energy. This was the best part of weddings, the perfect release that happened later, after all the preparations, after the tension of the ceremony, after a few bites of food and more than a few sips of alcohol. It always seemed like it wouldn't come, but it did, eventually. We were at that point in the evening, that rare moment when our thoughts were drowned out by the music.

So when I saw Jesse standing near the bar, my first thought was that it was the alcohol talking. It couldn't have been him.

But then I realized that it had to be. Nobody else could look so handsome and so stupid in a black suit and thin black tie. Oh, and he was wasted. He was drunker than anyone should be at a wedding. He was throwing his arms around everyone. I felt like the only one who understood just how far gone he was. When I caught his eye from across the room, he looked at me with mock suspicion and then grinned widely.

I looked away. I spoke to Maya in a whisper, leaning forward. "Um. Jesse is here?"

"Oh . . . yeah," she said hesitantly. "He's friends with Charlie. . . . Kate didn't tell you he would be here?"

"Ummmm . . . no!" I said.

"Well, I guess she's been busy, but . . ."

We agreed. She probably should have told me. But that was just like Kate to assume that because she would be calm and collected in such a situation, everyone else would be too. Maya would have sat me down months ahead of time, and then booked me a three-hour session with a psychiatrist specializing in crisis management.

"I'm going to go outside and get some air," I said.

"Good thinking," she said right away.

I made my way through the crowd with a purpose, through a tunnel of dresses and suits, trays of empty glasses, the guests hovering and dancing in a circle around Kate and Charlie. I grabbed a glass of ice water off a table and gulped it down, feeling the cold liquid down my throat and then expanding across my chest.

The door, once I reached it, was my savior. It wasn't the main exit but rather one off to the side that we'd been using all afternoon, going in and out for photographs. Once I got outside, I closed my eyes and stood there in the cold, rubbing up and down my arms with my hands, waiting for the water to work its way through my system and make me feel a little less light-headed. I texted Ben, urgently: *Miss you.* He didn't reply. I had to steer my mind away from this place.

My phone remained silent and it made my insides sink. *Why not I miss you too? Of course. Of course he's not responding. He's probably going to break up with you. He's probably sick of your shenanigans. He's planning his way out right now. That's why he's not responding. Because he's busy planning his escape. Why did you have to go on like that earlier? About how bad the wedding was going to be? About how doomed Kate and Charlie were? Why would anyone want to be with someone who is so negative all the time? Bravo, Ben! He finally realized it! The jig is up! Good for him. Now he is going to find someone who believes that all weddings are happily-ever-afters. In Prospect Park that day, he'd realized it. We are different sorts of people. Maybe telling me then about his father was actually his way of getting me to break up with him. He is smart enough to orchestrate something like that, something that wouldn't seem like his fault.*

I stared at the phone for the next few minutes, willing Ben to call. But the phone wasn't ringing. And Ben wasn't disproving anything. He was just like the others. How had I trusted him to be so exceptional? I looked down the street. There was a bearded man holding court among a group of homeless people, a woman walking by them with her hands in her pockets. I tried to lose myself in the action. But I couldn't. I was frozen. I felt like I was twenty-two again, so strong was my association between this feeling of insecurity and the Lower East Side. The streets sent me back in time. I was that lost girl again. The ground beneath me began to tremble.

And then, he found me.

"Congratulations!" he said, standing behind me. I turned around. Jesse, with a smile so cynical.

"What?" I said.

"I don't know. I've just been saying that a lot tonight. It's gotten into my head."

I nodded and then got a chill; the hair on my arms stood up. I brushed my hands up and down my arms.

"You want this?" he said, and then gave me a look that I knew. He started to take off his jacket. I shook my head, but he handed it to me anyway.

"You look like a trophy," he said. The dress, despite its color, was actually somewhat flattering. It was strapless, and looked like I'd lain down and raised my arms and allowed someone to wrap three-quarters of my body tightly in shiny brownish-green fabric.

"I look like a bridesmaid," I said.

He considered me. "Yeah, well . . ." He eyed the space between my hips, like he wanted to touch the fabric. We stood there for a few seconds in silence. Seeing Jesse would not have been easy anywhere, but here, I had to remind myself that I'd grown up, that I was different now.

"I'm guessing you're not going to tell me how you are."

"Good guess."

"Can I at least get a dance?" he said. I'd imagined this moment for so long. I'd seen different variations of Jesse around the city for years, people who looked just like him but weren't quite right.

"No, thanks." I didn't look up.

"But you looked like you were having so much fun," he said, getting close to me. "You really did. You looked great out there."

"Oh . . . I doubt that."

"And it's another one of those Motown cover bands! How exciting is that! Almost never happens! Shocking wedding choice!"

I kept my eyes on the ground. I wanted to say, *Oh, don't be such a music snob*, but I decided that that would be reverting to old habits. Instead, I smiled and nodded, decided to rely on smiles and nods, the mystery of them, without any of those dreaded words. That felt like the safest way to carry on a conversation with him.

"So what do you think of all this?" he said, after a minute or two, looking up at the synagogue. "Another one bites the dust, huh? You look great by the way." He leaned down and whispered into my ear. "Did I say that already?"

"Thanks," I said to the smell of whiskey, his warm breath hitting the side of my neck. *I can talk to my ex-boyfriend. It isn't cheating.*

Just then, an ambulance came barreling by, the siren blaring, and Jesse instantly plugged up his ears with his fingers. He waited until it was a few blocks away, glaring at the back of it. When the noise fully faded, he explained. "I'm overly sensitive to sound . . . from being on tour."

"Oh, how was that?" I couldn't resist. Was it so bad to want to know? I'd been there for the beginning, the crummy gigs and perpetual self-doubt. A part of me was happy for him that it actually worked out. At one point, it had been our little project.

"It was insane. So many cities in so few days. I absolutely loved it in a certain way, but I also remember being in a place called Detroit but I had no clue where I fucking *was*. I always felt like I was going to die in a car accident in the middle of the night. Or that the bus was going to go off a bridge."

"Why?"

"Just so many miles on the road."

"Ah."

"Yeah." He widened his eyes. "One time, the wheels caught fire."

I paused. "Really? What happens . . . when that happens? Sorry. Car knowledge low."

He laughed. "We had to pull over and put out the fire so that the fire didn't reach the gas tank and explode."

I winced. "It must have been a little bit fun though, no?"

"Yeah, of course. Being onstage is a jolt of energy like nothing else, but it's also harder than I thought it would be. With your bandmates, you get on each other's nerves, and you're not always playing the music that you want to play. And the constant ringing in my ears . . . that was the part that really drove me insane. But I keep writing songs because I can't stop writing songs, even though part of me wants to stop."

"Well, it sounds very glamorous to me," I said, sounding cheerful for the first time all night. "In a nonglamorous sort of way."

"Yeah, anyway . . ." He leaned into me to say, "I hate to sound like a cliché, but do you want to get out of here?"

"I'm not leaving with you. I have a boyfriend." *I am not cheating. I am saying no to cheating.*

"I know," he said, smiling. "I have a girlfriend."

"You don't care though, do you?" I said, my eyes zeroing in on his.

He leaned a little backward and looked melancholy. He stood there in silence for a few seconds. "My brother killed himself," he said.

A shiver passed through me. "What?"

"Don't make me say it again." He seemed genuinely sorry, like he'd said something too quickly that he hadn't meant to say at all.

"When?"

"Two months ago."

It was as if all my past feelings for him became present, shattering every stupid thought about how I was supposed to behave in that moment. I had an urge to reach out and pull him toward me, and I did. I no longer cared about this conversation, about what had gone on years ago, who won or lost. None of that seemed important anymore. It all just melted away in an instant. As I hugged him, a sense of longing was spreading through me. It was possible to be several people at once, as it turned out. I had different selves. Sometimes, they intersected for a brief time. Sometimes, it was peaceful. Other times, it was a bickering storm.

"You should have told me," I said, even though it made no sense. We weren't on friendly terms. But in that moment, I wanted to be. I wanted to go back to that time when we owed each other something.

"You never called me back," he said, as we released each other.

"I had no idea this was what you were calling about. I thought that I was taking a stand." We both smiled a little bit.

"I wasn't trying to torture you. It just would have been nice to talk to you again."

"If I had known, I would have picked up."

"Yeah?"

"Of course."

Our conversation was beginning to worry me. *But it isn't cheating. It isn't cheating to talk.*

"Are you all right?" I asked.

He shrugged. "Not really. Seriously, can we go somewhere right now? Just the two of us? I just want to take a break for a little while."

"A break from what?"

"Everything."

"I don't think that . . . we can do that . . . anymore."

He bowed his head down and shook it in disbelief. "It's crazy. It's like, I'll be going along, living my life, and everything will be fine, and then I'll have this flash of something that reminds me of you, and I'll realize that I still have this vivid memory of you, and it's like we never broke up. And then I'll start to have random nostalgia, like about how we used to watch movies together and you used to hide behind me during the cheesy parts, like the way most people hide when there's blood on the screen. That's the way you reacted to, like, a cheesy line. Or how you always made me check the fire escape for murderers in the middle of the night if you heard some noise."

"You act as if we *didn't* find a person sitting out there once."

"One time!"

"Ummm, once is enough! And you weren't very reassuring. You'd check, but you never gave me a straight answer. You'd just say, 'Yes, there is someone out there, actually, but I didn't want to disturb him.'"

He laughed. "I had to fuck with you. I just *had* to."

I put my hands on my hips. "I don't see it that way."

"See. I think of those things for five seconds and it's like I have this *gaping hole* of missing you inside of me and I can't do a fucking thing about it. Do you know what I mean?"

I slowly nodded. *I can talk to him about anything. It is just conversation. Reminiscing. Reminiscing is not cheating.*

"You do, right? Okay, good. I'm not crazy."

"You're not crazy." As long as he was going out on a limb, I wasn't going to make him stand there by himself. Especially when I *did* know. I *did* get it. It wasn't like I thought about him all the time, but . . . every now and then.

"Look. If you won't leave with me, that's fine. Let's go back inside." As we walked back in, he snatched the back of my dress and whispered to me, "I've always wanted to take you to church."

"It's a synagogue," I said, way too flirtatiously.

"Details."

We started to walk through the crowd. Out of the corner of my eye, I saw Charlie standing with Kate. They looked like the top of a cake, except they seemed to be having some sort of disagreement. I couldn't tell over what. She looked confused, wide-eyed. Eventually, they went their separate ways. The vows hadn't miraculously solved everything. I had a blunt feeling in my stomach, a growing pit of concern, for her, for me. For all of us.

The dance floor was packed with people now, sweaty and shoeless girls, and men with their shirts unbuttoned and ties tied around their foreheads. When we were fully immersed in the crowd, Jesse took my hand and held it low, so that nobody could see, and it was as if all my nerve endings were suddenly located in my right palm. My other senses were shut down. I ordered myself to let go of his hand. I was screaming inside my head, *This is not real,* but I couldn't quite pull it away from him. *What am I doing? I am not cheating.* A slow song came on, the melody working its magic, and his face was next to mine. It occurred to me that I felt exactly like I did before we slept together for the first time. I remember sitting across the room from him and feeling this need for him welling up, this rush of feeling that I couldn't control. I wanted him, even though we weren't touching, the anticipation was doing me in.

"Do you feel bad about it?" he whispered.

"About what?"

"The fact that you still think about me?"

I paused. "Sometimes. Do you?"

"Yeah. Same. Sometimes. I should feel worse."

"I know. I should feel worse."

"That's the thing though. *Sometimes* I can be that nonchalant about it. I can say, 'Oh, at another time, in another set of circumstances, we were together and now we're not.' And what can you do? I don't believe in that one-person-for-everyone bullshit. I've never believed in it. The fact that I feel this way goes along with everything that I've ever believed about the human race. It's all a mess. One connection doesn't obliterate the chance of another connection. How could it? But then other times, I feel *wrecked* at the thought of the situation being reversed. If my girlfriend felt this way, I would want to kill the guy. I would not understand. I would not sympathize. I would not say, 'Well, life is messy!' I would say, 'What's mine is not fucking yours.' Do you see how unbelievably hypocritical that is?"

"Yeah."

"And at the same time, I can't have you. I can't really *have* you, not the way that I used to. And while that may be for the best, or whatever, it also really fucking hurts, you know? But I also get hurt thinking about my girlfriend, who would be pretty upset if she knew how much pain it was causing me not to be with you right now. Isn't that fucked up?"

"If we all knew the truth, like if we all knew every little thing that went on in each other's heads, none of us would ever speak to each other again, not even husbands and wives."

"Oh, it would be the end of civilization as we know it." He smiled. "I guess I should apologize to you then," he said, leaning closer to me. "For all the dirty things I've thought about you."

"It's okay," I said, smiling.

"No, but really. There's been some filthy stuff."

"Stop," I urged him. *But go on.* "You're making it worse."

"Sorry. Sorry. But you know what, maybe she has her own . . . situations . . . that I don't even know about. And maybe it's like this double-blindness thing that we all do. A chosen ignorance. Is it the same for everyone? I have no idea. People never talk about this shit. It's always the same story—the boring wife and the exciting affair, right? Like you can never love both at the same time, like it's mutually exclusive. What happens when you really fucking love your girlfriend and you really fucking love your ex-girlfriend too? What do you do then? You just shut up about it, right? You swallow it. That's what everyone else does. But here's the problem with the two of us. Are you ready for it?"

"Probably not, but go ahead." I had the impression that he was thinking something over carefully, choosing his words.

"You and I are messed up inside."

"What's . . . that mean?"

"It *means* . . . let's say you get handed this glass with smoking-hot boiling lava in it, or something like that, and you're allowed to hold it but you're told that if you spill any of it, it would be really fucking bad. If nobody were watching, you and I would both tilt the glass, just slightly. We'd do everything but let it spill over. We'd come close."

"So you're saying that we like to play with fire?"

"I'm saying that we're interested in the fire, or the potential for fire, and yeah, sometimes we're going to play with it. Not every-one is like this. And I'm not saying they're wrong and we're right. I'm not saying, 'Yay us!' It's not necessarily good, and good for those other people who would just hold the glass as instructed and not do a fucking thing with it. Seriously. Good for them. So many people just feel shit and let it go, or they think about it for a few minutes and then it's over. I like to look at it more, and so do you. If I didn't come close to spilling that glass, or if I didn't know what it was like to have hot lava all over the fucking floor, I'd have exactly zero songs to write."

I wanted to understand how it was that he was changing the chemistry inside of me. Why were all my old feelings coming back to me now? Talking about what made us different from other people, I felt rooted to him, with all my selves. I was like Jesse, and I didn't want to be lonely for my whole life. Was this my only chance? My heart felt curled into his in a way that it might never be with anyone else's. It felt a lot like safety. It felt a *whole lot* like safety.

He looked down, and then put his hand on the side of my dress. The people dancing on all sides of us kept us in the dark. He stayed away from what was visible to those watching. Every-one else would see a friendly moment. I kept my eyes wide-open, fighting back against every molecule inside of me that wanted to buckle under. He had a deep pull on me, the same one he'd always had. It was no different now. It was a compulsion that I couldn't ignore, a fallibility I didn't know I had. Suddenly, I re-alized that we'd been hand in hand this whole time. *We could hold hands for a minute. I'd held Kate's hand before. It isn't nec-essarily romantic to hold hands. It isn't cheating. Ben is going to leave anyway. If not now, then eventually. And what would I be left with? Nothing.*

He led me across the dance floor and out of the main room and down an empty hallway. "Fast," he said, and then pushed a door open into a dark room and slammed it shut behind me. I could hear his steps. I couldn't see him, but I had his hand in mine, his thumb running across my palm. The darkness changed everything. *It isn't cheating to be alone in a dark room.* But we were available for each other now. He began to feel for my stomach, before I could see him, when he was just an outline of his hair and face and hands. I felt suddenly his lips on mine, as he pushed me toward the opposite wall, with so many objects that I couldn't see jangling and falling out of the way. *His tongue*, and all at once I remembered how it moved against mine. It was like a familiar song I hadn't listened to in so long, but *man*, it sounded good. He reached for my waist, held it with both hands, and then unzipped my dress. It fell to my ankles but stayed straight up in a column surrounding me. "Take off your heels, sweetheart," he said, like always. He used to give me gentle directions. *Don't torture me, sweetheart. Sometimes it hurts, sweetheart.* I took my shoes off. He bent down to his knees and felt my strapless bra. He reached back, unhooked it, and touched my left breast with his mouth open, inches away.

As soon as I felt his tongue on me, I touched his head and then pushed him, held him away with one hand. I saw his face. He breathed in and out, heavily. I didn't expect to start crying. *God knows* it wasn't the time to start crying, but I was feeling so much inside my body, so many conflicting emotions, that something had to break. Also, I must have known. I must have realized, somewhere inside of me, that I had royally fucked up.

"What's wrong?" Jesse said.

"Nothing." *Nothing. Nothing. Nothing.*

"Are you okay?" He must have seen the tears, even in the dark, even though I fought hard to keep them silent. He stood.

"Yes." *Yes. Yes. Yes.* "I can't," I said, and then started to move away from him, bent over, retrieved the bra from the floor, zipped the dress.

"Yeah, we've already established that." For the next few minutes, we were silent. He kept looking at me. I felt like throwing up. I willed myself not to throw up.

"I love somebody else," I said.

"I do too, Eve," he said, sighing, and then he started to walk toward the door. "But I love her because I love her. Not because I'm desperate to feel that way."

EVE

WHY DID THE PIGEON CROSS THE ROAD?

I was praying for the sound of his voice. I had my phone in hand, pacing up and down the red steps in my black shoes, ten steps up, ten steps down, waiting to hear the sound of his voice. I felt like if I left this place, I could no longer be sure of what reality was, of what actually happened. I would lose the chance to take it all back, or to at least alter something. Across the street, there was a school and a fenced-in concrete area with lines drawn, a basketball court. There were three trees. Above me, two stained glass windows. At the bottom of the steps, I decided to turn right and go to the corner and back. I passed the yellow speed bump sign, yellow school-crossing sign, fire escapes, red door, fire escapes, red door, green building, gray bricks, corner of East Houston Street, then quickly turned back around. Green building, red door, fire escapes, red door, fire escapes, crossing sign, speed bump, red steps. I was anchored to the steps by an invisible thread. I kept walking the same way: around the corner but I never left the block; always returned to where I'd started, at the top of the steps. I tried calling Ben again, and listened to the phone ring and ring with no answer. I kept praying for that steady voice of his to interrupt the endless vacant ringing. *Pick up pick up pick up.*

I stopped moving when a stranger passed me by. He was rolling a suitcase by his side, and for some reason, I pictured him going home to his wife and two children, kissing their sleepy heads good night, reheating his dinner in the kitchen. He stared straight at me in the dark, with curiosity. It must have looked strange from the outside, the scene: a narrow street, so quiet at night, no lights, a girl in a green bridesmaid's dress, visibly shaken; the clicking of her shoes up and down the steps. When he was out of sight, I went back to my phone. I called again.

"Hey, it's me," I said. "Call me back. I need to talk to you." It wasn't my usual course of action to leave·a voice mail, but it was the closest I could get to him, and it wasn't very close. I was desperate and starting to tremble in the cold, but I found comfort in the suffering. Inside of me, it was much worse. I had an energy that I couldn't get rid of or put toward anything. There was no place to turn, nobody who would feel sorry for me, not a chance.

In need of a distraction from my own thoughts, I started to watch a pigeon along the sidewalk, pecking away near a gutter, a stream of water at the edge of the street. We were both moving back and forth down the road, in the same aimless way. I kept my eye on it as I paced, as it inched farther and farther away from the sidewalk and toward the center of the road. I refused to leave those steps. I would wait there until Ben called back. If I left this place, I would be even more alone in the city, disconnected from everything. I needed an anchor more than ever, and with Ben gone, I had only this wedding and my friends inside. Without this place, I was tied to nothing.

I had a passing memory of Ben holding on to me as I slept; he'd always done this, even before it was required, even after the first drunken night on Saint Marks; yet somehow I'd managed to throw it all away. I felt like something permanent had changed, like there was something spoiled inside of me, capable of ruining whatever lay in its path.

I clicked my phone to check it again, and in that second, a truck whizzed by and crushed the pigeon to death. All at once I heard the snap of countless small bones. I gasped. I moved forward, slowly, peeking at its flattened body, the black, gray, and white feathers against the street. I recoiled backward. I kept thinking about how all it took was one wrong move, just one false step, and it could all be over. You could gain or lose everything. Wasn't that why Ben felt so guilty about his father? Even he knew how easy it was to alter the course of events.

Maya came outside and I looked at her, not masking my alarm.

"I just saw a pigeon die," I said. "It died right in front of me. A truck ran over it, and it was like, *whoosh. Death.*"

She seemed confused but hugged me. She didn't ask any questions. I didn't tell her about Jesse's brother, or Jesse's roaming hands in the dark, the kiss, what I'd done to Ben. I just held on tight and she did the same. After a few minutes, she loosened her hold on me.

"So was this like . . . a pigeon pigeon?"

I smiled at her. She put her hand on my shoulder and went back inside and brought me my coat and a pile of tissues.

"Apparently, we've reached the Kleenex portion of the evening."

I put on the coat, closed it with both hands, and held it that way, too concerned with staring at my phone to deal with zipping it up properly.

"How's it going in there? Do you think Kate's noticed that I've been gone?" I asked her.

"No way."

"Are you sure?"

She nodded emphatically. "Kate doesn't even notice who she married," she said. "Why don't you go home?"

"I can't."

"Why not?"

"I don't know. I just can't."

"I have to find Erol," Maya said, and turned to go back inside. I nodded, kept pacing. I didn't know how much time had gone by, but eventually, I heard the sound of a few wedding guests, too drunk and done for the night, saying their good-byes. *Is it over?* The first group of departures flung themselves into taxis, the yellow lights on and waiting. After the cab doors closed, somehow, miraculously, my phone rang.

Once I heard his voice, everything else went black. The city was gone. I heard no car horns or bits of conversation from the people walking by or music from inside. I heard nothing but the sound of his words.

"Hey."

"Hi."

"How was the wedding?"

"Fine."

"See."

"Oh, Ben, *I just don't understand.* I don't understand why you wouldn't tell me something like that. Something so important like . . ." My voice cracked and tears came spilling under my eyelids. "Something so important like that."

"This again? I'm sorry. I should have. Right away. You're right."

"You can't just go silent on me. You're so silent sometimes.

And there's nothing that scares me more than unexplained silence."

"I know."

"And it's all fucked up now. It's all so fucked up." I was sobbing into the phone, uncontrollably.

"*Why?*" he said. I'd never heard Ben sound so alarmed. It
broke my heart even more.

"I . . . I did something bad."

"Okay. . . ."

"I did something really bad."

"What is it?"

"I saw Jesse at the wedding."

"Okay."

"We kissed."

"What?"

"I know. It was the stupidest thing."

"Yeah."

"There's something wrong with me."

"Okay."

"I can't believe I did this, because *I love you. I love you so
much*, Ben. But you really threw me . . . when you told me that. I
was just so surprised. I never ever thought you would hide something from me. You were supposed to be the one who fixed . . .
who fixed . . . this hole inside of me. You weren't supposed to
create one."

"Okay."

"But even so, it was such a mistake. Do you believe me? It
was a big mistake."

"Okay."

"Say something other than *okay*, please. "

"What do you want me to say? Look. I say everything I need

to say. There's nothing bubbling under the surface. What you see is what you get. What is the point of all your words? They don't get us anywhere. For example, I was a lot better off before we had this conversation."

"I don't know, but please say more than just one word. I just want to talk to you. I feel like sometimes you aren't very expressive, and it's hard to tell what's going on in your head when I can't see you. So, if you could just say what you're feeling. . . ."

"EVE. Take a wild guess. Take a wild conjecture as to how I might feel. What's going on in my head? How do I feel? I feel exactly how you'd imagine I would feel."

And then the line went dead.

BEN

New York City is a phenomenal place to be pissed off. You fly into JFK from wherever the hell you were, doesn't matter now, because once you get to New York, as it turns out, your whole life has changed shape. Once the plane descends lower and lower toward that dizzying display of yellow and white lights, twinkling amid the blackness, the Empire State Building in the foreground, the bridges linking all the landmasses that look as if they might otherwise float away from one another, you're back to reality. Except this time, what you're back to is not the reality that you left behind. Because reality would have been sitting on the A train, calm but also pretty stirred up inside, in a good way, because you were going to see her soon, and that was always a little bit exciting. Reality would have been passing by Fulton and Chambers and Canal and getting off at the West Fourth Street stop, and then walking a few blocks to her place, or what had certainly become our place.

But instead of getting off at West Fourth, you watch everyone shuffle past you, *West Fourth Street, this is the West Fourth Street stop,* and you sit. You sit, and you wait, and you move your suitcase closer so that nobody kicks it square into your shins on their way out. The doors close. Somewhere below Times Square, you make the decision to keep riding. Because you are having trouble moving the way you used to, and you feel like maybe being a lump of useless mass on a subway seat suits you pretty well at the moment. Also you don't know where to go. You don't want to be alone, but you don't want to talk to anyone either. The subway is great for this purpose. That, and if you want to see a bunch of people whose lives are worse than yours. People go through some shit. Just sit on the subway for a while and you'll practically see them going through it.

The A train is known for the long express ride from 59th to 125th, with no stops in between, so maybe that's perfect, for now. For an express train, it is slow in downtown and midtown, relative to other express trains like the 2/3 or 4/5, but what's your rush? For riding it all the way uptown with no destination in mind, it is the way to go. After 125th, there is 145th, and then 168th, which is Columbia Medical Center. You smile to yourself about the idea of getting off there, because isn't there some sort of psych ward, the New York Psychiatric Institute or something like that? And isn't that where it makes sense that you'd end up, after all this? Yup. At a mental institution.

No. No. Come on. Seriously? Look at all the people getting on and off the train. Do they look happy? Do they look like they are having the greatest fucking time of their lives? No. They look somewhere on the scale of fine to miserable, for the most part. And I'm sure they have their reasons. Reasons better than mine.

I kept thinking, *Why?* Why bring someone else into a good situation? I guess it wasn't good for her. What other conclusion could there be? But how was it possible that I'd misjudged it so much? I knew nothing. I didn't understand her. That was the only answer. And what was it really to be with someone who you didn't understand? She and I . . . we weren't like apples and oranges. Because those belong in the same category, the same universe. Look at a fruit basket, for Christ's sake. Fruits mingling. Eve and I . . . we were like apples and . . . a book? A backpack? A metal pole? I don't know. These were just things that were surrounding me. She'd be better at this. She'd smile and say, *Oh, have you not heard the tale of the apple and the metal pole? That's right! You haven't. Because they don't hang out together!* And then it would just absolutely kill her with joy that I'd thought to make this analogy in the first place.

A soaring pain will run through you when you think of something she'd say or that you'd like to tell her but it feels like the sound of the wheels cutting through the tracks beneath you. That screeching sound is just about right as you arrive at . . . where the hell are you? 175th Street? End of the line is 207th. They'll repeat it a few times, so that you have no hope of going farther, no hope that you don't have to make some sort of decision. *You can't just do this forever, buddy,* says the MTA and everything else about this city that is unforgiving.

Next stop is 207th Street. 207th Street is the last stop.

part four

THREE MONTHS LATER

EVE

THIS IS PARK AVENUE

As soon as I heard the water stop trickling through the pipes in the wall, that gentle swooshing noise that came and went in the mornings, I knew that I had to make my move, and fast. I had about ten minutes to get some coffee, eat breakfast or at least assemble it, and then hustle back into the guest room. I forced myself awake, up out of bed, and put on thick socks so that I could cross the living room without the creaking of the wood floor.

The kitchen was dark. I flicked on the lights and went for the coffee first, then got a bowl from the cabinet, careful not to clank the bowls against one another. I grabbed the cereal and opened the box, gently, *gently*. Over the past few months, I had learned to open and close a cereal box like I was defusing a bomb. I reached into the fridge for milk, and then froze. *Were those footsteps?* I listened. I couldn't hear anything. I waited for another sound. I heard shuffling. *Shit!* I started to panic. *How could he have gotten out of the shower and put clothes on so quickly? He always takes ten minutes! Always!*

The footsteps got louder—low, heavy steps. *Shit! Shit! Shit!* I was screwed. There was no place to run. The best I could do was stand with my back to him, take an extra few seconds to plan my next move. This morning routine was becoming a ritual, but it seemed reasonable. The whole absurd dance wasn't so absurd, under the circumstances. I was trying to get along better with Arthur, but before 9:00 a.m., it was tough.

"Morning!" I heard Arthur's voice from behind me—always loud, always sociable. I poured milk over the cereal and then placed the carton back inside the fridge.

"Morning!" I uttered, as boisterously as I could, which wasn't very boisterous. Arthur's disposition was easier for him. It was as dependable as his wardrobe—a series of short-sleeved collared shirts in turquoise and orange with two pockets in the front and tucked into khaki pants. I watched him take a mug from the cabinet—he was wearing his orange number that day—and head to the coffeepot.

"How's the writing going?" he asked. Arthur always had questions, and asking them was not something he reserved for when I was wide-awake. Once he asked me about the state of the music industry before seven o'clock in the morning and I almost burst into tears. I decided this time to answer quickly and then take my cereal into my room, as if that were where I typically ate it. The good thing about Arthur was that he wouldn't take it personally. He was not the type who assumed that it was his company that drove people away. His nature was too sunny for that line of reasoning.

"It's going all right," I said, attempting to follow that with something resembling a laugh but which came out much more like a cross between a hiccup and a guffaw.

Arthur then laughed a much more legitimate laugh, and sat

down with a bowl and his box of chocolate Cheerios. He filled the bowl to the brim with the dark brown loops. *No judgment.* Really, no judgment. But I wished that he would just *tell me* that he knew that it was a weird breakfast, that it was almost like having dessert, and not quite normal for a sixty-five-year-old. With Arthur, I was genuinely concerned that he didn't know, that he thought the word CHEERIOS on the box implied health and whole-grain goodness. I was generally indifferent to the breakfast choices of others, but *this*, for some reason, really got to me. *Oh, the agony*—of watching him shovel the Cheerios into his mouth every morning with those large hands and the milk running down his chin. I silently wished that my mother were there to witness it. She would have made it less awkward, this cereal standoff.

His cell phone rang, and I heard his ringtone, the first few notes of 'Stayin' Alive,' which were all too familiar now. I took the opportunity to skip away, back to the guest room, pretending that I didn't want to disturb him. *So polite and considerate!* It was the first of Arthur's client calls. His phone rang constantly, allowing him to deploy with regularity his unique brand of chitchat. I wondered if there wasn't some electronic, or more up-to-date way for these people to find out about their stocks. But I had the feeling that all his clients were over seventy, and that they were just like Arthur, always wanting an excuse to chat. I imagined that his was the only call these people received all day, though I had no evidence.

"So, are you bored yet of looking at pictures of the baby?" I heard Arthur say on the phone, a faint voice now, before I turned the knob on the guest-room door. A few seconds later, he said, "I tell ya! It's hard work to be such a loving grandparent!" And then his signature laugh.

He never answered the phone with a simple hello. And he never said good-bye either. Instead, he got off the phone with, "All right, well, enjoy the crossword puzzle! Is it easy or hard today?" or "Call your mother!"

He was just being a nice guy. Three months of living with him and I was finally starting to master that certain live-and-let-live serenity. His apartment was Grand Central Terminal, but I secretly relished the distractions that it provided—the calls with his clients; his housekeeper, Camilla, a quick-tempered Colombian woman who tended to get into fights with everyone she encountered. She had a particularly contentious relationship with one of the doormen, Santiago, because she felt that he didn't arrive to take her down in the elevator fast enough, when she called for it (I assumed they were also in love and carrying on a secret affair, but again, there was no actual evidence of this). One time, their yelling got so bad that Arthur had to get off the phone with a client. I heard him say, "I have to go. My housekeeper and my doorman are fighting. A house divided . . ." And then the laugh. I enjoyed this. I decided that it was a very Park Avenue problem to have.

With my hands full of breakfast, I closed the door with my hip and went to the window, where I had a bird's-eye view of Park Avenue, women walking up and down the street in heels and men in suits, walking dogs or yanking children by the arm. A swarm of joyless workers crossed the street, with hard hats in their hands. Double-parked outside the building, there was a black car, its driver reading the newspaper and leaning against it. I looked out at the figures below, the glances at the sky, the briefcases and cups of coffee moving up and down the street. It was one of the many charms of being in that apartment, on the seventh floor, the view of Park Avenue and with it, a sense of luxury. Being this high up meant I was free from the prying eyes that I was used to in New York. To be seven floors above the traffic, to have nobody see me but the birds in the sky, it was a pleasure that explained so much. It was wonderful to be rich, but especially in this town.

I got back into bed, sat with my knees to my chest, and ate my hard-earned cereal. Across from me, there was a flat-screen TV. The other walls in the room had a few new, framed pictures—a print of Fred Flintstone, an abstract painting of Michael Jackson, a photo of a roll of Life Savers—all meant to convey the art-appreciating and yet fun-loving nature of Arthur. There was a photo of Arthur and my mother in a heart-shaped frame next to the bed. They were dressed up, at a wedding. Arthur was wearing a three-piece suit, with a gold chain dangling from his pocket. *Oh, the pocket watch.* My mom had begged him not to wear it that night, told him how old-fashioned it was. But he didn't listen. He said it reminded him of James Dean. She said it reminded *her* of the rabbit from *Alice in Wonderland.* Those were the kinds of fights they used to have. I was always grateful that there was nothing larger at stake.

I sank down into the four-poster bed, stared at the CD player above the dresser, which had a catalog lying on it, open to a page of silk handkerchiefs. There was a stack of CDs— Billy Joel's *Greatest Hits*, The Eagles' *Complete Greatest Hits*, The Beatles' *1*—Arthur didn't waste time with the lesser titles. When I asked him about it, he said: "The hits are hits for a reason!"

There was a sharp knock on the door. "Eve?" I heard his voice. When he came in, he looked around the room, at the untidy ball of clothes on the floor in the corner, books at the foot of the unmade bed.

"You're eating cereal . . . here?" He half smiled.

"Yup! Breakfast in bed!" I answered. I had that one locked and loaded, for whenever he caught me.

"Why not in the kitchen?"

"You were on a call. I didn't want to disturb you."

He nodded, seemed pacified.

"Eve," he said, his face screwed up like he was about to tell me something that was difficult for him to say.

"Yes?"

He lowered his voice and closed the door behind him. "Don't you think it's time to find your own apartment?"

"But I like it here!" I replied.

It could have been a depressing state, living at Arthur's place, but lately, I'd been trying to bond with him. We went to the movies together sometimes. Plus I had a job that I loved. Unfortunately, the job didn't pay enough to allow me to keep my apartment once the rent went up. And so, until I found a new place, I didn't see what was so wrong with seeking refuge with the fourth member of the Bee Gees.

"I'm trying to find a place," I ventured instead. I started looking down at my phone, scrolling through e-mails, but I could feel his eyes on me. The truth was, I was milking this and Arthur knew it. It was far from my childhood bed, but it was someplace to rest comfortably. The apartment was nice and spacious. There was a constant stream of distractions. I had company at night when I was feeling lonesome and missing Ben. My salary didn't get a huge chunk taken out of it for rent each month. The only downside was that every now and then, I had to shake off the underlying feeling that I was a pathetic loser.

"Are you really looking? What have you seen lately?" he asked.

I looked up at him. His hair was still wet from the shower.

"Everything is too expensive. You said that you wanted me to live here for a little while!"

"It's been . . . a while now."

"Well, you didn't specify a time limit. I've been very productive!"

"It's not about that, Eve. I know that you have a great job. And don't get me wrong, I like having you around, but it's time. Nobody likes to be alone. After my first marriage ended, I slept with the lights on in the whole apartment every night for a month. But you have to force yourself to be a little bit brave. You're just scared, that's all."

"Of course I'm scared. I ruined the only good relationship I've ever had. But the good news is, I do my best work when I'm scared shitless!"

A part of me was still recovering from the night of Kate's wedding. Ben had moved out of our East Village apartment. My first night there alone, I woke up at 3:00 a.m. in a massive state of panic. Sitting up in bed, I tried to focus on breathing. I counted to ten with every inhale and exhale and concentrated on each number as if my life depended on it. To get my brain to slow down and to break the endless loop of terrible thoughts, I listened to a few songs on my computer, the ones that always soothed me right before going to sleep. But that night, it wasn't doing the trick. It simply wasn't enough. So I took a pile of blank paper into bed with me and wrote an article for *Interview*.

When I was done, it was five o'clock in the morning, and I still couldn't sleep. So I packed up some of my belongings and left. I bolted out of the apartment with my heart beating rapidly and my shoes barely on. I was in such a rush, with no idea why, no idea where I was going. It was raining very hard, but I couldn't stay where I was. I was too afraid of how I felt inside, of what might happen if I remained alone there. So I stood outside, getting soaked as I hailed a cab. In my head, I heard my mother judging me. She hated cabs and often condemned people who took them as a form of transportation. "How much time do you lose sitting in traffic?" she would say. I was soaking wet by the time a cab pulled over, but I didn't care. The worst danger was that my problems might get washed away. I threw out Arthur's address to the cabdriver, automatically. I didn't want to call Kate or Maya or my sister. They would all indulge me too much in examining the details of the situation. I didn't want to talk. I wanted sleep.

The rain hammered the top of the cab as it made its way uptown, so much so that I couldn't see where it was going. Water sputtered inside. I closed the window, which had been left slightly open, and saw my reflection, my face dizzy with emotion, my eyes glassy and mad-looking. I must have looked strange to Arthur, at the door of his Park Avenue apartment, soaked through and shaking with cold but also fear. I felt an overpowering need for company. But he wanted to know first if I was in some kind of trouble, and then once he figured out what had happened, he considered it to be nothing that we couldn't sort out in the morning. He brought me into my old room, which had been converted back to a guest room, and opened the drawers full of clean and dry towels, while the rain came down outside. He produced a toothbrush. He offered me hot water for tea and then retrieved it. I was surprised to hear the voice of a woman in the hallway, even though I knew that Arthur had started dating again. We both pretended not to hear it.

I slept for only a few hours that night, and the nights after were no better. I awoke each morning with no idea where I was and what had happened to lead up to this place. Then, before my eyes were open, before I was fully awake, I had the sad job of explaining to myself what had occurred. It was a little recap that I did: "On last week's episode of . . ." *Ben's gone and it was mostly your fault. Funny how you wanted to be broken and now you are.*

I had a hard time going back to my East Village apartment. Somehow, it was the apartment itself that became impossible for me to handle. I couldn't settle myself down there anymore. Whenever I went back, I felt a sense of insecurity boiling up inside of me. I returned to the same place, but I was frightened now, of every bit of it, frightened that it would prompt that panicky reaction all over again. All the good moments that came before had been replaced by this one monumentally bad feeling. I could feel it when I walked around the space, opened the door, looked at the bed, the kitchen. I told myself that it wasn't the place that caused the panic, but it didn't matter. They had become too closely linked in my mind. I had to give it up. The only good that came from that night was that I sent my insanity-induced article to my editor at *Interview* and he loved it. Apparently, it was my best yet.

"Eve," Arthur said now, smiling at me.

"What? You're kicking me out?" He was the one who'd wanted me to stay there after I opted out of renewing the lease on my apartment. He thought it'd be best for me not to be alone.

"Sort of." He put his hands on his waist. "Consider this your two weeks' notice." His eyes lit up, like he was offering me the chance to play a fun new game.

"*Well, I've been kicked out of finer places.*" I got out of bed, shoving the sheets out of my way dramatically.

"Oh, have you?" He laughed.

"Of course not," I said, in a huff. "This is Park Avenue."

Would you look at that, I thought to myself, as I got dressed for work. Arthur and I were finally developing a rapport.

- - - -

The dark-wood-paneled elevator opened into the lobby and four doormen came to attention. The two who were sitting down on a leather bench stood up immediately. All four always greeted me, but I felt like they were forcing it, like they knew that I didn't really live there and there was no reason to be friendly to me, some temporary visitor. I nodded and said good morning back. My mother had always talked to them about the weather, especially with Dennis, who had an Irish accent. "They say rain, but I don't know, Dennis—what do you think?" she'd say. Or he'd tell her, "They say *sixty-five* degrees by Sunday," and she'd say, "Oh my. I'm going to hold you to it!" As if conversation with doormen about the weather was something she'd done all her life.

As I walked out onto the street, I noticed that the traffic was already building, going down Park. I preferred the atmosphere downtown, the vaguely bohemian nature of the Village. The Upper East Side was more uniform. Whatever didn't belong stood out. It was moms in exercise clothing with big leather bags, talking about their renovations. "There is nothing more difficult than doorknobs."

"I redid my bathrooms and people said, *You're crazy.*"

Young girls were on their way to school and dressed in matching skirts. They carried backpacks with tiny stuffed animals hanging off them, bobbing up and down as they walked.

"I'll text you and it's possible we'll be able to squeeze in a playdate!"

Everyone was finely dressed, no matter age nor gender nor ethnicity. Even old men who walked their dogs in the morning in sweatpants appeared semihomeless, but upon closer inspection, like their sweatpants might actually be really expensive. I watched the couples on the street—the women wearing long coats with fur accents, the men in suits and shiny loafers and pocket squares, often speaking French or Italian to one another. I didn't feel like I had something to offer them or them to me, but I was enjoying the look of their nice shops, the apartment buildings with matching awnings, the trimmed rows of bushes and potted flowers. My work was downtown and it wasn't high-powered and it wasn't something that people on the Upper East Side would find impressive, so once I got on the subway, the Upper East Side and I parted ways.

But first, I went to Madison Avenue for a pit stop. I sidestepped the puddles created by doormen watering the streets, and weaved through messengers carrying shiny shopping bags. I went to the same overpriced restaurant for overpriced coffee every morning, but I'd be lying if I said that the coffee wasn't delicious and that the pink cup it came in didn't make me feel like I was on a luxurious, Parisian vacation. Standing outside the place, I saw a guy who looked a lot like Ben's friend Glick. He was standing with his back to the wall. As I got closer, I realized that it was Glick, and my heart started racing, just at the thought that Ben might be nearby, that Glick might have seen or spoken to Ben recently. Glick was wearing a pale gray buttoned-down shirt that was buttoned up one notch too few, a triangle of his chest hair showing.

"Hey!" I said, sounding excited, perhaps overly so.

"Oh, hey," he said, with a more appropriately muted level of enthusiasm.

"What are you doing at this fancy-pants place on a Friday morning?" I said, looking at his pink coffee cup, which suited him even less than mine suited me.

"Just met with a client," he said, his voice groggy, ducking down to take a sip from his cup.

"A client?" I said, impressed.

"Yes," he said. "Is that so hard to believe?" He gave me an amused look.

"Yes, yes it is." He stuck out his leg, presumably to kick me in the shins, but he was too far away and didn't make contact. "What are you up to these days?" I asked.

"I'm selling real estate."

"What a coincidence!" I clasped my hands together. "I'm looking for real estate! To rent . . . an apartment." I cringed, for no apparent reason other than I was suddenly reminded of why I was looking for an apartment and that Ben's friend might find it a bit distasteful to help out Ben's cheating ex-girlfriend.

"What can you pay?"

Or not.

"In terms of money?"

"No, in terms of experiences," he said bitterly.

I looked around and whispered, "I figure I can pay about twelve hundred dollars a month."

He blinked hard and shook his head. "And I figure you've gone mentally ill."

"I won't find anything?"

"Were you figuring on New York?"

I laughed and rolled my eyes. "No. Any city will do!"

He opened his mouth and then closed it. "You know what, I have a place on Sixty-Ninth and Third that's for rent. You might like it."

"Third as in Third Avenue? In Manhattan? I'm sure that's out of my league."

"Wait and see the apartment first. It has some . . . liabilities. But what doesn't in this town? So when you flush the toilet, water comes out of the ceiling? Is that really so important to you?"

I laughed. "Um . . ."

"I'm kidding."

"Oh." I looked down at the ground. "So what's the rent?"

"I can show it to you now, actually." He raised his eyebrows.

"Now? I have to get to work."

"What time do you have to be there?"

"Ten."

"Ten! Jesus." He looked at his phone.

"Yes, I write for a magazine, which means I can get there at ten but I can't afford an apartment on the Upper East Side. You haven't even told me the rent yet. I probably can't afford it."

"What are *you* doing in this fancy-pants neighborhood, then?"

"Oh, my stepfather lives at 750 Park." I didn't explain the particulars of the situation.

He raised his eyebrows. "Oh. Then you'll be *fine*," he told me, and then said that the rent was something like twenty-one hundred a month. I knew right away that I couldn't afford it. But I had the sneaking suspicion that if I spent a half hour with Glick, I might be able to find something out about Ben. So I lied and said it was a doable number, that maybe I had undershot the runway and it wouldn't hurt to see the place.

Together, we walked down to Sixty-Ninth and then the three long avenues east. There was a crisp, fall breeze in the air. Colored leaves from the trees were scattered across the sidewalk. We passed by a blond woman pushing a baby in a stroller, a bag attached to the stroller with the word FORD written on it, in blue script.

"Ford," Glick grunted. "Perfect name for when you're having a baby . . . or a president."

I laughed.

"I'm sorry, but that baby was wearing loafers! I don't think I had a pair of loafers until I was twenty-five."

"Yeah, but you're special," I said.

I started asking him about his friends, pretending to be curious, innocently curious. I asked about Danza and Julian, their jobs, their apartments, waiting for the right moment to mention Ben.

"Let's see, there's Danza, Julian . . . who is my third friend? Who else am I friends with who you might ask me about?" he teased me. "God. You know what, I can't think of it. This is a real head-scratcher."

"All right. All right."

He paused for a few, long minutes. I did my best to be patient, to wait for him to say something, and then he did. "He has a new girlfriend, you know."

"Oh yeah?" I said, feeling my heart sink.

"Yep. She works for a nonprofit and runs marathons."

"Wow."

"So she's *definitely* a good person." He snickered.

I didn't know what to say. "Well, good for him."

"They'll probably end up engaged within the year." He sighed. "Any day now, I'll be buying them a pizza-making kit or a mango pitter or a picnic basket."

"Ah, the picnic basket," I said, with a slow nod. "Why do people register for those? Do you think they really use them? I've never heard any of my friends express the slightest interest in going on a picnic, and yet, evidence suggests that picnics are a big part of marriage."

"Also, how often are you eating mangoes that you need a *specific instrument* for them?"

"I agree. I feel like mangoes are a very once-in-a-while type of fruit."

"I don't know, man," he said, sounding tired. "Seriously, being almost thirty is just finding out which of your friends who you used to throw up with in the street is now registered for a picnic basket."

We stopped at the corner of Sixty-Ninth and Lexington and waited for the light to change. "So, not into the whole marriage thing?" I turned to him. His hands were in his pockets.

"Oh, I don't know about that. Haven't found the right girl yet is more like it. Not everyone can handle me, Eve."

"Yeah, well, join the club." We crossed the street, dodging a dog walker with six or seven small white puppies jumping at his ankles.

"Eve. You didn't do anything *that* bad," he said. "You just wanted to blow up your life."

"What?"

"You wanted to blow up your life," he repeated.

"I didn't *want* to."

"Oh yes, you most certainly did. People do what they want to do, and you wanted to blow up your life."

"Did Ben say that?"

"No. Have you met Ben?"

I smiled in spite of myself.

"It happens to everyone. Well, it happens to some people. For whatever reason, sometimes you just want to fuck shit up. I'm sure you had your reasons."

"Yes, well, I've thought about it and I've thought about it and I've come to the conclusion that it was just all going along *so smoothly*, and, I don't know. Every relationship I've ever been involved in has been so tumultuous and . . . I guess, rather than wait for it to get messed up in some unexpected, out-of-the-blue way, I took matters into my own hands because I think on some subconscious level . . . I'm an idiot."

"No, I know what you mean though. It's like that feeling on a roller coaster when you're slowly going up higher and higher and nothing bad is happening yet but the fact that something is coming totally fucks with you. And sometimes, you don't want to wait for it. Sometimes, you just want to get it over with."

"Yeah," I said. "Maybe." I decided that Glick had an okay side to him, when he wasn't drunk and destroying a fax machine that he found on the street.

"Ben's a good friend though," he said. "Ben's like an anchor and . . . I'm like a buoy."

"Yeah, I'm kind of a buoy too. Wait, aren't buoys also tied to something?"

"I don't know, man! This is my first maritime analogy. I thought they just floated around aimlessly, no?"

"Oh, maybe you're right."

"You know who would know the answer to this question?"

We both said it at the same time. "Ben."

I looked up at the white brick building that took up half the block. "Is this it?" I asked. He nodded. When we got upstairs to the apartment on the seventh floor, I pretended to check everything out, the way I would in a realistic situation. The place had big windows overlooking Third Avenue. The bathroom and kitchen looked recently redone. That was why I couldn't afford it. I'd never lived anyplace in New York with a bathroom or kitchen from this century and I had the feeling that I never would. But it was okay. I'd come to appreciate the black-and-white-tiled floor, the quirky fixtures, knobs and cut-off pipes sticking out of the wall for no reason.

"I'm going to tell you something," he said, standing in the middle of what would be the living room. "But only because I feel like we've bonded now."

"What is it?"

I could tell that he was fighting off a smile. "Ben may not be headed to the altar as soon as I implied earlier," he said.

"What do you mean?" I went over to the kitchen, opened and closed the fridge, then the oven, launching a fake investigation of all appliances.

"He had a fight with his girl. We were making fun of him about it."

"Oh? What about?" I crouched down to look into a drawer below the oven. *This is where the wrapping paper could go*, I thought to myself, to make sure I had the right facial expression.

When I lifted myself back up, Glick was tapping his fingers together, under his chin. He was enjoying this.

"What?" I demanded. "The suspense is killing me."

He looked me up and down. "He said your name."

"Huh?"

"He said your name." He winced. "During . . . sex."

"Shut up." I put my hands on my head.

"You're welcome." He laughed and walked over to the window. I could see his reflection, squinting into the sun.

"I can't believe he did that," I said. It was like a door that had been slammed shut now had a tiny sliver of light showing from underneath.

"I know. And she flipped, obviously. It was pretty unwise. But classic Ben, right? I swear. Outside that iron-clad smart brain of his, there is a fluffy layer of marshmallow stupidity."

I nodded, knowing exactly what he meant. The kick under the table at my father's apartment. The yellow roses, gently used.

"I just can't believe he was talking, let alone during sex," Glick said.

"I wouldn't call that talking."

"True. Anyway, she threw him out of her apartment. But I think they've recovered."

"Wait, but this is great news!"

"Why?"

"Because it means I'm in his head! It *means* I still have a chance."

"Maybe . . ."

"Well, Michael, this leaves me no choice."

"What? What do you mean?"

"I have to go to the airport."

"What airport?"

"To find Ben, of course! I have to chase him down and tell him that I love him and try to get him back."

"He's not at the airport." He gave me a puzzled look. "He's at work, you dingbat."

"I know." I smiled. "I was just kidding. I watch a lot of television. Everyone is always making big declarations at airports. And it's always raining."

"Blue sky." Glick pointed out the window.

I shook my fists in the air. "I can't catch a break!"

"So what have you done so far? To get him back?"

"Just a lot of calls and e-mails and one borderline insane handwritten letter. But I stopped about a month ago. I was trying to give him space, but not so much space that he could find a new girlfriend."

"Eve. We're almost thirty. How hard do you think it was for Ben to find a girlfriend? Factor in that he has a job and a pulse."

"But I knew him back in his hooded-sweatshirt days!"

"Oh, come off it." He shook his head. "You didn't like him back then either."

"Whatever!"

"How about this." He paused, paced around the apartment for a minute, deeply entrenched in thought. "I go out to a bar tonight with my boys. I know. I know. Very unusual occurrence for us on a Friday night. It'll involve an elaborate scheme of deception I'm sure. Anyway, I get Ben to come, and you show up."

I paused. Glick and I had never been close, to say the least. I'd always gotten the sense that he'd merely tolerated me, for Ben's sake, but he often looked at me like he couldn't quite place what I was doing there.

"Why are you doing this for me?"

He thought about it. "Because you made him happy, and then you made him miserable. But at least he wasn't going on any picnics."

We walked out of the apartment and toward the 6 train stop on Lexington and Sixty-Eighth. I was descending the stairs to the subway platform, thinking about how Glick had really come up in the world, when he called after me, "And about tonight . . . wear something sexy."

- - - -

Glick texted me later that afternoon with details and, that night, I showed up to the bar on Second Avenue and Seventy-Eighth

Street, in a black slinky dress, ready to ambush Ben. It was clear that I had somewhat lost my mind. If Ben had wanted to reach me, he certainly knew how to do that. And you couldn't force someone into something. I knew that. But I didn't allow myself to think too much about the weirdness of what I was doing. I realized the depth to which I'd sunk, but it was no greater than the depth of my mistake. That had been way more embarrassing, way more wrong than this. I had to break it down into small pieces. *I'm just going to a bar.* I told myself that this was a coincidence, a coincidence that happened to be orchestrated. It wasn't a lie if you really, really believed it.

Before searching for them, I went straight to the bar and got myself a drink. The bar had TV screens everywhere with sports playing. The place was filled with the abstract faces of men talking, streams of them moving toward the bar or sitting at tables. They were of all ages, and I passed through the crowd, with them whispering to one another. I had a strange feeling of being talked about, as they stood in small circles, wrangling one another. The voices made me ache for Ben, as I always did, among other men.

Once I had downed some of my drink, I looked for them—Ben, and the three others—Glick, Danza, and Julian. I spotted them at a table in the back corner. A waitress walked over to them, observing first and then getting more involved. They were a familiar unit to me, but there was some strange feeling sinking in, a sense of power that they now had over me. I got very nervous for a few seconds, and then, I thought, *Act. Do not think. Act.*

I went over to their table in a bit of a trance. Ben lifted his face when he saw me walking toward them. He looked innocent, slightly afraid. It reminded me of how he had looked to me in college, before I really knew him. Him watching me. I was received in silence. The others rose from the table. There was a confused pause. Glick tried to smooth it over.

"Well, if it isn't the devil herself," he said.

Ben then got up to greet me. He hugged me solidly. It wasn't distant. It was friendly. *It feels so good*, but I thought to myself: *Dismiss this thought.* I was getting ahead of myself. I knew that, objectively, I had a long way to come back. *But he said my name! And the hug! Quiet. Quiet.* I thought of trying to call Ben while standing outside the synagogue that night, and it had a calming effect on me. *It was a long way to come back.*

I sat down and the five of us talked together about some mutual acquaintances from college. After the first twenty minutes, things started to feel more normal. When Ben laughed at something I said, it was the best sensation I'd felt in a while.

"Eve and I were just talking about your hooded-sweatshirt days," Glick said.

"That was a great hoodie," Ben responded.

"Yeah, except you wore it *all* the time," Danza added.

"My other clothes weren't as comfortable."

"As what?" I said, laughing. "The pajamas you were always wearing?" The alcohol was kicking in. I was feeling unguarded, careless.

"Hey, Ben. Why don't you tell Eve about the fight with your girlfriend," Julian said. Apparently, he was feeling the same way.

Ben looked down, smiling slightly. "I'm not going to dignify that with a response," he said. There was a moment of unbearable silence when the three of them got up. "Okay then, you two. Talk among yourselves," Glick said to us.

We sat there, watching them go to the other side of the bar, drifting farther and farther into a pack of people. "How's it going?" Ben asked me.

"I'm good! How are you?"

"Pretty good." He shrugged.

"How's work? Hey! I read something about glass panels being installed. . . . That's a good sign, right?"

"Yup. They've been doing that for about two months."

"That's excellent!"

"Yeah, it's pretty cool. What about you?"

"Me? Nothing new . . . except, I'm all grown up now." I motioned to myself and then smiled.

"So you're not writing songs about your socks anymore?"

"Listen! I just think . . ." I looked down at the table, blushing. "I just think that the Laundromat must be a stressful place for socks. They could get left behind. . . . They could lose their other half. . . . I'm just trying to make the whole process easier for them."

He nodded, his mouth in a straight line.

"Sorry. I know. It was a lot of craziness."

"Actually, I didn't mind the craziness."

"You could have done without it."

"No," he said, thinking it over. "That was just you. If I'd lost that . . . I would have been too afraid of what else I might lose."

"That's a nice thing to say," I said, and then shifted my dress and sat up on my knees all excitedly. I put my hand on his arm and my head on his shoulder as if that were a perfectly normal thing to do. I could feel him shift a tiny bit toward me, bend his head in my direction. I looked at him and noticed that his eyes were slightly closed.

After a few seconds, I took my hand off him and sat back down, properly. "Anyway, I was reading this article about the Freedom Tower and I learned all this stuff about shoring and false work! Like what you do when something is unstable and might collapse, expanding the foundation to make it structurally sound. I learned what *underpinning* means!"

"What's it mean?"

"When a building is collapsing, you put a new building next to the existing building so that when you create a basement level, the building next to it will fall over into the hole."

He smiled. "Not even close."

"What?"

He stood up suddenly and put his hand on my bare shoulder and I felt the movement of his fingers. It was nothing, and yet it made me miss him even more. My body went completely still. His fingertips felt warm. "Do you want another drink?" he asked, looking a bit exasperated. I was wearing him down. Maybe. *But in a good way?* Maybe.

"Sure," I said, looking up at him. *My name. The hug. Another drink. This is going to be okay.*

He tapped my shoulder two times and then walked toward the bar. I sat there for a few minutes, looking at the table, both taking in what had happened so far and in a frenzy to plan my next move. I decided that I couldn't waste any more time. When he came back, I was going to put all my cards on the table. I felt a sudden burst of bravery about what I might say. I was spinning inside, like my thoughts couldn't fit inside of my skin for much longer. I couldn't wait to be sitting next to him again, how good it would feel to be next to him. For the first time, it all made sense. I believed that I could get him back. It was only a matter of getting him alone again, just one more time, and that was all. *Another drink.* He'd asked about another drink and that was a good sign. I could work with that.

After a few minutes of waiting, and then a few minutes more, Glick came over to me looking guilty. I could hear my own heartbeat. I don't know why I had such a bad feeling from the second I saw his face, but I did.

"I'm sorry, Eve," he said. "Ben left. He told me to say good-bye to you for him."

I was dissolving inside. All my hopes fell, in a single instant. All I heard was *Ben says good-bye*.

BEN

I had one last drink, standing at the bar, then got out of there, and kept walking until I got to the west side. I had to just get away from Eve. That was my main objective. To physically get away from her. The rest would follow. Sanity would follow. She was like a stimulant. Seeing her was like a shot of espresso to my system. And I didn't want that, the way I used to. I wanted to go back to my natural state of calm.

Natalie and I had been together for only a couple of months, not exactly "show up at the door drunk" territory, but I felt the need to be in her vicinity. Eve was not going to suck me back into her dysfunctional world, where nothing meant just one thing or whatever the hell you thought it meant. I texted Natalie as soon as I got outside the bar. She texted back that she was in bed but that she'd leave the door unlocked for me.

Great. Perfect. All I really needed was the ability to get in the door.

The block where she lived, Eighty-Second and West End,

was deserted. Natalie's neighborhood, in the evenings, was like a refugee camp for recovering from the city and the madness that was life in the East Village with Eve. It was quiet, no traffic, few noises, no matter the time of day. It was like looking out at a lake with water that wasn't moving, not even a ripple. A little strange for the city, but I'd take it.

The lobby of her building was lit with half-hidden bulbs that released an amber glow. I took the elevator up to the fourth floor. Once on the landing, I examined myself in the hallway mirror. I was dressed for work, pulled together from the outside. The only thing that gave me away was that my eyes were red, the way they got when I drank.

There were five apartments on her floor. Her door was the only one propped open by a sneaker. I pushed the door in and felt my way through the dark entranceway. I was hit immediately by the smell of oranges. Natalie's apartment always smelled like that, like some perfume she'd just sprayed, citrus-scented. All I could comprehend was the light from the living room window. The walls of her apartment were cream-colored but they looked darker now. My eyes were adjusting to see the fireplace with a long mantel, and framed pictures lining it. She had sheer, gold curtains, which made the living room a place of dignity, with a brown velvet couch and an old piano that had been left by the previous tenants of the apartment but that Natalie said she couldn't bear to give away. I took off my shoes and locked the door quietly behind me. I went into the kitchen and drank a glass of water, quickly.

I went into her bathroom. Everything in Natalie's bathroom had her name written on it in tiny script—the towels, the tooth-brush holder, the soap dish. A tissue box was inside a tissue box cover with her initials on it. Who knew that tissue boxes weren't meant to be exposed to the outside world? Natalie Williams. That was who. It was ironic that I had said Eve's name, hovering above Natalie that night, because Natalie's name was everywhere. *Natalie. Natalie. Natalie.* As I looked down at the tile floor, it shifted in and out of focus. I rubbed my eyes a few times, and then washed my hands with a bar of dark green soap that smelled like olive oil.

I was more careful once I went into the bedroom, took off my clothes noiselessly and slinked in next to her. I lifted up the cream-colored blanket and put it over me. The slight movement against the mattress made her shift positions on the other side of the bed. I looked over there, at the outline of her face. *Natalie was good.* Natalie worked for the Alzheimer's Foundation of America, and she didn't even know anyone with Alzheimer's. Natalie made dinner, cooked it herself from ingredients. Natalie always smelled like vanilla and kept flowers on her windowsill because she believed that flowers gave people a sense of well-being. She used logic when discussing anything. Her household management skills were unparalleled. It seemed as if she'd been preparing for adulthood since she was a little kid, like back then, all she'd wanted was to hurry up already and be an adult with e-mails to answer and bills to pay and vegetables to chop. I slept turned away from her, so that we were facing opposite walls, so that I could, despite everything, despite every fucking thing that made sense, imagine Eve in the dark.

It happened most nights, especially when I slept in Natalie's bed. I had no control over it. My mind just went there. That night, it was this time with Eve when it was snowing outside and we spent the entire day in her bed watching a *Star Wars* marathon, not because either one of us particularly liked *Star Wars* but because it was on TV. We were so snug in her bedroom that day, as the snow piled up on the frame of the window. We literally could not get out of bed. The outside world held no interest. The sun came and went and we were still in the same position. I fell asleep smiling, thinking about how much Eve hated the action scenes and her absolute favorite moment was when R2-D2 swiped a muffin from a table. That, for whatever odd reason, thrilled the hell out of her. Leave it to Eve to watch *Star Wars* and focus all her attention on that little robot and the one random scene with a breakfast buffet.

Before I knew it, I was out cold.

I woke up to the sunlight heating up one side of my face and Natalie standing above me.

"Ben," she said, patting my leg. I took a few seconds to orient myself. *I saw Eve. I am in Natalie's apartment. I came here last night after seeing Eve. Natalie is okay with it. Natalie doesn't know about it.*

"What?" I croaked. Then, realizing that I'd drunkenly showed up at her place without much warning, I tried to be nicer. "Hey, good morning," I said, feeling for her arm.

"I'm going for a run. Do you want to come?"

I still wasn't out of my dreamlike state. "A what?" I opened my eyes wide, not entirely sure whether I was imagining this, but there she was above me, all dressed in her stretchy workout gear, her dark hair pulled back in a ponytail, her skin pale and just washed.

"I'm going for a run," she said. A smile appeared on her face. "Would you like to come with me?"

Natalie went running in the park every morning. She did not miss a single day. She kept a calendar and marked her times and checked off tiny boxes. She had a great deal of discipline when it came to keeping herself active. On weekends, she dragged me with her, but I craved an exception on this particular Saturday morning. It may have been too late to apply for one.

"Okay . . ." I said, wanting to be hospitable. "You sure you want company?"

"Yes, because I know that if I leave here without you, I'll come home and you'll still be sleeping." Her face was passive, not angry, just matter-of-fact.

"That's not true."

"You're right. *Maybe* you'll have woken up and then migrated to the couch, where you'll be about five minutes away from taking a nap."

I closed my eyes and then opened them again. "You always think I'm taking a nap."

"You almost always are," she countered.

"That's an unfair characterization," I replied, smiling with my eyes closed.

I tried to drag her back into bed with me but she got away too quickly, and out of my reach. I grasped at the air, and then got up, mostly because I was afraid of pissing off two women in a twelve-hour time period. Maybe running would be good for me. Sure, it felt like the last thing on earth I wanted to do *now*, but once I got out there? The wind in my hair, my feet pounding against the pavement? Instant clarity. Maybe.

While she waited for me near the door, I put on the shorts and T-shirt that she'd left on the bed for me, something old and too big for her. Maybe belonging to an ex-boyfriend. I didn't have sneakers, so she said that I should just put on my dress shoes I'd been wearing the night before.

"Dress shoes?" I'd gone to the bar straight from work.

"Better than nothing. And it's actually a little bit cold this morning," she said. Natalie's running outfits were always coordinated and changed depending on a five-degree difference in the weather.

I looked at her blankly. "I don't have anything to put over this."

"Don't you have some jacket here?"

She opened her closet and took out a fleece that I must have left at her place one time. I put it on and looked down. She laughed at me.

"What? No good?"

"It's fine. It's fine. Not the ensemble of the century, but it's okay." She said it was fine. I thought I looked like I was missing a pair of pants.

It was a sunny, windy day. Red, green, and yellow leaves were spread across the road and blowing over the grass. Central Park was looking pretty magnificent. We ran along the mesh fence at the side of the road. We got to the Great Lawn and ran around it three times. There were children on the grass playing soccer. I watched as a little girl knocked down a boy and then spat in his face. *Eve.*

We ran until I could feel my breath burning in the bottom of my chest, until I could feel last night's alcohol rising in my throat. I looked over at Natalie, who appeared to be moving at a steady pace, with no need to stop. When I couldn't go any farther, I made her take a break with me. I sat on a bench, pretending not to be sucking air into my lungs, as she stretched her legs.

"Weren't you some kind of college athlete?" she said, grinning.

"Yeah, ten years ago," I said, coughing and then blaming it on my lack of proper footwear.

"You don't need sneakers to run," she said.

"Yeah, but it sure as fuck helps," I replied.

She was marveling at me just as I was at her. Natalie was the most well-functioning person I'd ever met, maybe a little shrill when she was busy with work, but she was numb to the harm of everyday occurrences. She threw parties at her apartment. She had a ton of friends. She was always setting up dinners with people visiting from out of town. I'd never seen someone get so many visitors from out of town. How did she know all these people? I couldn't figure it out. Her calendar was filled with social engagements and she never broke them. Once it was in the calendar, it was set in stone. It didn't matter how tired she was on any given Friday night, if Natalie Williams made plans, she stuck to them.

She wanted to run the reservoir, so I told her to do the loop without me and then come back. I'd still be there. Recovering.

She seemed more than fine with it. "Okay . . . but we're not finished!"

"I know. I know."

Once she was gone, I sat there on the bench and reached into the pockets of the jacket, protecting my hands from the cold. I could see the tops of the buildings on Central Park West, each with its own unique outline, set against a clear blue sky. Central Park was remarkable in that it couldn't be defined by just one part of it. It was meant to be a moving experience, a passage of scenery, not repeated or uniform but unpredictable, like nature itself. It was the designers' intention to make it seem limitless, a great expanse of green. The Great Lawn was a green oval in the center of it all. Back in the day, it was a precious work of art, and people fought against the placement of baseball fields on the grounds. The diamonds were introduced in the fifties, and they confined recreational activities to this area, meant to be "a place for play."

The wind blew against my legs. My fingers felt a square

folded-up piece of paper in one of the pockets. I took it out and examined it. *Ben.*

It was her handwriting, and I remembered right away.

Eve had left it at my door about a month after we'd broken up. When I saw it on my doorstep, a sad little folded square of paper, I knew what it was. I assumed that it was yet another apology or explanation. She hadn't been thinking clearly, et cetera, et cetera. Back then, I was on my way out for the night, and put it in my jacket pocket without reading it. I went to meet my friends at a bar, all pissed, not throwing the thing away, but *definitely* not reading it. That was the night I met Natalie, and then deliberately forgot that the note existed. It got warm outside. I left the jacket at Natalie's place. I didn't look for it again all summer.

Sitting on that bench, I watched people pass by and played with the folds of the paper, unfolding and then refolding, still with no intention of reading it. I kept looking over my shoulder, for any trace of Natalie. Eventually, I unfolded it enough times to see the words *potato chip incident*, then refolded it, then put it back inside my pocket, then took it out again and thought, *Potato chip incident?* I opened it. It was two pages of writing, in Eve's customary lettering, part script, part print, less neat as she went along, *i*'s never dotted, halfhearted *e*'s that never quite seemed to close their loops. I checked over my shoulder one last time.

I started reading.

The Potato Chip Incident

You know how you hate it when I eat chips in bed? It makes sense that you hate it. It's a terrible idea. But I was doing it anyway. Because you were gone and I was nervous

and I heard something somewhere about
carbohydrates being relaxing and I could
pretty much confirm that as a medical fact
since I've had more than my share of soothing
moments with a french fry. Anyway, I wasn't
paying attention while eating them because,
as usual, I was writing at the same time,
and half a chip got caught in my throat.
I couldn't breathe and I got really scared
for a second or two. I ran over to the sink
and cupped water in my hands. As soon as
I started coughing and breathing again, I
realized something. This near-death (I can
actually hear you thinking NEAR DEATH? But
yes) experience taught me that anything can
happen in life. You can live to be a hundred or
you can die of a freak potato chip mishap.
So there is no point in hanging on to something,
there is no way to really hang on to anything,
at least not in the way that I was.

I used to have this fear of people leaving.
I feared the discomfort, the sheer hurt of
it, and none of that happens without the
beginning part. None of that happens if you
don't have that crucial beginning, where you
trust, you love, you hope, you rely. I have
spent my whole life thinking that I have this
limitation: my father left when I was young,
my mother died, my sister and I were left all
alone, so I have a fear of people leaving.
But I always wondered whether it would be

true forever. I wondered, once you and I got together, whether I would get over it, simply because I felt that there was nothing I could do that would make you leave. That was how I felt, finally, amazingly, like you were really there and would always be. Well, it turns out that wasn't true. I tested it, and you left, and it hurt every bit as much as I had anticipated, maybe more.

But, I'm still here. As it turns out, I'm stronger than I thought I was. I now realize that there is no such thing as an unblemished childhood or a perfect family. There's always some form of pain or loss. And I feel like this impulse to avoid discomfort is not compelling to me anymore. I stopped believing in it. It's illusory. It is like walking past an apartment that you have moved out of. The apartment still exists, but what's the difference what has happened there, since you left? Basically, my fear no longer has structure. It no longer has substance. When I was on the Lower East Side and saw Jesse again, I didn't just go back to that place, I really... really... went back to that place. I went back to being twenty-two. Back then, I had this feeling like I was protecting myself, like I might be able to prevent all the bad things in life that I couldn't control, because I wouldn't be able to handle them. I went back to feeling like I was a certain type of girl, who was very fragile and needed a certain type of boy. But I went back to a place that no longer existed. I went back to something that I could only see from a distance. I got so wrapped up in my pseudo-traumatic past and my most definitely present stupidity that I forgot to factor in something important: other people. Our relationship changed me. And not just because I felt that you wouldn't leave, but also because when you did leave, I got through it. It was painful, of course, but it was something that I could withstand. It was something that, of course, I could withstand.

I can't predict the future, but I can tell you that based on the evidence at my disposal, I feel fairly certain that it can still work between us. And, Ben, that's all anyone can give you. That's all you'll ever get. It's the best that you can ask for. I hope that you know how sorry I am. I hope that you can forgive me. Not because you're perfect or I'm perfect or because of any promises made for the future but because we are in the unfortunate position of being in love. And I hope that we can eat chips together again sometime, because for certain people (who shall remain nameless), eating them alone is a dangerous, dangerous proposition.

GODDAMNIT, *Eve.* I read the letter again. It wasn't like I was *missing* something with Natalie. You know what it was like? It was like I was sitting down to a full dinner, and yet I couldn't stop thinking about the fucking ice-cream truck parked outside. I couldn't stop thinking about shoving my fucking face with shitty ice cream.

Why couldn't I get her out of my head? I'd sulked for weeks over her betrayal. I hated her. I got drunk, played out various scenarios in my head, what I would say or do if I saw her. But the bottom line was I never really let go of how I felt about her in the first place. Always on the verge of sleep, in the darkness, and replaying happy memories with Eve in my head. In dreams, in walking down the street, she was there unless I told myself not to think about her, which I didn't. *That* was my problem. I didn't stop myself.

And the name mistake, well, that was poetic justice at its best. I guess I always felt like I would see Eve again, even as my memory of being with her began to fade, made the wound less fresh. I couldn't stop feeling like everyone else who I encountered was a substitute. Eventually, I wouldn't see or hear from her. She'd give up trying. I would unwind myself, and then I would be free. Except, I didn't want to be free. If I wanted to be free, it would be easy. I was never one of those people, never the person who thought I was supposed to be with someone who gave me *vertigo*. But this was what she wanted, right? To be the most frustrating and exasperating person I couldn't live without?

GODDAMMIT. I was starting to yearn.

- - - -

Natalie found me after her run and we walked together for a few more minutes. Thankfully, eventually, she started to get tired, and so we went back to her place. I sat on the couch in a daze as she handed me a plate of carrots with a lump of hummus on the side and a glass of orange juice. She turned on the football game. She left me there, went into the other room, to do her Natalie things—refold her clothes, keep up with her acquaintances. Everything in her apartment was so neat that I was almost tempted to knock over the glass of juice, just to see what would happen, just to see what kind of lawlessness might unfold.

I hadn't said anything about wanting to watch the game. But it didn't matter. It was fall. It was Saturday. Natalie liked to hear the sound of football on television. She said she'd grown up with it. Her father was always watching sports. She found the sound of the games comforting. And come to think of it—wasn't that what she liked most about me? That I used to play hockey? That I was some semblance of a guy who was into sports. That I was some semblance of a guy who Natalie imagined herself with. But was I? Well. I don't know. Not fully. Yeah, I liked sports, but so did a lot of people. It felt like she'd made an error in casting.

So I just stared at the TV screen for a while, with my glass of juice, holding up a plate of carrots, wanting to leave, and feeling like an asshole.

Something was wrong here. That was all I knew. I put down the carrots. I walked into her bedroom, where she was organizing her sock drawer.

"Ah. So what's your sock strategy over there? Standard matching or free-for-all?"

"Huh?"

"I assume you're going to keep each sock matched up with their standard partners?"

"How else would you do it?"

"Well, there are multiple ways. . . . So what do you do with your leftover singles? Is there a singles' mixer?"

"What are you talking about?" she demanded.

"What do you do with your leftover socks? You know, when one is worn out and you have to throw it out, what do you do with the second sock?"

"I throw them both out. Once one is worn out, they both go in the garbage."

"Really?"

I stopped myself right there and thought, *Wait, why do I care about this so much? What am I even saying? Socks? A singles' mixer? Leftovers? What have I become?*

"I have to go," I said to her finally, knowing what I had to do.

"Why?" She looked genuinely surprised. She was quite capable of ignoring this random non sequitur. She was a better actor than I was, or would ever be.

"I have to disprove a theory," I said.

"Work?"

Yes, she certainly was.

I looked Natalie in the eye and she looked away because she knew but didn't want to face it, not with me around anyway. She'd sort it out after I left, on the phone with her friends or her mother. I'd receive a very well-crafted e-mail in two to five business days.

- - - -

I waited for the elevator to come with such impatience that I almost started banging on the doors. I felt like everything around me was moving in slow motion. Once I was outside, I got on my phone.

"Where does she live?" I said to Glick.

"Who?"

"You know who. Where does she live now?"

"Are you about to make some magic happen?"

"Fuck off."

He told me the address. Park Avenue. Not exactly where I expected to find her, but it was convenient. I crossed Amsterdam Avenue and headed back to Central Park West. I went into the park, taking long strides. Surrounding me was the pond, lying still in the sun. I went over a small bridge built of cedar timber. On the right, I could see the skyscrapers of Fifty-Seventh Street in the distance, the sun low in the sky and falling lower. On my left were small rocks and larger stones, the water splashing faintly in the breeze. During the warmer months, there were often ducks, people rowing boats, their figures leaning toward each other. But today, the only people out there were crossing their arms and standing on the embankments surrounding the pond.

I started to feel a tiny vibration near my heart, like it was about to spring out. I walked faster, straight through the Ramble, making sure to avoid all the meandering trails that would have taken me out of my way. I stayed straight on my course, through a maze of dense woodlands, a web of jagged paths and planted woods. There was a sense of mystery to the Ramble. It was tall trees everywhere and wild shrubs along the ground. The terrain wasn't smooth, and the crops crowded one another in disorder, vines and ferns and then, suddenly, I was out, and passing by a lawn with a single magnificent tree, its autumn leaves scattered across the grass beneath it. Once I hit this point, I actually started to run, just like they do in the movies, dress shoes and all. It was a good thing that girls made you watch all those romantic comedies, otherwise I would have no idea that this was normal, that this was what I was supposed to be doing.

Throngs of people on Fifth Avenue overwhelmed the sidewalk.

There were artists displaying canvases and paintings and vendors peeking out of their carts, an ice-cream cone attached to an outstretched hand. I crossed the street to the less-crowded side. Traffic wasn't moving. I weaved through cars to cross, past a policeman blowing a whistle. An army of children crossed next to me, a few adults, exhausted and shuffling them along. I pushed past them, was almost to Park Avenue. The feeling that I would see her again was suddenly palpable. I could hear my pulse.

In front of the building, there was a man in uniform with red cheeks standing by the door. His eyes fell on me. *What the hell was her stepfather's name?* It wasn't coming to me. *Arnold? Maybe?*

"Hello, I'm here to visit my friend Arnold." It sounded wrong the second I said it out loud.

"Excuse me? Arnold who?"

"You don't know Arnold? Yeah, gosh, Arnold, can't believe he's been living here for fifty years! You must know him! I'm here to meet him for our annual . . . golf outing."

His face was empty of any recognition. He looked at his watch, signaling his impatience. *I was tracking her down. Out of the blue? Hello? This was romance!* He took a long pause. He didn't look like the type of guy who would let me into the building based on romance.

"Arnold!" I said. I was desperate and on the verge of shouting rich-person things. *Cigars! Cuff links! Monocles! Whiskey! Boats!*

"You know what, I'll just call him," I said, making a big show of digging my phone out of my pocket. They let me into the lobby and I sat in one of the two chairs facing a mirror. I considered it a small victory. If I waited there, maybe she'd come down. I pretended to be on my phone as I listened to the doormen talk to each other. Nobody seemed to find it strange, or suspected any bad intentions about the fact that I was sitting around for so long. Eventually, they seemed to forget that I was there. I interrupted their conversation to say that I'd spoken to Arnold and that he was delayed upstairs due to some fluctuations in the stock market but that he'd be down momentarily.

And then, like a miracle, when I was out of ideas and my wait had lasted an hour and was verging on dubious, Eve walked into the lobby. I stood up, walked toward her in such a dreamy condition, reeling inside. She didn't look surprised to see me. She wasn't blinking. It was like there was something alive in her eyes, something very alive. She seemed to be seeing through me. And then she stopped looking at my eyes and looked down at my shoes.

"Why aren't you wearing pants?"

I felt like reaching for her face. This happened once in a lifetime, I was sure of it, if you were lucky. It wasn't like another one just came along. I held up the letter for her and then put it back into my pocket.

"I'm just here to tell you that there's no way you could have choked on that potato chip," I said. "It would have disintegrated long before killing you. Your esophagus would break the chip in half. It might hurt, but you'd still be able to breathe."

It seemed to register with her that I had only just read it. She had a slightly hurt look on her face, involuntarily, but she pushed past it. "Maybe so," she said, looking down solemnly.

"And you are the only one in the world who would refer to that as a potato chip *incident*."

"It was scary!"

"For you? I bet."

"I know what you're thinking. *Am I okay now?* Well, it's been a few months . . . but the recovery time is always longer than people tell you it's going to be. Plus, let's not forget to factor in post-traumatic stress. . . ."

"Oh yeah. Let's not. We'd be remiss."

Her face fell into a smile and my mind raced as I tried to settle on what to say next. Our conversation felt delicate, like we were both maneuvering on glass that might crack. She asked if I wanted to take a walk, so we went outside and walked a few blocks. Eventually, we settled on a bench on the park side of Fifth Avenue, next to a car with its windows open and seats reclined, a man in the front seat playing salsa music. As we sat there, a group of children in brightly colored running clothes passed us by. A small crowd began to accumulate near the bus stop. An ambulance wailed. A woman smoking a cigarette stopped to fix her shoe in front of us, her hand leaning against a big tree. We watched the activity on the street for a while, the people walking by in twos and threes, with backpacks and with red shopping bags from the gift shop at the Met. Everyone was returning home from Saturday activities, hands in their pockets and faces directed toward the pavement ahead. Most people were headed downtown. An ice-cream truck started playing "Pop Goes the Weasel." Eve's head remained bowed, with a dangerous smile that I could see, even though she was trying to stifle it. She appeared to be holding her breath. I knew that there were things I should have done differently too, that I wouldn't mind a fresh start. I wanted to see her again, and again and again, and that was that.

My mind was chaos. It was breaking over me, this feeling that my heart was bursting and beating fast. This girl broke down some wall inside of me—she must have broken it down a long time ago—and being without her now was unthinkable. A thrill ran through me as I reached out and touched her arm, like I was smashed into fragments. I wanted her face next to my face, to clasp her hand in mine. I touched a few of her fingers just then and it was pure bliss. But also torture. Incomplete. Nothing else mattered now besides the fulfillment of this sensation.

"I don't know what happened to me," I said. "I honestly don't know."

"You became a big sucker," she said, closing her hand around mine, more firmly now. Those eyes, staring right into mine. She leaned forward. "Just like the rest of us."

EVE

- - - - -

112 MACDOUGAL STREET, APARTMENT 5C, WEST VILLAGE

"I can't do this anymore!" I yelled, and threw the shriveled tube of toothpaste down onto the floor.

Ben looked at me, as usual, a little mystified.

"Can't do *what* anymore?"

"*This.*" I pointed at the ground.

"Just squeeze from the bottom."

"I've *been* squeezing from the bottom! I've been squeezing from the bottom for *weeks*! There's nothing left. Can I please have one of the new toothpastes that we bought?"

"Not until the old one is finished. There's plenty left in there."

"*Plenty?*" I stomped past him. "Clearly, you've gone insane." I tore open a box on the floor in the kitchen and started rifling through, putting aside rolls of paper towels and toilet paper.

"*What are you doing?* That box is organized and ready to go!"

"I need new toothpaste and I'm not going to live under this puritanical regime any longer!"

Bottles of hand soap dropped onto the floor, one after another, *thud, thud, thud.*

"Get out of there!" He grabbed hold of my waist, attempted to lift me out, but I held on to the box so that he couldn't pull me away. "You are . . . nothing . . . but . . . trouble," he said. As I rifled through, Ben held me by my feet, but my hands were still inside, so the box went sliding along with me, around the floor of the apartment.

"Get . . . OUT!" he said, part struggling, part laughing.

"Where is it?" I shouted. "*Where* is the new toothpaste?"

"I will give it to you. . . ." He grunted. "Jesus, Eve. Once we get to our new place. New apartment, new toothpaste."

He wrestled me away from the box and to the floor. I squirmed out from under him, stood up. I walked back to the bathroom and pointed to the toothpaste that had been banished to the floor. "*That one* is done." I started to laugh. "You can have that toothpaste or you can have me but *you can't have both.*" I put my hands on my hips. "MAKE A DECISION."

"Then I choose the toothpaste," he said, going to pick it up. He pinched the flat tube, from the bottom to the top, rolling up the tube as he went. Blue liquid appeared at the opening.

"See," he said, and then handed it to me. "Plenty."

I took it into the bathroom, brushed my teeth, but with added gusto, a slight resentment. I almost didn't brush them at all, *out of spite.* But then I got over myself. I wanted to brush, after all. Regardless of who won the argument, true victory was about choice. Or something like that.

I went into the bedroom to ready myself for the monumental

dinner ahead, our last dinner in our neighborhood, as residents of Macdougal Street.

"You know, I'm going to miss this place." I came back out and looked around the apartment we had rented for the past year. All our possessions were now in thirteen boxes, labeled one through thirteen in thick black marker, because Ben insisted that numbering the boxes would make it easier to keep track of them. I wanted to label the boxes based on room in which they were most frequently used. That's when the marker got taken away from me.

"I'll miss it too," he said.

"You're taking that?" I asked. Ben was holding up a ten-year-old can of Campbell's clam chowder. He'd kept it over the years, because of some sentimental attachment that I didn't understand involving his friends from the hockey team. "Are you sure?" I said. "What if it leaks? I think it's too difficult to transport."

"We're taking you," he said, shoving the can into the corner of a filled box. "And you're difficult to transport."

The apartment didn't look the same anymore. We'd covered every bit of wall space, and now the walls were bare. We didn't have much furniture, just an old armchair and an Indian-print carpet and a bookshelf that Ben built himself on one of those days when he took out his toolbox and listened to songs like "Takin' Care of Business" and "Working for the Weekend" and felt the need to fix things around the apartment. All our books were in boxes now, haphazardly, as if they'd never been given a careful order. The apartment was small but compensated for any deficiencies by being on a quiet, tree-lined street. It was a couple of blocks from Washington Square Park.

We'd discussed the move at length. It was the best possible decision for the future. We needed more space. We were never meant to live in this apartment forever. We had taken it as a short-term solution. Once Ben and I decided to live together, it seemed that we needed to live together right away. Logistics like where to put our possessions once our one closet was overflowing and the oven was full of plates and lesser-used pans . . . well, that could be worked out later. And later had come, though it was impressive watching Ben put his engineering skills to use, to see him staring into the closet with extreme focus and rearranging it until we had a legitimate spot for that bottle of Advil that used to fall to the floor whenever we opened the door.

We hadn't lived there for very long, and yet there was something about it. We were very much there. It was the happiest time of my life so far. It was where we'd gotten back together, and where we knew we'd never be apart. It was where we took a break from the world, which was, in the city, never very far away. We only had to peek out our window to see into other peoples' apartments, each square with its own points of interest. Through one window, there was an old lady who lived alone, who liked to come outside to her patio on Saturday mornings and sweep the leaves into a dustpan. In another, there was a young guy who was always sitting near the window behind his computer. He had a rotating cast of roommates. In the apartment above us, old music and movies were always playing. The couple who lived below us liked to watch sports together and then get into screaming fights about whether they should have children.

The next day, the movers would come. I got to work on my last task, which was folding and packing up our bed linens. They were all white and immeasurably soft, purchased for us by Arthur at a store on Madison Avenue. I nearly fell over when I saw the price tag, but Arthur insisted. "Your mother would have wanted you to have them. She loved this store. You know she believed that the key to happiness was soft sheets." I nodded and accepted the gift. As I folded them carefully, corner to corner, end to end, I thought, *She would have loved these sheets, but mostly, to see me so comfortable beneath them.*

Ben was working up until the point when we left for dinner. He promised that he would start getting nostalgic with me then, at dinner, but not a moment before.

"Hey," I said, looking around for my phone. "Do you remember when I said I was going to make a video about our time in this apartment and *you said*, 'It's three o'clock in the morning, go back to sleep'?"

He continued staring at his computer screen. "Like it was fifteen hours ago."

I removed my phone from the windowsill. "Okay, well! Now is the time!"

Ben was sitting on the floor with his computer on his lap and paid no attention to me as I started the video, walking throughout the apartment, talking to my phone about all the different parts of it. I wanted to give it one last good lookover before we left. Its appearance was much worse without all our stuff in place, but I didn't care. I still loved it, every corner of it. I explained our brief history there to the phone, holding it in front of my mouth and basically walking around in circles (there really wasn't very far to go).

For dinner, Ben requested that we go to Pluck U, a "restaurant" that specialized, unsurprisingly, in chicken.

"Really? We can go?" he said, energized and a little alarmed, when I agreed. "I always want to go there, but you never do."

"That's because the online reviews are terrible. More than one post mentioning food poisoning is the rule," I explained.

"One is an outlier. Two is a pattern. But I'll do it this time, because relationships are all about compromise. And I want it to be noted on the record that I am a great compromiser."

"You're a great compromiser. I asked to go to Pluck U twenty thousand times, and we went once."

"Exactly."

"Whatever," he said, yanking long strips of brown tape from its dispenser and wrapping it around a box. "If I left you to your own devices, you'd eat potato chips and Junior Mints for dinner."

Outside, it was clear that winter had come to New York. The snow had buried everything. We walked on West Third Street, past Sullivan, until we hit Thompson, our boots clomping along the sidewalk. We walked past all the bars, packed with a mix of college students and older couples.

Pluck U was the brightest establishment on the block—a port in the storm, with its yellow awning, and painted yellow walls— it radiated its golden hue all the way down Thompson Street. Once inside, the smell of french fries hit me in the face. There were only two tables, and one was open. I hung my coat on the chair, to save it for us. I wasn't going to eat our farewell chicken dinner standing up. Ben gave the menu above the cashier a serious look.

As we sat at the table a few minutes later with our respective chickens, I was expecting some kind of shift, for this dinner to be different from every dinner we'd ever had before, but it wasn't.

"So does Pluck U stand for Pluck University?" I asked Ben. "Because the chickens are in college now or something like that?"

"Yeah, but it's just a play on words. They're not, like, making a statement about the education of their chicken."

The song "Rockin' Robin" came through a speaker in the corner of the ceiling.

He rocks in the treetops all day long . . .
Hoppin' and a-boppin' and singing his song . . .

I looked up. "Wouldn't it be funny if every time they played this song, a guy in a chicken suit came out and ate everyone's food?"

Ben dunked a fry into a pool of ketchup.

"Why would a chicken eat other chickens?" Ben was often in the position of questioning the logic of my jokes. Before I presented an idea at work, I usually ran it by him, just to make sure I hadn't gone too far off the deep end.

"I don't know. Maybe he's one of those self-loathing chickens?" I thought about it for a few seconds. "Or maybe he comes out and knocks the food off everyone's tables?"

He nodded. "See, now that makes sense."

I got a secret thrill from his approval, from coming up with an idea that would satisfy even an engineer.

"I guess it's appropriate that we came here on our last night in the apartment, since we had that 'moment' on Saint Marks, over chicken wings. Chicken seems to be a common theme in our relationship."

Ben didn't respond. He took a sip from his soda.

"What? You don't think so?" I asked.

"Does our relationship need a theme?"

"It does if we don't want to confuse our future wedding planner!"

The expression on his face was like he sensed a trick. He stopped eating. What I said was *that* important.

"Oh!" I added. "They can play the 'Chicken Dance' at our wedding! 'The Way You Look Tonight.' Give me a break. Actually, do you think they could do the 'Chicken Dance' but like a

Sinatra-esque version? Arthur would love that. He loves Sinatra.
He always says, 'That Sinatra has got star power,' as if he's the
one who discovered him and Sinatra were still alive. Oh God.
Would Arthur be the one to walk me down the aisle? I think I'd
be okay with that, actually. As long as he doesn't wear that hideous pocket watch. Oh! Emma could be the maid of honor. Ugh,
she'll probably sleep with one of the groomsmen. What do you
think? Have any friends whose lives you'd like to ruin?"

His eyes went wide. "Are you finally saying yes to marrying
me . . . *in Pluck U?*"

"You know what," I said, cheerfully. "I am."

Ben seemed to give it a second thought, and then looked satisfied. He went back to his fries, grinning. "And by the way, the
'Chicken Dance' is played at baseball games, not at weddings."

"Are you sure?"

"I am."

– – – –

As we walked back to our apartment on Macdougal Street for
the last time, I asked Ben whether he thought that our next
place would feel as much like our real home as this one did.
The correct answer was, yes, of course, that our real home was
us together, that was all. There was no need for the structure
itself. It was about that feeling of safety in the world, that
was what people wanted most of all. Everything else in life
revolved around getting to that point. I told him if that were
the case, we should have gotten together a long time ago, saved
ourselves some trouble. But Ben said that he believed in the
process.

"The city exists in contrasts," he said. He explained that

it was true here more so than anywhere—people were always throwing themselves into the feverish streets and then seeking shelter from the madness. He said that was what made New York so great, that you couldn't fully appreciate a sunny day unless you'd come in from a storm. If that were true, then I could only be glad I didn't yield to him earlier. I didn't realize the visionary I was when I involved myself with the very wrong people who came before him. *That* was really my most brilliant move—to find every bright love interest who wasn't quite as bright as I imagined. I wouldn't even recognize them now, with how falsely and powerfully they existed in my memory. But, I was thankful for them. They were each a promise of something greater. And if things really do exist only in contrasts, then how wonderful to feel disappointment, to be not quite right, to feel confused and not always adored. How important it was to be able to say I was quite the heartsick girl, once upon a time.

In the morning, the movers arrived. I thought it would be a long process but the boxes disappeared quickly. I took one last glance around, looking for something to take with me, but I couldn't find it. I knew I would never see the apartment again. If we were to come back, in the years to come, it would be a distorted space. I wanted to remember it the way it was at that moment. That was how it would always be, in my mind. I had the video from last night. And I took some photos, before we'd torn it all apart. I tried to remember a few moments, because I just needed a few moments to come back to me.

The side of Macdougal Street that Ben refused to walk on with me because he walked on it alone during the week and it reminded him of going to work.

Sneaking over to our neighbor's doorstep when we knew he

*was away so that I could look through his mail while Ben kept a
lookout.*

*Walks through Washington Square Park when it snowed and
watching kids go sledding down a hill that was only three feet high.*

*The Italian restaurant on Ninth Street where we went once but
everyone was over seventy years old so we felt kind of uncool and
decided we couldn't go there again (because of our self-esteem), but
we could definitely have it delivered (because it was pretty tasty).*

*The hallway outside our apartment where we practiced doing
the lift from the last scene of* Dirty Dancing *because I'd just made
Ben watch it and said it didn't seem that difficult to me until we
tried it and I kept laughing so hard and running toward him and
then chickening out before he could lift me.*

*The NYU kids moving into their dorms in August and their
parents unloading the cars with worried expressions on their faces
and eyeing the older NYU kids with piercings and tattoos like*
What is to become of my child?

My hair clips and earrings on the night table.

*His socks under the bed, hidden like snakes so that I couldn't
see them and nag him to put them away.*

*The kitchen where Ben made hash browns on Saturday morn-
ings and reheated pizza on Sunday nights and invented "spice-
cabinet chicken" a.k.a. chicken that he seasoned with every single
spice we owned.*

*The hallway outside the kitchen where I said things like "Stop
micromanaging my ice-cream situation!" And Ben said things like
"Did you know that the Italians have only been cooking with toma-
toes for the last one hundred years? Christopher Columbus brought
them from the Americas."*

*The couch where I sat while he cooked because I'd been ban-
ished from the kitchen for giving too many unnecessary directions.*

The Korean restaurant on Carmine Street we went to so often that I said that when we have a child his or her first words will probably be not dada *or* mama *but* bulgogi taco.

The TV that stopped working one day and we didn't do anything to repair it and then a week later it started working again and we looked at it, astonished, and Ben declared, "Fixed itself!"

The closet where Ben's shirts hung and he wore them in a rotation and he was a slave to this rotation, so I changed the ordering of the shirts once, which caused him to have a short but acute psychological breakdown.

The living room where Ben came home with the final sketch of the Freedom Tower and I told him that it was the most beautiful thing I'd ever seen and he was all excited and proud and said, "OF COURSE IT IS. BECAUSE YOU CANNOT FUCK WITH THIS CITY, EVE. YOU CANNOT!"

The Laundromat on Thompson Street where we took our clothes and I made fun of Ben for never emptying his pockets before washing his pants and the machine would start to clank because Ben was accidentally washing pennies and his credit cards.

Suddenly I had a genius idea. I went looking in the bedroom closet. Something was written there. I'd seen it months ago. I opened the closet door and looked down. It said *112 Macdougal Street, 5C* in black, thick marker on one of the pieces of wood near the floor. I bent down, ran my finger along the words. There had been places I'd lived, but this one was different. We'd built something there that would last. It would last forever and nothing would destroy it. Underneath *112 Macdougal Street,* I thought about writing *Ben & Eve,* but something stopped me. The reality of our names on the wall seemed trivial, and the result was nothing, without context. I thought about the strangers, the future residents, who would see it. I wanted the apartment to pass into its next episode unscathed, the way it was when we found it, like a continuous, vacant sphere, filled and then emptied, filled and then emptied. It wasn't about that anyway—our names. It was about what had transpired there, and all over the Village. But I couldn't recall so much of what had taken place. I hadn't written anything down. I'd made a huge mistake.

"We're not dying! We'll go out and make new memories," Ben said later, when I told him, to make me feel better. "We will always be here, in a sense," he added reassuringly, as he closed the door. He knew that I needed a lie, a fairy tale, a happy ending.

But I believed him, and so it was.

ACKNOWLEDGMENTS

I have been writing this in my head since I was a little kid, when the prime recipients of my gratitude were a stuffed monkey named Triple-Dip and a penguin named Icing. But because I am older and wiser now and the very essence of maturity, I will refrain from . . . oh what the hell—thanks guys! Couldn't have done it without you!

Okay. On to the humans. My friends are the inspiration for every warm, honest, funny, crazy, complicated female character I've ever written. Monica Sethi, Kristin Soong, Ellen Fedors, Erica Temel, Logan Fedder, Sandra Rose, Marisa Zucker, Shelly Kellner, Emma Zuroski, Priya Ravishankar, Kasey Fechtor, Madeleine Root, Nattha Chutinthranod, Anna Christodoulu, Caroline Fairchild, and Jamie Joseph, thank you for the brilliance.

I am indebted to the Columbia University undergraduate Creative Writing Program, where ridiculously impractical dreams are made; and to Professor Michael Seidel, hawker of literature that has stayed with me always.

I have been lucky enough to work at two of the best literary agencies in town. Thank you to everyone at Levine Greenberg Rostan for being the happiest home for an intern new to the world of publishing, and especially to Kerry Sparks. Thank you to my friends at Writers House, and to Simon Lipskar, for pushing me to write but better. The day you agreed to read my manuscript inspired one of the best victory dances my apartment has ever seen.

Many thanks to the looney tunes of the Writers House Softball Team: Dan Conaway, Ian Kleinert, Amy Appel, Ashley Collom, Mickey Novak, Christina Fodera, and Sean Fodera. Hanging with you Bookies in Central Park on summer afternoons is the greatest. To my council of men, who provided endless and sometimes frightening insight into the male psyche—Henry Ginnay, Colin Farstad, and Daniel Meredith—you guys are so dreamy. Clare Reeth, beautiful genius, unique snowflake (said in the voice of Leslie Knope to Ann Perkins). And to my best frenemy, Kevin Meredith, who makes my jokes funnier and my life better.

Michael Miracle, my first boss who ruined me for all future bosses. Chris Sweetgall, for his knowledge of all things rivets and bolts. Camille Rankin, for my first by-line, which consisted only of my initials in tiny print but it was still glorious. Lila Coleburn, for her much needed guidance. Phillip Rosen, trusty legal advisor and cool uncle. Gitta Rosen, Leslie Mintz, and Wendy Sarasohn, for the perpetual cheerleading. Danny McEneaney, my brother-in-law, for keeping my spirits up. Marc Philippe Eskenazi, for insights into the rock-and-roll lifestyle (p.s. do they still call it rock and roll?). Christine Benedetti, my Colorado stories would be nothing without you.

My friend David Siffert—I've never had a brother but I assume it means someone who watches out for you even though they find you mildly annoying and who sits across from you at various diners throughout Manhattan while you experience a wide variety of breakdowns? Sif, I would only eat waffles with wine in front of you. You're welcome.

My agent, Andrew Blauner, has the soul of a Jew and the charm of a WASP, which means he's pretty much unstoppable.

I remember when he first sold this novel, he told me that it was "an absolute, unconditional high" for him. What kind of person gets an absolute, unconditional high from making someone else's dream come true? A really, really good one, that's who. My thanks also to David Duchovny, clutch hitter extraordinaire, for coming in with encouragement at just the right moment. Andrew and David are basically the kindest, classiest, most well-educated guys who do what they want and don't give an F. When I grow up, I want to be just like them.

Elana Cohen—I could not have asked for a more perfect person to edit this book. Sometimes I felt as though I dreamed you up and I wanted to storm into the S&S offices and make sure that you were real. Nina Cordes, for taking over with such enthusiasm and grace. Jennifer Bergstrom, for giving me the very special gift of Elana and Nina. And to Kate Dresser, Meagan Harris, and Molly Gregory—thank you for joining my team.

My Russian parents-in-law, Yuly and Roza Verbitsky, for their support and for never allowing me to go too long without pickled cabbage.

My father and Diane for always believing that my choices are the best choices.

My sister, Ali, who is my public relations director, social media expert, stuffed animal consultant, and constant compadre. What I would be without her is alone in old family photos, and while one person dressed in a hideous floral ensemble (complete with matching hat!) is a bit pathetic, two is most definitely a crowd.

My husband, Dave, who ten years ago requested the role of leading man in my life and has been crushing it ever since.

And finally, to my mother, for reading so many drafts, for seeing me through so many catastrophes, and most of all, for teaching me how to write and love.

THIS
LOVE STORY
WILL
SELF-DESTRUCT

LESLIE COHEN

INTRODUCTION

Columbia University, 2005. Ben meets Eve. Eve meets Ben. And not much of anything happens between them, until one day, they meet again, and it changes the course of their lives forever. Follow Eve and Ben as they navigate their twenties in the midst of New York City's twisty-turny streets, through first jobs, first dates, and first breakups; through first reunions, first betrayals and, finally, possibly, first real love. A timeless tale reimagined for the millennial era from two unapologetically original points of view, this is the story of what it means to find love in today's modern world.

TOPICS AND QUESTIONS
FOR DISCUSSION

- - - - - - - - - - - - - - - -

1. Cohen introduces us to the impassioned, quirky Eve in the opening chapters of the novel, before revealing her tragic past. How did your impression of Eve evolve as you learned her backstory?

2. One could argue that New York City is the third protagonist in this novel, one whose characteristics shift dramatically at various points in the story. Eve's description of living in the city ranges from feeling "like an ant trapped amid a towering maze of buildings, waiting for a giant shoe to crush you to death" (pg. 109) to the "damn city fit like a glove" (pg. 118). How does the setting both impact and reflect the characters' emotional states throughout the novel?

3. On pg. 169, Ben says to Eve, "We've come into each other's lives over and over again, and that's fine. No big deal. But because we have, we begin to feel a destiny with each other . . ." Discuss the moments of serendipity that

connect Ben and Eve. Do you think these coincidences are random, or are they, as Ben believes, a matter of "synchronicity"?

4. What do you make of Ben's decision not to immediately tell Eve about the connection between his father and her mother? How would you have handled the situation?

5. Discuss the significance of Eve's mother dying on 9/11. Do you think Eve's experience of this significant loss would be different if it were not linked to such a public, large-scale tragedy?

6. On pg. 248, Jesse tells Eve that she's in love with Ben because she's "desperate to feel that way." Do you agree with this statement? If so, does it minimize Eve's relationship with Ben?

7. While discussing his job on pg. 136, Ben says "there is a certain satisfaction in bringing order to the ideas." How does this sentiment hold true in his relationship with Eve? Ultimately, do you think Ben helps Eve bring order to her life, or does she accomplish this on her own?

8. Both the novel's opening and closing scenes take place in Eve's apartment. How does her definition of "home" change over the years? What major turning points shape her perceptions about where she lives, and where she wants to live?

9. On pg. 1, Eve recounts, "Let us not judge hastily the actions of the young for fear of neglecting the importance of the journey." Ben echoes her on pg. 313, claiming that "you couldn't fully appreciate a sunny day unless you'd come in from a storm." Do you agree with them? Has this statement held true at any point in your life?

10. Reread the prologue and discuss how your interpretation has changed now that you've finished the book. Would you consider either Ben or Eve reliable narrators in these opening passages?

11. What future do you envision for Ben and Eve beyond the last page of the book?

ENHANCE YOUR BOOK CLUB

1. In the prologue, Eve describes "the streets, apartment buildings, bars and restaurants . . . A part of the story will always remain in those places, as if stranded in time" (pgs. 1–2). Ask each member of your book club to bring a photo or memento from a physical place that triggers a memory for them, and share the stories that stay "stranded in time" for each of you.

2. Cast the film version of *This Love Story Will Self-Destruct*. Which actors, living or dead, would you chose to play the novel's characters?

3. Host a New York City–themed book club: discuss *This Love Story Will Self-Destruct* over brunch or happy hour, snack on bagels and lox or pizza, and decorate accordingly.